THE
COLOUR
OF
THUNDER

SUZANNE HARRISON

Legend Press Ltd, 51 Gower Street, London, WC1E 6HJ
info@legendpress.co.uk | www.legendpress.co.uk

Print ISBN 978-1-78955-9-392
Ebook ISBN 978-1-78955-9-385
Set in Times. Printing managed by Jellyfish Solutions Ltd
Cover design by Simon Levy | www.simonlevyassociates.co.uk

Suzanne Harrison is an Australian journalist and editor who has lived in Hong Kong since 1999. She most recently worked freelance, writing lifestyle and news features for the *South China Morning Post*.

Follow Suzanne on Instagram
@suzannejs.455
or on Twitter
@suzannej123

If you're going to seek revenge, dig two graves.
Chinese proverb

Hong Kong is a former British colony and – since 1997 – a special region of China, located in the South China Sea.

Ethnic Chinese make up more than 93.6 per cent of the population of roughly 7.4 million. Expatriates account for 4.6 per cent, representing countries from all over the world.

Hong Kong is a highly significant global financial centre. Its people enjoy some of the longest life expectancies and the highest national IQ estimate in the world. It is generally safe and peaceful.

However, there has been significant political turmoil in recent years, marked by democratic reform protests, some of which have resulted in violence and mass arrests.

There are many diverse and intriguing characters that have made their fortune – or are planning on it – in this vibrant city. As is often the case with those seeking the excitement of riches, some of them will do anything to get the results they want.

CHAPTER ONE

Sunflowers Orphanage, Tianjin, Mainland China.

The recent past.

Only bad things happened when it was this hot. Bathed in sweat, Li Wei felt a sense of dread in the pit of his stomach as he ambled towards the office. Once inside, he knew his gut was right.

His boss, Miss Beverly, and her co-worker Nick had already mentioned the little things: a dripping tap, a squeaking ceiling fan, the ripped curtain that let in too much sun. Wei was doing his best to fix them all before someone boiled over. The faster he worked, the hotter he got. The sweat dripped into his eyes. No one noticed.

It was a Tuesday morning in August. When his handyman work was done, Wei did the usual thing and collected rubbish from the kitchen. As he left the building, he heard the tapping of keyboards and the shuffling of paper coming from Miss Beverly's office and hoped the sour mood had passed.

But then the telephone started. It kept ringing, all morning, which was very unusual. He could hear its shrill cry from outside and whoever answered it – probably Miss Beverly – kept slamming the receiver back down. When he went back inside to fetch his rucksack, the frustration in the office was as thick as the air was humid. As he left, Wei's footfall on the parquet floor seemed louder than normal and he willed it to be silent, just this once, worrying the noise would be the final straw for Miss Beverly.

Summer fever, his mother used to call it. Now he knew why. There were omens everywhere.

That evening, when the damage was done, he blamed himself for all that went wrong; for not acting sooner.

Just before lunch, Wei had skulked away to prune the bougainvillea clinging to the chicken-wire fence separating the orphanage from the alleyway behind. Even then, he could still hear the office phone ring and ring, over and over. Someone slammed it so hard that Wei jumped, pricking his finger on a thorn. He watched the blood swell and bubble on the surface. It was the same colour as the flowers he held in his other hand.

Wei went back to work, but not long after, he heard Miss Beverly yelling in Mandarin, then English.

Wei saw an old utility vehicle parked outside the front gates. That was nothing unusual. Deliveries came throughout the day. Clothes and toys, from charities mostly.

The deliveryman was standing very close to Miss Beverly. She pointed a finger and the man squared his shoulders. Wei stood taller.

"No, no, no," Miss Beverly said in a calmer voice. "Do you think I'm stupid?" She tried to say something to the deliveryman in Mandarin but reverted to English.

"We warned him," the man snapped.

The deliveryman was tall, with a large chest that he pushed out as he towered over Miss Beverly. He had very short hair and Wei could see the sparkle of a gold watch on his left wrist. He also wore thick-rimmed black glasses, like Superman. Wei had watched the movie on a DVD.

Wei had seen such trouble brewing when he was growing up. Once, in his rural village, a heatwave caused his best friend's grandmother to go mad. She had stabbed her daughter-in-law for overcooking breakfast and then killed herself, in front of her entire family. Wei's mother was sure the heat had created a devil, although his father disagreed. He said the woman had been insane since birth.

The door to the orphanage squeaked open and closed. Nick came outside holding a cup of coffee. He stomped over to Beverly and the man, Nick's blond hair shining like a lantern in the sun. They all talked at once in English, but much of it was lost on Wei. All he *could* tell was that Nick was trying to keep the conversation calm, as was Nick's way. Maybe the man had forgotten to deliver something important. They were low on toilet tissue and vegetable oil, for one thing.

Wei shrugged and decided it was too hot to stand there in the sun listening to them argue. He took a bottle of water from his rucksack and sat down under his favourite tree, to the left of the courtyard. In front was the main gate and, to his right, the arched doorway to the orphanage, painted bottle green by Wei himself just days before.

It was pleasant in the shade and he felt the stress of the morning fade away. Even better, if he sat very still, a light sea breeze was making its way through the tall buildings that fronted the orphanage.

Wei closed his eyes and listened to the children singing a morning song. He smiled to himself at their innocent words.

Tài yáng dāng kōng zhào. The sun is shining in the sky.
Huā'ér dui wǒ xiào. The flowers are smiling to me.

Being around children was comforting. Wei had never had much of a childhood. He was left to his own devices from the age of six or seven while his parents worked. He escaped to the city as soon as he'd turned fifteen and took the handyman job in the orphanage within a week. Miss Beverly said he was their oldest child. She hugged him sometimes, despite the fact he stank of rotting vegetables and nappies from carrying bags of rubbish all day. One day, she told him he was kind and that this made him special. He liked Miss Beverly. Her smile always reached her eyes.

He would never leave the orphanage. It was his home now.

Wei had just nodded off, a fresh dream of tall mountains and a speeding car edging its way into his subconscious brain, when he heard Miss Beverly. She was yelling, very loudly. He had never heard her shout before.

He sat up and rubbed at his eyes. He heard Nick's booming voice.

"That's it!" Nick said. "No more! Go!"

Wei stood too quickly, almost falling over. He saw Nick put up a fist in front of the man's face. The man pointed something at Nick.

"You have no business here!" Nick yelled at the man in Mandarin. "Put that away!"

That was when Wei saw the new girl, Nick's friend, come out of the orphanage door, edging the older children inside as she did. Ever since she'd arrived to visit Nick at the orphanage the day before, Wei had been mesmerised. She was in frayed denim shorts and a T-shirt, and Wei kept his eyes trained on her long, lean legs.

"Get back!" Nick called to his friend.

"Why?" she cried. "What's going on? Nick?" She had reached him and was trying to grab at Nick's shirt, but he shrugged her hand away and hissed something in her ear.

Miss Beverly took the new girl's arm and the two walked backwards very slowly. Wei followed them towards the schoolhouse.

It's the heat, he wanted to say.

Wei caught up with Miss Beverly and the new girl.

"Do you need help?" he said, a little breathless. They had stopped near the doorway.

"Wei," Miss Beverly said to him in a whisper, "go inside and call the police station. Now. Okay? I'm right behind you." She smiled at him, a kind of annoyed grimace, as though he wasn't moving fast enough. He widened his eyes and ran.

From Miss Beverly's office window, he could see the far side of the courtyard, but the gate was hidden from view unless he leaned the top half of his body out of the window.

He hoped the deliveryman had gone. Nick was respected. He had done a lot of good. Maybe Nick had paid the man off.

But just as Wei hung up the phone, the new girl screamed. She called out Nick's name and, a few seconds later, Miss Beverly stumbled into her office with the new girl in her arms. The two of them were sobbing.

Wei smelled a musty heat coming off their bodies and wanted to be sick. Outside, he heard the front gate slam against the broken metal lock and the roar of the truck as it drove away. Miss Beverly told the new girl to sit down. She slumped to the floor, her head in her hands.

Wei bent down and gently rubbed her folded arms. But then he saw the blood. A sticky cobweb of deep red staining her shirt. Wei gasped and pulled his hand away, but it was too late. The blood had coated his palm.

"I think he killed him," the girl whimpered.

Wei shook his head. "What do you mean?"

The new girl stayed silent. She was shivering.

"Stay here," Miss Beverly said, rushing back outside.

Wei went to the window and pushed at its timber frame. He inched himself through it. Surely Nick had hurt the bad man. Surely Nick was stronger.

But lying on the ground like a discarded jacket was Nick, his blond hair soaking in a pool of black blood. The pale-blue coffee cup lay cracked into two perfect halves next to one outstretched arm. Miss Beverly kneeled over him. Her body heaved before placing a hand over her mouth. Behind her, several of the older children were weeping loudly, their cries shrill in the still air.

"Bring the children in, Wei!" Miss Beverly called out in between sobs. She didn't take her eyes off Nick's body. Wei did as he was told.

* * *

A week later, the new girl had gone. The police had spoken to Miss Beverly not long after the ambulance had taken Nick's body away. Miss Beverly made Wei promise to never tell anyone what happened or what the deliveryman looked like. And he didn't.

Sometimes, Wei heard Miss Beverly talking about Nick on the phone, but she always whispered. Afterwards, she'd whimper a little.

Over time, life went back to normal, for Wei and the children anyway.

But Miss Beverly, she stopped smiling.

CHAPTER TWO

Snake Bay, Sai Kung, Hong Kong.

Three months later.

She knew as soon as she saw him that it was time. He stood not far from her, but even from there, she could see the darkness of his eyes, their murky depths.

Everyone was drunk or close to it. She watched as champagne fizzed, corks popped and colourful canapés appeared on silver trays carried with lightning speed from galley to deck. Occasionally, she heard the heavy splash of bodies as the braver ones jumped from the boat's roof into the olive-green waters below. It was heady, and despite herself, Scarlett was caught up in the rising excitement as the boat gently swayed against a light breeze.

Seated to her right was a girl from the UK called Alice. She was tall and slim, with beautiful red hair and a calm voice, as though everyone around her was slightly less intelligent than herself. Scarlett had spotted Alice on first arriving and – noticing she too was alone – sat next to her immediately. Alice had her legs tucked neatly under her, nose turned up as others walked past.

But Scarlett didn't find this off-putting. Maybe it was Alice's curiosity. As they talked, Alice didn't pry but was interested, and shared snippets of her life story without rabbiting on like most people when they've been drinking on a boat in the sun all afternoon. For Scarlett, it was light relief, considering she knew no one and could not make an excuse to leave until the boat docked.

A man with a booming voice stood and clinked a spoon against a glass. He had a red face and a beer belly, a pink-checked dress shirt stretched tight across what appeared to be a hairy stomach. His cheeks wobbled as he spoke.

"We are gathered here today…" he started.

Everyone laughed and told him to sit down and shut up.

Scarlett asked Alice who he was. Alice replied, in that smooth, soft voice, that he was Mark Bignell, the owner of the boat, a long-time Hong Kong banker. He loved to throw lavish parties and was very generous with his money. He was infamous for once being caught red-handed in leathers at an S&M dungeon in Central Hong Kong, a place the police had raided after a tip-off that the occupants were heavily involved in illegal drug use. Naturally, they were. It was all over the papers. Mark Bignell was married with three teenage children.

"But Johnny knew people who helped him," Alice explained with a slight smirk.

"And who is Johnny?"

Alice pointed. "Be careful," she said. "I'm serious."

Alice could be helpful. Very helpful.

"Who invited you here today?" Alice asked with a vague wave of her hand around the crowd.

"My new boss, Vivian." Scarlett tried not to blush. She reminded herself that she was lucky enough to get the job as an executive at Vivian's highly regarded PR company. "She's been very… helpful. With information. About Hong Kong, I mean. I knew nothing when I got here. Nothing and no one. It's… amazing."

Alice had offered a small smile, her eyes lingering on Scarlett's, before glancing away.

The party roared into life, with a rising frenzy that was palpable with every passing hour. By dusk, there were some who could barely stand, grappling with railings and benchtops as the boat keened and rolled back to Sai Kung Harbour. The waiters still served canapés with patient smiles, the music pounded and thumped along the polished teak deck, fine wine flowed like water from a fountain and some of the younger girls in bikinis were dancing on the bow. Scarlett felt her head might explode, but it was now or never.

She could see that he was a little drunk for sure. But he had his wits about him. He kept his gaze steady as he talked and his voice was not raised three octaves, as was the others'. He was steady on his feet despite the choppy waves.

Scarlett watched as he leant against a railing near the stern, a quieter spot away from the throbbing speakers. The girl talking to him was tanned and petite, with long, light brown hair, loosely plaited. Scarlett thought it best to hang back for a bit and sip at her drink. The cocktail was sickly-sweet and she felt a wave of nausea. She'd already had too much to drink as it was and, being racked with nerves, had barely eaten. Maybe now was not the right moment after all. She needed a sign. That, or go home and try another time, although the thought was depressing.

Singing started from behind her. The boisterous, rousing bellowing of football stadiums. *I love you, baby, and if it's quite all right, I need you, baby!* They were oblivious as they shoved and pushed against Scarlett, heading for some other section of this massive floating party boat, a junk, summer's favourite day out in Hong Kong. She felt a wash of something ice-cold drip down her right arm, the spilled contents from one of the singer's sticky cocktails. She wiped at it, glad for the distraction from standing there alone in a sea of social animals.

In the comparative quiet after they moved away, a seagull cried and Scarlett turned to watch it sail above the thundering music and off into the perfect nothingness of a clouding sky. Scarlett wondered if she too would one day be able to do the same, to find that kind of peace.

"You okay?"

And there he was, standing over her, smelling of cigar smoke and gin, or was it some kind of exotic bottled scent? Scarlett felt her pulse race as she automatically inhaled. The combination was strangely exhilarating. For all the times leading up to this – when she thought she would have to feign happiness – she surprised herself by beaming the most warm and genuine of smiles.

Scarlett nodded and said yes, laughed her throaty laugh. She introduced herself and he took her hand in his. The heat flowed from her arms up to her cheeks. The heavy late-afternoon sun beat down. The music faded into the background.

Johnny didn't take his eyes off hers, and Scarlett felt a cold rush of panic rise from her stomach to her temples.

It was, she later thought, as though he knew too.

CHAPTER THREE

Central Psychology, Hong Kong.

Five months later.

"I hope I'm not late."

Carolyn Burnside looked up from the papers on her desk and took in the pleasing sight before her. A tailored, charcoal-grey suit, white shirt and a navy tie being loosened as he walked, as though arriving home to a loving wife.

He headed for the lounge chair facing Carolyn's desk and sat slowly before lifting his gaze to make direct eye contact. Lightly tanned, with just the acceptable amount of laugh lines for a man she guessed was in his late forties, Carolyn thought all her Christmases had come at once.

"Hello, Mr Humphries. How are you?" she said, repressing a desire to flirt a little. His easy, masculine manner was hard to resist. "Weather cold enough for you? Hope you didn't have to travel far to get here."

He leant back in his chair and pointed out the window in the direction of Victoria Harbour. "Work right across the road. Grabbed my usual chicken and quinoa salad from Oliver's before coming over and the queue was a little longer than I expected, so…" Carolyn blanched internally. *Quinoa. Since when did men not eat old-fashioned carbs?* She'd been divorced two years now and still no luck. "But, yes," he folded his hands over each other on his lap, "this is the coldest winter I've experienced for some time in this city."

She nodded. "Don't I know it? Been here since 1994. Came over from the US to work at the university. And I don't recall anything like this."

He smiled. His teeth were white and uniform.

"I arrived here around then, too; early 1995 I landed." He sat forward and pulled a deadpan expression. "You can call me FILTH."

She laughed. FILTH was an acronym from the old days of British expatriates in Hong Kong – *Failed in London, try Hong Kong.*

"I doubt that, Mr Humphries."

"Well," he jokingly raised one brow, "let's hope not."

They took each other in, both nodding slowly. Johnny uncrossed one leg and slowly recrossed it over the other, wincing a little as he did.

"Are you okay?" Carolyn said.

He shrugged. "Not really."

"I'm sorry to hear that." She glanced at her notebook. "Now. What's brought you here this afternoon?"

He sighed deeply. "Well. I'm in a bit of pain, to be honest."

She frowned.

"I am actually far from fine." Carolyn watched him carefully. He bowed his head, glancing at his hands, two fists he was clenching and unclenching. She noticed he was wearing a signet ring on his pinkie finger. "But it's not really me I'm here about. Well..." He relaxed back into his seat. "It affects me, so, selfishly, I am here about me."

Carolyn sucked on a mint to keep her in the present, a trick she'd been taught at some conference or other.

"It's my girlfriend. My partner, I suppose they say these days. We live together," Johnny said and looked away. But still, Carolyn could see tears welling. "First time I've ever lived with a woman." His hand shot up and he rubbed his chin. "I know what you're thinking. How can a man of my age never have lived with a woman before?"

"Okay."

She waited. Johnny composed himself.

"So I am… Was… Well, let's say it took me a while to grow up. I got bored easily. God knows what I was looking for, but anyway…"

"Well, at least you're honest about it," Carolyn replied.

Johnny offered her a little smile back.

"Scarlett is quite emotional."

"I see," Carolyn said, while adding notes to the pad in front of her.

Johnny shook his head. "It's more than that. For weeks, she's been taking prescription drugs. Her behaviour has become wildly erratic. I don't even know why. One minute, she'll be watching me like a hawk, the next, sneaky and distant. I mean, I've said she doesn't have to worry about money, if she wants to get another job, but she says it's not the job; that she's struggling with some demons from the past. But she won't tell me what they are! How can I help?"

Johnny was almost out of breath. He flung an arm in the air, then pushed a perfectly neat fringe from his forehead.

"She's hardly ever home. Her best friend, Alice – who used to be a good friend of mine – won't tell me anything. And just recently, I found out that Scarlett's taking pills from some dodgy chemist."

Carolyn reddened slightly. She regularly bought sleeping tablets from Faldo chemist down the road. No prescription required. How else was she supposed to sleep, now that her husband of twenty-five years had run off with the music teacher from their son's school?

"Then last night, out of the blue," Johnny continued, "she… she kicked me in the shin. Twice. When I tried to… you know, get the pills away from her."

He reached into his briefcase beside his chair and pulled

out a small bottle of medication: Tranquid. *That's a new one*, thought Carolyn.

"She punched me on the shoulders when I lifted her to the bed to calm down. Then she kicked out at me. I've got huge bruises all over my thighs and lower back."

Johnny started rolling up a trouser leg to show Carolyn what he described as two angry, purple bruises. Carolyn tried to focus on the garish-looking bruises rather than the slender curve of his calf muscle.

He rolled the trouser back down. "They're quite sore, as you can imagine. I was going to report it to the police this morning I was so angry with her. It's… it's…"

He fished for something inside his jacket and unfolded a piece of paper. "Look. Then I found this note. This morning, I left for work and realised halfway down the Peak that I'd left my second phone at home, the one I use when I'm in China. My driver raced us back up and when I got inside, it was quiet."

Carolyn tried to picture his house on the Peak and her mind wandered to a lavish spread in *House and Garden* magazine. She'd love to see it. *Focus, Carolyn.* She moved the mint to the other side of her mouth.

"The maid said Scarlett had just left, and then I walked up to our bedroom to get my phone. Next to my side of the bed was an empty cup of tea, the cup Scarlett always uses. Very old, thin china, with some kind of Australian bush bird hand-painted on it. She's very territorial of that cup."

Carolyn leant forward and took the note from Johnny's outstretched hand. She squinted at the piece of paper. In exaggerated, rounded handwriting, the numbers *140375* had a bold line through them. Then under that, the words *Ask B?*

Johnny rubbed at his chin again.

"Where was the note?"

"Screwed up, on my side of the bed."

"Why'd you look at it?"

"Pardon?"

"Why'd you read it?"

Johnny blinked a few times and shook his head a little.

"With the way she's been acting, I just had some kind of… feeling. Does that make sense? You know how you hear about people sensing something's up and then they check their partner's phone and, bam, there's a message from the husband's lover. You know the story."

"Sure do."

"I mean, what the hell is all this supposed to mean? I know that's my birthdate, but so what?"

Carolyn made a *tsk-tsk* noise. So far, the story was quite unusual. She had female clients come in and talk of physical attacks and strange behaviour, but handsome, tall and well-dressed men? This was a first for her. She felt a stab of admiration that he was admitting to the seriousness of it. She took another long suck on her mint.

"The thing is, the note is not important. What is, however, is what she did to you. And what you do next. Because you've got to see this for what it is. Abuse. Plain and simple."

He nodded and glanced out the window. The heating must've been too warm as his cheeks had flushed pink above his stiff white collar.

"Johnny." He jerked his head back to look directly at her. "Tell me more about you. Take your time."

Carolyn wrote most of it down: *Only child of a short-lived romance between aristocratic entrepreneur and Chinese mother. Had little contact with father. Brought up by mother, father paid for best schools. No contact with father. Johnny now in finance.*

As he talked, Carolyn ran it over in her head. She felt he was real, but you never knew. He looked real, smelled real and he was holding back what appeared to be real tears. But there was something more, something she couldn't quite put her finger on. Having said that, Carolyn reminded herself, it was too early to be diagnosing, if at all.

Carolyn kept writing. *No siblings. Seems largely negative*

about father but loved his mother. Both deceased. Carolyn paused as she wrote his name again, this time with a question mark next to it. Johnny talked, his eyes averted to the window and trained on the middle distance. *Johnny Humphries. Johnny Humphries. NAME FAMILIAR? Check.*

* * *

THREE WEEKS EARLIER

Scarlett had been doing laps in the limestone-bordered swimming pool at the bottom of the garden. The cold didn't bother her. It never had. She had swum almost every day in the sweeping grounds of her childhood harbourside home in Sydney's eastern suburbs, no matter the temperature. There was some brief talk from a sports teacher about her trying out for a semi-professional swimming team, but Scarlett didn't swim for the competition. She swam to be alone with her thoughts.

She surfaced and felt the sudden cold rush of crisp morning air. Her ears stung in the breeze as she dried off, but the shock of the icy wind was invigorating, and she smiled to herself as she watched the sampans puttering on the melee of Aberdeen Harbour below. There was, she often told people, no better way to get you going at the start of the day. Every bad thought, every moody dream, every worry could be erased after thrashing through cold water. And after her behaviour the night before, she needed a bit of a mind cleanse.

In the kitchen window, high above the garden, Scarlett noticed the maid, Lily, peering towards her, frowning as usual, and most likely wondering why the hell someone would choose to swim outside when the temperature had barely reached ten degrees. Scarlett raised a hand to wave at her. Lily immediately motioned for Scarlett to come inside before making elaborate gestures that Scarlett took to mean her breakfast was ready.

"I'm coming!" she called out, running on tiptoes up the stairs, through the games room underneath the house and into the cool winding internal staircase that led to the hum of the main house. She stopped outside Johnny's office and peered around the heavy timber door. She'd been in Hong Kong for nearly five months now, living with Johnny for a month. She was feeling time slipping away from her.

Think, Scarlett, think.

"Ma'am Scarlett? Your phone is beeping!"

"Coming!"

My own mother didn't even care for me like Lily does, Scarlett mused yet again, as she entered the soothing warmth of her heated hallway. *Having Lily in the house keeps me sane.*

As it had been in recent days, the table was heaving with breakfast cereals and tropical fruits, jugs of fresh juice, toast in a silver wire rack. There was a pot of coffee and another of tea, a jug of milk, a bowl of yoghurt, a butter dish, side plates, bowls – all yellow and white to blend harmoniously with the eggshell blue of the linen. Through the glass French doors to her right, a weak sun settled across the table, creating a calming halo around Scarlett and her feast as she sat down to read the *South China Mail*.

"I won't have time to eat all this!" Scarlett called to Lily, as she clanged pans in the kitchen. "Did Johnny eat anything before he left?"

"You worked too hard!" Lily said from the hallway that led to the kitchen, a room Scarlett entered rarely and only in the middle of the night. "You won't have babies! You will become old and get sick and die!"

Scarlett raised her eyes to the ceiling and sighed. "I don't want babies, Lily. You know that."

Lily crashed a few more pans together. Scarlett checked her phone, saw a message from Alice about a dinner that weekend and closed it down. She glanced at the front page of the newspaper. The Hong Kong democracy movement was the front-page headline again. Hong Kong was once under British rule, but since 1997, it was returned to China under the One Country, Two Systems arrangement. Hong Kong still had some autonomy and its residents more rights. However, alarm over the voting process for the Chief Executive of Hong Kong as well as now-scrapped plans for a controversial extradition law between China and Hong Kong meant that regular protests rocked the streets for months.

Scarlett took a keen interest in such events, particularly when it came to China. She'd been intrigued by politics once she left school and had gained a degree in political science at university. Her old boyfriend was particularly involved in student-led protests and she often went with him for support.

She turned her gaze back to the news article. Anything to take her mind off her current problems.

On page three there was talk of more protests, ones much like the Umbrella Revolution in late 2014. Back then, thousands of democracy supporters had taken over downtown Central for two months. To Scarlett, it showed they had a voice and were not afraid to express it.

But it seriously displeased Johnny. As he explained, keeping Hong Kong ticking along nicely – the way it always had – was vital to his business.

A minute or so later, Scarlett's phone beeped again, this time a message from Johnny: *Can we have dinner tonight? What's going on? I just want to talk.*

Scarlett smiled, her lips tightly pressed together. She tapped away at her phone. It rang a few times before a woman answered.

"You were right," Scarlett whispered.

"Good to hear." The woman sniffed a bitter little laugh. "It was a matter of finding the right balance."

"I can't believe this is happening."

"It's for a greater good."

"See you soon."

They said their goodbyes, just as Lily walked in carrying a platter with bacon and eggs, grilled tomatoes and hash browns.

"Oh God!" Scarlett gasped.

"You're too skinny. Too stressed. Eat some proper food. Maybe you ask Mr Johnny to eat with you. Okay?" Scarlett frowned.

"Have you noticed?" She picked at some blueberries. "Of course you have."

"Love is like that sometimes. Now eat. You're like a sulking baby. Okay? And put on warm clothes and dry your hair. You will catch cold!" Lily smiled and patted Scarlett's shoulder. Scarlett knew it was a gesture to show she felt sorry for her. "Mr Johnny has never had a lady live with him. You're the first. You should talk to him. *Talk*. Okay?"

Scarlett smiled graciously at Lily as she picked at a few berries.

"I will. Thank you. *Again*." Lily went to walk away, but Scarlett cleared her throat. "Lily?"

"Yes, ma'am?" She folded her hands across her front.

"Have you ever, you know, seen what Johnny puts in that safe of his, under his drawer? In his study?"

"Not me." Lily shook her head, reaching down to take a side plate dotted with a few fruit pips. "I never touch anything that isn't mine. Okay?"

"I know!" Scarlett reached out and gently patted her arm. "Just wondering. You know. Men. Secrets." She tried to giggle.

Lily gave her a wan smile and backed off.

"Thank you for a delicious breakfast."

Lily threw a hand in the air as if to say no problem.

It was important to Scarlett to be grateful for those who really cared. The burden of her cold and confusing childhood still weighed heavily on her shoulders. She tried not to dwell on it, but it came upon her in fits and starts, like a sudden stormy breeze before the rain starts.

"Where's Mum?" she had often asked her father, her voice echoing against the marble tiles in their cavernous living room. "Not home," he'd say, refusing to look at her. "When

will she be back?" Scarlett had tugged at his sleeve. "Never.
Now go to school and study. There's nothing else."

Upstairs, Scarlett riffled through Johnny's bedside table. There was the old black-and-white photo of him with his friend Brian, their arms placed protectively around each other's waists and standing in front of what looked like the ruins of an old brick house. It was not good quality and their faces seemed almost whited out with time. On the back of the picture, Scarlett read, again, the words *Brian and Me. Free at Last.* She walked to her desk, grabbed a piece of paper from her notebook and wrote the same numbers she'd tried before, but in a different way, *140375*, then angrily crossed it out. *Johnny's birthdate*.

"Shit." Scarlett had already tried that, among others. She was looking in the wrong place. And she knew it. Maybe Bobby could help? Like she did at the office, she wrote his initials down as a reminder on the same piece of paper, then realised even that was a long shot. He was always so busy. It'd take her ages to find a night for him to meet her. She screwed up the note before shoving it in her dressing-gown pocket. Or so she thought. It was time to get to work. Scarlett threw the gown over the bed on Johnny's side by the window and forgot about the note.

* * *

Johnny turned his head to take a good long look at Carolyn. She was finishing her notes and sitting very straight; dancer straight. Her dirty blonde hair was tied in some kind of messy bun with a bright pink silk scarf wrapped around it, her skin fair and unfreckled, hazel eyes warm and thoughtful, which was lucky for someone in the counselling game. She was about his age, he guessed. Hard to tell these days. He'd never heard of her until two days ago, until he bit the bullet and did a quick online search of the city's best Central-based shrinks.

Maybe he'd said enough. The notes were taking her ages.

"Sorry," Johnny said. "Have I gone on a bit?"

"No. Please. I like to be thorough, that's all. Talk away. That's what you're here for, right?"

Scarlett had changed his womanising ways, he said with a small upturn of the corner of his mouth. She had drive, wit, charm, beauty and a genuine kindness to top it all off. He thought they could make it. But now, her dark mood was threatening to break their happy union.

"Johnny," Carolyn said softly, "it's great that you've come to see me, but I think if Scarlett is the one having the problem, then she probably needs the help first. It'd be a good idea to get her in to see me. Here."

Johnny's mouth opened and closed. He looked at his feet.

"Yes," he said, but Carolyn could tell it was said reluctantly. "I suppose you're right. Maybe I'm... overreacting. I should've taken my colleague's advice and just walked away from her."

He hung his head in his hands.

"I am so, so sorry," Carolyn said. "I can see how distressing this all is for you. I feel that Scarlett really is the one who should seek help. Of course, in the meantime, if it happens again, you must take a different kind of action."

"I don't know." He shook his head. "She's unapproachable these days."

He sighed, ran his fingers through his hair and sat back heavily in the chair.

"I mean it's a bit silly, really. We met only a few months ago. She was so new in town she didn't have a place to live. Almost immediately, she was resident in Chez Humphries. I mean..." He pushed out a curt laugh.

"These things happen, sometimes." Carolyn knew only too well how chemical attraction robbed you of logic, which was why she was now single.

"Not to me. Normally, I got bored. The girls wanted me to commit. I ended up pushing them away."

This piqued Carolyn's interest.

"But with Scarlett? Why have you stayed with her and not the other women?"

Just the mention of her name and his face lit up.

"She was... *is*... different. She needed me, at first. I mean, she landed here from Sydney to work for Vivian. All she could afford at first was a single bedsit in a cockroach-infested walk-up, you know, grates on the windows and metal doors, like an institution. I met her on a junk, something Vivian had invited her to. She'd just got a job at Stealth, Vivian's PR firm. She had absolutely no idea about where to live or ID cards or whatnot. And I, I suppose I enjoyed being her... her saviour, so to speak, although saying it out loud is embarrassing." He glanced at his hands. "But she started to pull away from me, only after a few weeks of moving in. That was – and I mean this in all honesty – a real first for me."

"I see," Carolyn said, her internal warning system firing. "And how did you handle this... pulling away?"

"Well, it made me want her more, I suppose. I did whatever I could to please her. But then, it's got worse. Well, with the moods anyway. She goes out without me, won't even sleep with me anymore. She asked me to be patient and I have. But, you know, I am a man." He blushed slightly at this. "Is it me?"

Carolyn shook her head.

"We all know that saying, as clichéd as it may be... It takes two to tango."

* * *

A bout of intense drilling outside Carolyn's office finally stalled. She relaxed; unclenched her jaw. A waft of lavender from her oil burner drifted under her nose just in time. After she'd hit her late forties a few years back, the old nerves had become even more easily jangled.

It was unsurprising really. One of the reasons she'd studied psychology all those years ago in South Carolina had been to get to the root of this jittery side to her character, alongside an innate interest in the workings of the mind. A sense that there had to be something more drove her curiosity and when it bit, she couldn't let go.

Turned out being a psychologist was a good career choice. When immersed in clients' issues, she felt a smugness that was strangely calming. Carolyn wasn't blind to the fact this no doubt had something to do with how she'd handled her glass-half-empty mother throughout her childhood, which had given Carolyn plenty of emotional intelligence when it came to helping others. That, in turn, made her then feel better herself.

Okay. She hadn't had it exactly tough as a child. Her family were middle-class, she'd gone to a good school, her bedroom was the requisite pink and purple and they once had a poolside holiday to Maui (hula dancers at sunset, piña coladas, robotically joyous staff) when she was fifteen. But overall, her father was always busy as a medical rep in cities that weren't theirs. When he was around, he'd peck them both on the cheek and, after simple niceties that Carolyn worked out were for her benefit, watched the news while nursing neat vodka and occasionally saying, "atta boy" at the sight of anything to do with Ronald Reagan. Her mother silently read faded Harold Robbins paperbacks at the dining table in a dim, yellow light, Carolyn as familiar with the hiss of a cigarette tip being heavily dragged by her mother's rouge-red lips as she was with the gaping silence that filled every timber crevice.

At school, Carolyn had a couple of basketball pals and, not irregularly, some male attention that ended with a clumsy fumble of her burgeoning bosom and a promise to call.

The first real guy who came into her life was Greg, a former high school dropout. After a few years working as a tennis coach, he'd got it together to graduate before Carolyn met him in his first week as a gloating mature college student. Greg had Mick Jagger hips and a sun-kissed face that set off glow-white teeth. When he slunk towards Carolyn in ripped denim jeans, she mistook attraction for a possible soulmate, or some other such drivel, as she thought of it now.

Not long after they met, Greg had told her of his visions of tropical adventure, far, far away from mundane suburban life. It was music to her ears. As Carolyn had only ever experienced Hawaii, she imagined canoodling under date palms, culturally rich dinner dances and flaxen-haired children sharing great half-moons of pink watermelon on sweeps of thick green lawn. Marrying young to a slightly older man who promised international thrills was a no-brainer.

Before what was to become her last Christmas living in the US, Greg had applied for a job as a fitness instructor in Hong Kong and before you could say "kettlebell", there they were, Greg puffing up his chest like a prize peacock at a new chain of fitness studios, while Carolyn found work as a trainee counsellor for a GP clinic. It surprised them both, how much they took to the crazy work-work-work buzz of Hong Kong life. Later, she supported Greg as he retrained as a PE teacher and it wasn't long before Greg took to other things as well, like his female colleagues. Basically, Greg let her down and she had told him to leave when she found out. Leaving him was another no-brainer. Still, she had two great kids, so Carolyn heeded her own psyche advice and kept busy. Time would heal all wounds, et cetera, et cetera.

She put down her pen and looked at Johnny.

Despite his distress, Carolyn noticed he still seemed contained, not a hair out of place, a healthy sheen to his cheeks still visible above sharp cheekbones.

Carolyn tapped her pen. A shiver had run down her spine for reasons she couldn't fathom.

"Johnny. May I ask... Why are you here? With me, seeking help? I mean, I would say – from what you've told me – that you've had a lot of experience when it comes to women. So why now, with me, here? I get you have some bruising and that might have tipped you over the edge, but..."

He waited. He looked to the ceiling. He lowered his eyes to

hers and they stayed very, very still. A coffee machine gargled in the background. Carolyn's wind chime dinged pointlessly.

"I… um," he started. "I suppose," he was still slightly flushed, "I need someone to talk to. I don't have any true… friends. Only Phil, my business partner. And he isn't someone you'd take advice from." He slapped a hand on his thigh. "And it's because of my mother. It's what she would have wanted." He rolled his shoulders up and down. "To be honest, I think I've changed recently. I'm sick of my way of life. It's been quite troublesome at times. And my mother wanted me to have a family. But she's dead, so let's move on." He flicked his right hand as though to banish a dark thought. "Do you recommend, Carolyn, that I… stay with Scarlett? Or that I forget all about her?"

The question hung in the air as his lips continued to move, but for a few seconds, no sound came out. "I've never sought help from a professional before, but I do feel it's time. It's strange. I truly loved my mother, crazy bat she could be, but I know she would want me to be happy, to get married and have children. She wanted what was best for me on all fronts and…" He turned his gaze, yet just before he did, Carolyn saw a shadow darken his eyes. "Well, I thought it would be Scarlett."

Whatever doubts Carolyn had harboured that he was speaking the truth began to fade. She leaned closer towards him, resting on her elbows, the waft of peppermint and lavender hovered between them.

"Only stay with Scarlett if you feel you are safe, but please bring her to see me. If she refuses, take a stronger line. Tell her she can't stay with you if she doesn't seek help. It might just scare her into wanting to make a change. But the bottom line is, I would not recommend you stay with a woman who is taking drugs, hurting you and refusing to change, nor love you respectfully."

He smiled, lips pressed together. Satisfied? Carolyn couldn't tell.

"Think you can do that?" she asked.

"Of course," he said. "I'll discuss it with her – calmly – as soon as I can."

"I applaud your determination. I'm sure most would simply walk away."

Johnny clasped his hands together. "I only give up on something I never really wanted that badly in the first place."

"Interesting." She nodded, sucking in her cheeks a little.

The drilling outside roared into life. Carolyn's stomach flipped. She would never get used to the intensity of that constant hammering.

Johnny stood, very suddenly and stiffly. Carolyn offered her hand. He followed her lead.

"Just quickly," she said, "you ever been on TV or in the news? Your name sounds…"

"Oh, no," he said, sharply. "I'm out of the public eye. It's one of those names, so I'm told. Sounds so snootily British, doesn't it? Kind of verging on being a bit like Rupert Bugger-Bollocks, or something or other."

She laughed. "Yeah, you're right." She steered him from the office. "It was nice to meet you. Good luck and please come and see me with Scarlett. I'm sure you can find a solution. And take care of those bruises."

The two shook hands.

* * *

Carolyn's assistant, Koffee, ran out from her desk to shake Johnny's hand as he headed for the lifts. Like many other young people in Hong Kong, Koffee's real name was something else – Fang, to be exact – but she had taken an English word she liked the sound of and modified it for fun. But despite her caffeinated nickname, Koffee normally scowled over her desk and shuffled her feet noisily, as though walking was a real hassle. A part-time psychology student at University of Hong Kong, Koffee recently told Carolyn that it wouldn't be long before she was putting up her own sign on the door of the office. Carolyn understood that with her own professional qualifications on the horizon, Koffee had grown tired of being the assistant, but Johnny's presence seemed to change Koffee's mood. Carolyn smiled cynically as she rearranged some papers on her desk.

When a client left her room, Carolyn often felt their energy still permeating the pale-blue walls that she'd painted one weekend with Koffee two weeks after her marriage broke up. *Fresh start, fresh paint!*

She could still sense her client's emotions vibrating within the tall polished timber bookshelves, filtering like smoke around the spiked indoor potted plants placed carefully on hardcover tomes with names such as *Heal Thyself* and *The Anger Within*.

As the battery-operated water fountain trickled into a pool of shimmery pebbles on her desk, she sat back and let it all sink in. Carolyn hoped she had helped the man, she genuinely did. She was sure she could get through to him and his partner, if they continued to seek her advice. However, as always with couples, she knew there would be a lot more to it, and she started writing a few more notes: *Girlfriend can't cope, takes over-the-counter drugs, gets aggressive. He still loves her – possibly a control freak. Need to see GF to confirm the story. Check name, or...?*

Carolyn had thirty minutes between clients and wanted to get some groceries. Standing to leave, she glanced at his name once more. Was she imagining things?

Koffee tapped on her door. Carolyn called her in as she fished about in her oversized handbag for her purse.

"There's something up with the lock on the bathroom door," Koffee whined. "I've cut my finger twice just trying to get out of there." She sucked on her pinkie and frowned. Carolyn was lost in deep thought. "Anyway. Here's the files on the next client."

"Thanks, Fang."

"Koffee."

"No thanks," Carolyn replied. "No caffeine for me after 3pm."

"No. I mean my name is now *Koffee*."

"Sure," Carolyn replied as Koffee walked away. "Sorry about your finger!" she called out. "I'll make it up to you!"

Carolyn rubbed at her eyes. *Johnny Humphries. Johnny Humphries. Finance guy. Eurasian.* Her obsessive desire to know everything about everyone was kicking in big time. She sat back down. A quick Google search showed two recent business news stories about a bankrupt car-parts manufacturing group; nothing unusual there. There was a LinkedIn profile for his firm's website and a few photos. After page two – and realising she had clicked on a Johnny Humphries who resided in Alabama – she closed it down.

That was that, Carolyn reasoned, taking out a red pen: *Fix bathroom door. Buy Koffee chocolate to make up for cut finger.*

She felt a little hot under the collar and loosened the scarf around her hair.

And then it struck her.

She knew exactly why she knew his name.

"Koffee… you're a genius," she muttered under her breath.

CHAPTER FOUR

Central, Hong Kong Island.

Outside, Johnny smiled to himself a little, in the vain hope it would make him feel better, then headed north towards Victoria Harbour, stuffing his cold hands into his pockets. As always, he felt a surge of confidence as he tackled the busy streets of this island city of just 80.4 square kilometres. The city rose from flatlands at the edge of a world-renowned harbour, overlooked by a mountainous rise known as the Peak, where he now lived. As a child, Johnny could never have imagined such luxury.

He was comforted by how well he knew such an impressive place as Hong Kong, one so different from the dour, mud-brown streets of his childhood. Every crowded path, every looming office tower, narrow concrete step, musty laneway, incense-scented temple, frantic street crossing. Furthermore, the inherent spirit of Hong Kong people would often take him by surprise. Just when he thought another large glass door to a gleaming building would be slammed by the person in front before he could reach it, a smart young office guy would be holding one open. Once, Johnny dropped his wallet outside a warehouse building in Chai Wan after some dull art-installation cocktail party and the day after, the police rang. It had been handed in. There was HK$5,000 in cash in that wallet. Not a penny was taken.

Yes, there was the harried impatience on the crowded

streets at lunchtime, but that was part of the city's no-nonsense attitude. Hong Kong people got things done. And its co-existent menagerie of diverse and educated people made him proud. You could be whoever you wanted to be here, and no one cared who you were before, as long as you contributed. Johnny felt a flash of remorse and pushed it aside. He was good at that.

As he walked, Johnny instead reminded himself that these streets were as etched into his being as the lines on his palm. The city's haphazard twists and turns overwhelmed new visitors. Yet to Johnny, his familiarity with its carnival-like craziness ensured a sense of control. He liked it that way. The problem was, since Scarlett had changed, he could feel his foundations starting to slip, as though he didn't know himself as well as he thought. Was he really in total control of his destiny, the way he'd always assumed? Perhaps that was arrogant. Actually, of course it was.

But in the past, this belief had worked. Every risk he'd taken had gone his way. Somehow. Now, he wasn't getting what he wanted, and nothing he did seemed to change that fact.

Despite the cold, his face flushed and he rubbed at his eyes to remind himself that this too shall pass.

Minutes later, Johnny boldly entered the hushed lobby of Berwick and Chan Investments on the fifth floor of Alexander House, a few minutes' walk from Carolyn's office. He winked at the receptionist.

"Blossom," he said, with a little grin.

"Mr Humphries," she giggled into her hand.

She had a thing for him and he knew it. Having said that, they all did. May as well enjoy it.

He sat down at his broad mahogany desk and buzzed the receptionist.

"Bloss. Can you please see if Phil is in? Ask him to pop his ugly mug in here for a minute?"

He sat back, surveyed the expansive view across the

harbour to the melee of Tsim Sha Tsui and folded his arms out behind his head.

"Yo." Phil stuck his head around the glass door. He was short, bald and chubby with a neatly trimmed, salt-and-pepper goatee that he often stroked lovingly. Phil walked with a waddle and had grown up minutes from where Johnny spent his early childhood. "'Ow'd it go?"

"Fine," Johnny replied with a sigh, motioning for Phil to sit down. "As fine as something like that can, I suppose." He looked at his hands. "To be honest, I never thought it would come to this."

Phil guffawed. "Who are you and what've you done with Johnny?"

"Thanks, mate. As always."

They sat in a brief, comfortable silence.

"To be honest," Phil finally spoke, "I never thought I'd see the day you sought help about a woman."

"I never should have mentioned it to you." Johnny half-smiled.

Johnny had met Phil, now in his mid-fifties, the day Johnny had arrived from London. Johnny had landed his dream job working for Phil's then boss, a successful businessman in the hotel and bar industry named Albert Chung, who had a cracking team and was revered for his business acumen. Phil was Chung's "minder", a former cop who had become a kind of assistant/heavy/security advisor. Phil helped simultaneously fend off bribes that the food and beverage industry invariably had to endure and also liaise with them to keep them on side. But mostly, Phil was Chung's bully when they were dealing with difficult clients who thought they knew more than Chung.

Chung had initially loved Phil for his tenacity and inside ties to the force, but over time, he eventually tired of Phil's erratic personal problems, namely, cocaine. Chung sacked Phil two years after Johnny arrived.

Still, Phil and Johnny had formed a kind of bond, initially

due to the fact they were both from the same part of London, but it was also a sense-of-humour thing, combined with a desire to make a fortune any way they could. After Chung sacked Phil all those years ago, Johnny watched him descend into an even worse personal situation and he decided to help him out.

Johnny was planning on starting up Berwick as it was, and thought Phil could be a good sidekick, so he brought him along for the ride. Plus, by that point they both hated Chung, albeit for different reasons. Phil now acted as Johnny's eyes and ears, great for being the tough-talking buffoon, particularly handy when the client was not exactly transparent. Phil did great research too, never asked questions and, despite his love for illicit substances, never missed a day at work. He knew a lot about Johnny – a rarity – and never said a word. Still, it hadn't always been easy , and keeping an eye on Phil had caused a few problems over the years.

"I liked the psychologist, actually," Johnny said. "Straight-talking Yank."

Phil was bored with the Scarlett talk. He cracked the knuckles on his right hand.

"Glad she helped," he muttered.

Johnny nervously checked his phone. *What is really up with Scarlett? Am I missing something here?*

"Don't mind me," Phil joked.

"Sorry. Got a few messages, mate. Be patient. I'm a busy man, remember?"

As Johnny pecked at his phone, Phil ranted about his current girlfriend, her annoying, overbearing mother and her habit of sucking her teeth.

"Honestly," Phil waffled, "I feel sick to the stomach. Is it legal to sew up the lips of your future mother-in-law?"

Johnny barely heard the rest. Deliberately. Phil was a good partner to have around, but he really was a bastard.

"Got to pay this, mate. Won't be a sec," Johnny said into his phone.

Phil – as always, trying to get a rise out of someone, or possibly simply unable to be still – reached across and picked up the square black bottle on Johnny's desk. Johnny's favourite bespoke scent. He'd worn it for so long it had become a part of him. It stayed on his desk like a good-luck charm. He never moved it. Sometimes, he could tell if Phil had had a go with it, a slight mark on the timber more visible if it wasn't put back perfectly in place. Funny the things you cared about when you had money, Johnny mused.

Phil removed the solid round lid with a dramatic flurry of his hands and liberally daubed it onto his wrists.

Johnny winced.

"Not *again*," Johnny said, frowning slightly. He'd hoped Phil would outgrow the desire to emulate him. But it reared its head every now and then.

"Hey. I've bought you endless bottles of this magic potion for your birthdays over the years. I always make sure you've got a full bottle."

"And we know that you always make sure to use it."

Phil sighed.

"I promise I won't do it again, sir. Just that you're sitting there and I'm waiting and, you know, *I'm a busy man and all that*."

"Sure, Phil. It's just, you know, let's move on. Put the bottle back, mate. There's a boy."

Phil bared his teeth in a broad, fake smile. "Fine with me."

Johnny placed his gold-encased phone down and turned to watch two large brown kites flying in wide-arced circles above the harbour. He loved this time of day in Hong Kong. Nearly dusk, the evening lights starting to flicker on the water, the promise of people, music, fine food. It never got boring. The city was alive, day and night. He could always, no matter what, find an escape. Johnny thought of Scarlett, the night they'd first met on that boat. Johnny hadn't seen her around town before. He'd been looking for something and someone who didn't have – he hoped – any preconceived notions about him or even the city itself, which wasn't easy. But most of all, she had something different about her, something almost ethereal. He thought he could do it, this long-term thing. But now it was all coming apart. And not because he wanted it to.

"We're different, men and women," Johnny said towards the window.

"No shit, Sherlock." Phil tapped the side of his temple with his index finger.

"You know what I mean," Johnny said with a forced smile.

Phil could be irritatingly basic, Johnny was again reminded. Not that he would ever show that this annoyed him. Phil had a truly nasty side that Johnny had seen first-hand. Many times.

"*You know what I mean*," Phil mimicked Johnny's accent, pinching his lips together as he spoke in a mock upper-class accent.

"You do that perfectly," Johnny smiled. "Pity you can't sound like that all the time, you low-life scum."

Phil blushed a little and the two laughed. Phil jerked his eyebrows up and down and tried to stay silent as Johnny mused on something private.

"You look worried, J," Phil said into the hovering silence. "And that's not a look I like. Waste your life worrying about crap that won't happen. Killed my old dad. I was stuck with an overworked mother, who's now dead from worry. Fat lot of good it did her." From his jacket he had pulled out a small plastic bag of white powder. He gave it a flourish and then placed it on Johnny's desk. "Come on. Dinner with Ken is like watching paint dry."

Johnny leaned forward to inspect it but sat back just as quickly. A big night out with Ken Chen – Phil's best mate and a part-time assistant in the office, if you could call it that – wasn't what he had in mind. Ken was born and bred in England to Chinese parents who'd also been born and bred in England. He didn't speak a word of Cantonese. He was British through and through. He had gone to public school, moved in the "right" circles and appeared to be working for

Berwick, but he never really had a head for business. He and Phil were peas in a pod, but Ken served no purpose for Johnny; he just quietly tolerated him. Ken had proved to be a weak link before. The less he was in the office, the better. In fact, being around him made Johnny's skin crawl. Besides, he was also hoping to have dinner with Scarlett.

"Not tonight, mate," Johnny said, swivelling to his left to pick up his phone again. "But if she cancels, I'll meet you at the Tequila Bar for a couple before dinner."

"Suit yourself," Phil sniffed. "Missing out, you are. You're going to be begging me for it later. Friday night and all that."

Johnny was getting impatient with Phil's mindless banter.

"By the way, I called you in here for a reason," Johnny said.

"Course, mate. Soz, as the kids say."

Johnny gave some brief advice about a client who had delayed the signing of a key document. Phil nodded a few times, daydreaming, Johnny assumed, about his first tequila slammer. Johnny watched him finger the plastic bag in his pocket, before he confirmed he would do what he could to get the document sorted.

"Sounds easy," Phil said with a forced chortle.

"Yes. Thanks, mate. Right up your street. Well, look, no offence, but got a few things going on. So get out, will you?" Johnny said, smiling to keep it jovial. "I'll speak to you tomorrow."

Phil sang a few off-key lines of Beyoncé's 'Crazy in Love', as he strolled out the door and down the hallway. Johnny couldn't help but smile, but then he noticed Ken rushing down the hallway, trying to catch up with Phil.

Johnny's phone rang.

"Hi," he said into the receiver. "Sure. Why?" He paused. "In person? I suppose." He nodded a few times. "Yes. Meet me outside Central Building in five minutes. We can walk. Don't have much time, though."

Just before he left, he riffled through his drawer, found an old Nokia phone with a pay-as-you-go SIM that hadn't been used. He dialled. A man answered.

"Old Miss V wants to meet," Johnny said.

"Hmmm." They fell silent for a few seconds. "Maybe it's time to go easy on her. She's been loyal and hard-working. She just wants her story to herself."

Johnny clicked his tongue. "Maybe not yet. I mean… you've got a point. But there's no rush. She's not going to actually do anything."

"I hope not," the other man said gruffly.

They hung up. Johnny shoved the phone into a plastic bag and placed it in his briefcase. He'd ditch the SIM later. Sometimes, he even threw away the phone, just for good measure.

* * *

Outside, Vivian was dressed in a soft grey coat that swamped her slim frame. In the early days, Johnny told her she reminded him of his mother, and Vivian felt a rising anxiety in her throat that stuck like a rock at the memory of the days when she thought he was her saviour.

Exposing her softer side was not Vivian's normal disposition. In her day-to-day life as the head of Stealth PR, she was a tigress, a powerhouse of planning, known for her focus and cool demeanour.

She steeled herself before turning to see Johnny saunter towards her. Just two old friends catching up.

Silently acknowledging each other, she and Johnny walked along Des Voeux Road, glimmering designer stores mirroring their every step, Vivian as tall as Johnny in her heels. Finally, they stopped, and he looked at Vivian.

"I just don't get it, Viv," Johnny said. She had a taut smile plastered across her delicate features. "She's so upset."

"It's quite simple. I told you." Vivian wiped at her eyes. She hoped Johnny couldn't tell if it was from the harbour wind; that they were real tears. "It was difficult, you know. Sacking her like that."

Johnny pumped his shoulders up and down a few times.

"Well. I suppose it had to be done. This is business." He looked suddenly very tired. "I know you would have kept her on, if I'd asked." Vivian knew he would have wanted to ask, but she also knew that he'd pushed it enough over the years as it was. And Johnny didn't really care if Scarlett had a job or not. Vivian was certain of that. It had ensured she'd settled in the city, but now she had Johnny to give her the *tai tai* life. It was laughable, really.

Vivian kept her gaze straight ahead.

"I know." She inhaled. "But I thought those days were over. You said years ago that by now, you would have—"

He nodded; raised a hand in acknowledgement.

"Listen. Sometimes, because of what happened in the past, we have to be careful how we tread. We were quite reckless in those days. You know that. I need an insurance policy. That's all."

Vivian firmly closed her perfectly applied red pout, afraid of what she might say. But she had to say something.

"Johnny, I have spent twenty years doing what you've asked."

They turned the corner. A sharp gust of toxin-scented wind shot down the narrow lane behind them. The harbour had become increasingly polluted. On certain days, its fame for being fragrant was far from the reality. Just now, Vivian felt like throwing herself in it. That's how bad her frustration had become.

"I don't understand, Johnny." She wanted to get this done with. "Don't you trust me anymore?"

He stopped walking and looked into the grey dome of sky above.

"I still have to be careful. That's all."

"But I'd like them back," she said through gritted teeth. "It still feels like I'm being… threatened."

They watched the passing parade of shiny Mercedes.

"But you're not," Johnny replied slowly. "You run your own show."

Vivian said nothing.

"Did you know that I'm trying with Scarlett? Actually trying? Never done that with a woman before. Getting help and all that. Not sure why. And then you went and sacked her. Maybe, if you take her back…?"

Vivian hugged her coat tighter around her waist. She knew this would happen and it gave her a brief burst of strength, enough to stay calm.

"Maybe." Vivian couldn't look him in the eye. She was, she realised, still scared of him. "But only if I have confirmation that you will return my things. So I can destroy them."

He shoved his hand in his trouser pockets and rocked back and forth on his heels as they waited for the lights to change.

"Really?" He said it with a fake smile, holding her elbow as they crossed.

She turned, only slightly. "Why," Vivian felt her teeth clench, "can't I have them back, without having to give in with Scarlett?"

"Is there a need for you to have them? I mean, surely it's best just forgotten."

Vivian bit her bottom lip.

"Like I said, I want to destroy them."

"But why? Rest assured, I'll never give you up if you're loyal to me. It's bad enough you've let Scarlett go. I mean, that's not the worst thing you could have done. But I know you have plenty of information in your head about things that very few other people do, so…"

Vivian stomped one foot against the cold.

"Oh, come on, Johnny. I'd hardly let it all out now."

The lights near the Mandarin Oriental changed. A tsunami of bodies threatened to engulf the road in front of them. Johnny bent down, gave Vivian's arm a good, tight squeeze and kissed her cheek.

"Viv. It's all going to be okay. We've all got what we wanted. The past is the past. Leave it at that. I'll get over you ditching Scarlett from Stealth, if you let me in on one little secret."

"Okay. Go on." She sighed inwardly.

"Is it me?" He looked straight ahead, as they walked. "Or is she the insane one? Do you think she'll leave me?"

Vivian was shocked.

"I mean," he continued, "what do you know about her? Who is she?"

Vivian cupped her chin in her hand and raised one eyebrow.

"I told you when you first met her that she's simply a young woman who came here to try her luck. I looked into her past. She's clean. No strings attached." Vivian paused. "But that's enough assistance from me. You've told me you won't help me out, so I'm sorry to say, I can't offer you any more either."

Johnny winked as he turned around.

Her lips parted as she watched him become swallowed up by the shadow of double-decker buses and delivery trucks.

Maybe he was right. Maybe she should leave it. Forget this crazy idea and live her comfortable, luxurious life.

But then, she thought better of it.

* * *

Johnny needed a drink and the soothing warmth of the Captain's Bar in the Mandarin Oriental was calling. The famous lobby bar was his favourite watering hole on earth. A stiff drink, a bit of jazz music and he'd be okay. He hoped. The truth was, the thrill had gone from his somewhat high-flying way of life. This desire to steer clear of the murkier elements of his past had started a couple of years ago and then, he'd met Scarlett. Loving her made him want to embrace his more conventional side. But now, even that was falling apart.

As always, the Captain's Bar was humming nicely. Just

the right amount of early buzz combined with a calm and cool sophistication, the kind of place in which, as a child growing up in East London, he dreamed of enjoying a quiet drink, like a real gentleman.

But as soon as he took a sip, there was a gentle tap on his shoulder.

Alice.

"Thought it was you."

He jumped, just a little.

"Hi. Wow. Alice. It's been ages."

"'Tis me. The one and only."

She was wearing a black jacket and skirt. The jacket was buttoned tight at the waist and a long gold chain had inched its way into rounded white flesh spilling from a cream blouse. As always when in office mode, Alice's pale red hair was pulled tight from her face into a fierce bun, giving her green-grey eyes a feline quality. They were either beautiful or menacing, depending on her mood.

"You here alone?" Johnny took a quick look behind her.

"Yes." She cocked her head to one side and gave him an uncharacteristic coy smile. "Got any good-looking friends coming along?"

"Not tonight, darling," he scoffed. "I'm all out of Hooray Henrys. There's been a run on them at Harvey Nicks."

She quickly changed her features.

"I'm only bloody joking," she said, sipping her champagne. "No need to get huffy." They fell silent. "What's wrong with you?"

He rubbed at his eyes.

"*You* ought to talk."

She sloshed her champagne this way and that.

"Well, you know, I'm in a good mood I suppose. No need to stay mad for ever."

Johnny felt a slight wash of relief. Alice was always cool with him. Had been for years.

"Sorry. I've just… I've just 'ad a gutful today."

Alice had a laugh like an ecstatic hyena. The three men and one elderly woman seated near them all turned to look as she squealed one out.

"'Ad a gutful? Is that *the* poshest man on earth, talking like the son of a shopkeeper? Whoops. Better not have any more whisky."

They'd known each other since they'd both first arrived in the city, but Alice could wind him up like no one else. She was clever – a talented linguist and a razor-sharp lawyer. But one minute, Alice had been his friend, the next, a stranger. When he mentioned it to Phil, he'd shrugged. Phil and Alice had never got on. Maybe in the beginning, but it was short-lived.

Johnny said nothing. He didn't want to rise to it. Her sudden friendliness was unusual and, as such, he was confused about how to react. She'd definitely been avoiding him – and for some time. Not long after he met Scarlett, she'd mentioned her new lawyer friend Alice. Small world this city was. But whenever Scarlett had met with Alice, they didn't invite him along for the ride. He hated to admit it, but he'd missed Alice. Even that manic laugh.

The two of them drank as the sultry musician sang about making love, finding love and losing love. He ordered another whisky. A double.

"Anyway," Alice said lightly. "Can we start again? Hi. How are you?"

Johnny paused ahead of taking a sip and raised his glass to clink it with hers.

"Sorry. Things are a bit crazy right now."

"Scarlett?"

He gave her a questioning glance.

"If anyone knows the state of Scarlett's mind, it's you."

She raised her brows and sighed.

"True."

The bartender placed two bowls of spiced nuts in front of them. They both took a handful. To his left, Johnny could hear the arrival of new hotel guests being greeted with typical

Mandarin proficiency and politeness, their holidays about to begin, excited about exploring the pearl of the Orient.

"Did you know," Johnny said into his glass, "that the doorman here has been working in that very same job for thirty-five years? Giuseppe. Came over from Italy and never left. He loves it. He's become a legend, just for opening doors."

Alice threw back the last of her champagne. "If only we could be happy with such a life," she sighed.

"But we're not like him, are we, darling? We wanted something else. We wanted more. And we bloody well got it. Now I almost wish I was—"

"You wish you were Giuseppe?"

Johnny laughed. "Maybe."

She raised her eyes to the ceiling. What a long neck, she had, Johnny mused, and not for the first time. Long enough to see more than anyone else in the room? He nearly laughed out loud at the thought.

"Remember when we first met? At that Christmas party at Bobby Ling's new restaurant? What was it? Red Devil? Something like that. I was so excited. I'd never been to such a luxurious event, for one thing. I'd only been here for a month and already I was living it up like a rock star."

Johnny smiled into his glass. "You were so young, too."

"But you saw something in me, right?"

He nodded. "Sure did. Same thing Phil and I had. Guess that's what brought us here."

"Well, not the same thing Phil had," she scoffed. Johnny stared ahead.

He knew how unpopular Phil could make himself, but he needed him. Or was stuck with him. For now, anyway.

"And here we still are," Alice added, as though trying to lighten his mood.

They laughed a little. To Johnny, it felt hollow.

"Cheer up, Johnny," she added, eying him sideways. He

stretched his lips into a cartoonish grin. "Oh, come on." She ordered two more drinks. "Now. Want to hear a funny story?"

Alice talked. Work, her new house, her new dog, a botched surfing lesson with a charming neighbour. Whatever had made Alice this friendly, he'd take it, considering the mood he was in. After a few minutes of chatter, Johnny felt his nerves finally settle. Maybe he would call Scarlett and see if they could plan something for the weekend.

He interrupted Alice. "You seeing my lovely girlfriend any time soon?"

"'Course."

"When?"

She shrugged. "Tonight."

"Hmm. I thought I was the lucky one tonight. Oh well." He swirled the dregs of whisky in his glass. "Well, please tell her I said—"

Alice turned.

"Yes?"

"Ah, nothing. Listen. Got to run. Business is calling." He kissed her quickly on the cheek. He was struck by the coldness of her skin. "Take care, Al," he said, throwing down a couple of notes.

* * *

Alice watched him walk away. So did half the bar. He was dashing, as her mother would say.

Alice took one last slug of her drink and stood to leave. She was meeting Scarlett in fifteen minutes and had to grab something from her office first. Scarlett was always complaining about Alice's tardiness.

"*Mai dang!*" she called for the bill in Cantonese. The bartender ambled towards her, unsmiling, an empty glass in his hand. Alice motioned for him to move closer. "That's your guy," she whispered to the bartender in flawless Cantonese, nodding her head in the direction to which Johnny was departing. "Watch him. All night. Watch him whenever you can. Okay?"

The bartender nodded, almost imperceptibly.

Alice put a large wad of crisp notes onto the silver tip tray and, on top, her business card. The bartender swiftly took it and shoved it in his pocket.

CHAPTER FIVE

Hong Kong Island, East.

From her top-floor apartment building, Felicity Cussler could see all the way to the olive-green hills of eastern Kowloon. Behind them, at night, the lights of the Clearwater Bay Golf and Country Club would create a dome in the sky. She often lay back on a rattan deckchair on her roof terrace at the end of a long day, smoking and drinking a chilled beer or a glass of vodka with lime, listening to the mournful horns sounding from far-off cargo ships and thinking how lucky she was to be safe and free, to have money coming in, to not be looking over her shoulder. Best of all, no one in her little world knew who she really was.

It was a small, seaside apartment in a touristy village on the southside of the island, which was a huge departure from her childhood home at the western face of the Peak. But not being home very often, she barely noticed its cramped corners. Her private investigator office, not far away in bustling Quarry Bay, was where she was most days, trawling for client information and making phone calls. A few years ago, after tiring of endless dead-end jobs, she decided to get her PI licence after studying a few related courses online. And once she had that, she set up a business, asked to join an international association and made a few "friends" in the Central police station. The industry was pretty unregulated in Hong Kong and the transition to being a PI was a breeze.

The police loved the idea of a lone female PI and she played it to her advantage.

Felicity described herself as being the only person she knew who truly had a "dual" personality – she was biracial, bilingual and bisexual. "Bihuman," she'd tell people.

Most didn't laugh. But she didn't care. Being misunderstood was the story of her life.

At least now, she had become as much of her own person as was possible. Her father had recently died; her mother lived in New York. Best of all, she had a new name. She had changed it by deed poll to Felicity just after moving back to Hong Kong under a year ago. She also kept a low digital profile on a personal front – technology was vital in her day-to-day work life – and had taken herself off all social media, using a post-office box for mail. Her mobile phone was pay-as-you-go, the number untraceable. Nothing smart about it all. She always had it on silent and rarely texted, just to keep things as simple as possible. Her society mother told her she was crazy, living back in Hong Kong. "People will talk," she'd stressed. Yet perhaps, as Felicity told her, becoming a private investigator was a kind of insurance policy; it ensured she was on alert.

The only "outside" work she did was as a freelance writer. Once a month, she wrote a column for the *South China Mail* about dealing with conflict.

She'd studied counselling and tried her hand at HR for one of those big faceless firms before deciding neither were for her, so sometimes, she'd use her real-life PI jobs as newspaper story fodder – wives spying on husbands, bosses spying on their employees (fake names of course). She worked under the pseudonym Faye Win and that was all the newspaper readers knew about her. Seeing her fake name in print – and living with a new name on top of that – always gave her a good laugh. Being anonymous was much more fun that she'd thought it would be. But sometimes, she did wonder. One person she could confide in would be nice. Just *one*.

When her office phone rang on a wintry Tuesday afternoon,

Felicity jumped. It'd been a quiet day and she was a little hung-over. The night before, she'd agreed to meet a potential client – a man, which was unusual – and he'd taken her to the Lobster Bar in the Golden Sun Hotel. It used to be her favourite as a kid. Back then, her father had owned the hotel chain and the bartender would give her all the Coca-Cola she wanted. But the previous night, with a sleazy client in a cheap suit, the nostalgia turned to self-pity, especially when the lounge singer broke into Billie Holiday. After three vodkas, Felicity was wallowing. Copious glasses of champagne followed. Anyway, the client was a waste of time; some guy who suspected his hotshot banker girlfriend was already married, or so he said. Felicity sometimes wondered if the rare male clients she did agree to meet with got off talking with female private Ds; that she was a kind of comic-book fantasy they hoped would become reality.

The phone had jumped into life just as she'd started to nod off, her head laying cradled in crossed arms on her desk.

She cleared her throat and threw back a glass of water.

"Starlight Services."

The business was listed in various newspaper and digital classifieds in English and Chinese, a simple black-and-white box, basic font describing her "very discreet" investigative services. Nothing exciting. But people noticed it. There was a lot of demand for what she did and, as far as she knew, there were few English-speaking women who did it. Not that she'd know, being what she thought of as a "shadow person" on the social front. That is, she didn't socialise.

"Hello. I'm uh…" The voice was soft with rounded vowels. Australian? English? Felicity couldn't tell. "I'm looking for Felicity Cussler, please. I mean, I hope I've called…"

"Speaking." Felicity had named herself Cussler after the thriller writer Clive. She'd been delayed in LA airport on her way to see her mum in New York, not long before she arrived in Hong Kong, and bought one of his paperbacks. Her real surname was Chung. At least they both started with a C, she had laughed to herself.

"I need your help," the woman said, a little stronger now. "I believe you might be able to help with, with um…" Her voice trailed off and Felicity heard her blow her nose.

"Start from the beginning," Felicity said in her best counselling voice. "And your name is?"

The woman coughed and sighed. "I need your help with my boyfriend," she said.

Surprise, surprise, Felicity said to herself, tapping an unlit cigarette on the desk. She noticed a cockroach crawling over her sandwich scraps and thwacked it with a heavy book, *The Hound of the Baskervilles.* She'd read it about ten times.

"And what kind of help do you need, Miss?"

"I need you to spy on him. Isn't that what you do?"

Felicity took a deep breath. Some depressed expat whose lover was doing the dirty. It was her bread and butter. It was a major reason why she decided to set up Starlight in the first place, even if it did sound like a Wan Chai hookers' bar.

"Sort of," Felicity said. "But we can discuss more of that in person if you'd like."

"I'll pay you very well," the woman said. "But I want assurance this is all totally confidential."

"I can assure you, it is," Felicity replied, hoping she didn't sound patronising. "To be honest, I am the most reliable in town on that front. I pride myself on it. Most people doing my work are paid to spy on the children of wealthy Mainlanders, to check if they are studying and not wasting their nights splattered in vodka shots in Lan Kwai Fong. Those kinds of detectives do not build a trusting relationship with their clients because the people they're spying on are so… obvious. They're not difficult to find and not difficult to implicate. The job's over very quickly. There's very little rapport between the client and the investigator."

"Yes, yes," the woman said, and blew her nose again.

"I, however, prefer to know more, about the person I am

watching, the things they have done, where they go. I'm dealing with adults, some who are quite adept at skirting around prying eyes. So, basically, I do need to meet with you. Of course, use a fake name for yourself if you'd like. I am fine with that. I will, however, need the real name of your boyfriend. I can't look into him otherwise. Which does probably mean that I will, through the simple act of digging around for facts about him, work out your real name anyway."

So far, so standard, thought Felicity. Thank goodness. Not for the first time, Felicity did wonder if she was any good at this job. But then again, it was fun, and, naturally, she was getting better with time. She rubbed at her temples. The hangover was a creeper.

"Oh, all right," the woman said, a little churlish. "Can we meet somewhere out of Central? Kowloon?"

"Sure," Felicity said, knowing what was coming.

"Great. But not the Peninsula." The Peninsula, being one of Hong Kong's most exclusive hotels, was not the place to be seen conferring with a private investigator.

"Of course not." Felicity finally lit her cigarette, opening her rickety office window to blow out the smoke. Of all the cigarettes she picked up throughout the day, she only lit one or two.

They agreed on a faceless mall with a café on the mezzanine, just off Canton Road, frequented by hairdressers and shop girls on their lunch break. Felicity had met many clients there in similar situations. It was off the beaten track for those who lived on the island and the client was highly unlikely to run into someone they knew. Still, going to Kowloon always freaked Felicity out a bit. Again, she'd have to grin and bear it.

"And may I please have your name? Or your pseudonym at least?" Felicity asked, one more time.

"Like you said, how can you follow my boyfriend if you don't know his name? If you're as discreet as you say you are, then I don't need to worry this will get out, I suppose." Felicity could tell the woman was saying this to herself more than anything. "My name is Scarlett, Scarlett Caldwell." Felicity curled her lip. Scarlett Caldwell. What an ambitious moniker. "And my boyfriend's name is Johnny Humphries."

Felicity jumped to her feet, becoming slightly dizzy in the process. *Johnny Humphries.* A hand shot to her mouth as her cigarette fell to the floor, and she sat down, forcing herself to take a deep breath.

She leaned her elbows on the desk, letting the red-hot shock of hearing his name cool a little. A long time had passed since someone had said the name out loud, and with it, her familiarity with the impact it had on her.

"You still there?" the woman asked.

Felicity mumbled a yes and bought a few seconds of thinking time with an off-receiver cough.

"Can you tell me a little about him?" Felicity finally replied. It was best she kept to her normal script. She'd think about it all later. "Just the basics. What does he do? That kind of thing."

"Um... he's in finance. He's in his late-forties. He's British-Chinese, been in Hong Kong since he left school."

"A banker. How *unusual.* Here." Scarlett tittered politely. "And he came here after school. Has he ever lived anywhere else in recent years?"

"No. Always Hong Kong." She was drinking something. Felicity's mind raced. "Hello? Is there something…"

"No. No. Not at all. Got to get my facts straight so I can do a bit of research before we meet. My main aim is to get you the best results."

"Sure. Yes. That is what I need. I am going stir-crazy here."

Felicity realised she was shaking. It was time to put the phone down and go for a long walk before she cracked up.

"Can we meet at three, tomorrow afternoon?" Felicity said.

"Yes. I suppose," Scarlett said, letting out a sad little sigh.

She took Scarlett's number and hung up, grabbed her jacket and keys, stamped on the cigarette, and headed for the elevator. It was quiet in the darkened hallway as she waited and Felicity rubbed her shoe against a tear in the worn carpet, her shoulders pinched and hunched.

Hearing his name had triggered all sorts of emotions. Last time she'd checked on Johnny Humphries was just before she'd decided to move back to Hong Kong. She had seen he was working with Berwick and Chan and was often photographed at fancy charity events. But for as long as she could remember, she'd been doing what the counsellors had advised and was moving on, keeping far away from her old haunts and letting bygones be bygones. She had avoided any research, despite the lure of what the World Wide Web may tell her, all these years later. Naturally, her mother told her there were too many memories in Hong Kong, and her mother was right. There were *plenty* of memories, some so bad it was terrifying. But for Felicity, it was still worth it. This was the only city where she felt truly at home. Her mother had hoped she'd stay in New York, where her parents had lived since Felicity was in her early twenties. Over the years, Felicity had tried, taking jobs in LA, Chicago, Boston, you name it. But none of them ever really gelled. The smells, the sounds, the entire mood was not embedded in her soul as was her home town. And then, her tough-talking Manhattan psychologist had stressed to Felicity she was now safe, no matter where she was. The men responsible for her ordeal in Hong Kong all those years ago had gone to jail. But there was one man she believed could have been involved and yet had slipped through the net. And *that* was Johnny Humphries.

Logically, Felicity understood that even if she ever did run into him in Hong Kong, there was nothing much she could do about it. She hadn't managed to get anyone to believe he had been involved at the time, so what good would it do to bring it all back up again? They said she was mad, even her own father intimated he felt the same way. Furthermore, the years had softened her memories, and with that, her conviction that he even *was* an evil liar. Part of her therapy had been to accept he was found innocent and get on with it. And she had tried. *She'd really tried.*

But, now, damn it, his girlfriend wanted her to spy on him. The temptation to see what he was up to – whether or not it had anything to do with Scarlett – might be too much to resist. Sure, she'd done a lot of digging in the past, but it revealed nothing. He was clean, as her father had kept insisting.

But he is probably a philanderer and getting him busted would be… fun.

Felicity was already dying for another cigarette. She'd given up a few months ago but, rightly or wrongly, decided cigarettes often served as company, a reprieve from the occasional bouts of night terrors and, often, a way to pass time when hanging around on the job.

Felicity clenched and unclenched her fists.

She was conflicted about what to do and what to think and that made her mad. Was it too much of a coincidence that Johnny's girlfriend contacted her? Maybe. Maybe not. Hong Kong was small like that. Coincidences did happen. In a way, she didn't really care. Her mind was on one thing and one thing only. To nail Johnny for something. Anything.

Her stomach knotted.

The lift clunked to the fifteenth floor. As she stepped in, Felicity felt it. For the first time in about ten years, the pinkie finger on her left hand ached, throbbed almost. What was left of it, anyway. She rubbed at the tip where the knuckle normally would be, a finger halved, no nail, just a stub. Cut off with a meat cleaver just a few months after her twentieth birthday.

* * *

A few days later, Felicity was sipping a beer at the buzzing Tequila Bar, a popular after-work hang-out at the end of a dark alleyway, lit faintly with strings of fairy lights and tiki torches. It was the day after her coffee with Scarlett, and, already, she'd tracked Johnny down, her entire body jangling with nerves. She'd waited outside Berwick's offices in the afternoon and, bam, out he came, just as she was about to give up. Felicity imagined it would be the case, but – damn it – he looked the same, apart from a few charming laugh lines. Felicity had felt the prickle of a tear, a nanosecond of nostalgic longing for the innocent young woman she used to be. Steeling herself, she'd hurriedly wiped at her eyes and peered out from under her baseball hat, saw him take the lift up to the tenth floor of a building that housed a shrink's office of all places. Now, a couple of hours later, here he was in a bar, living life to the full. *Good on you, Johnny.*

This time, she could see from her seat at a corner table a few metres away, just side-on to where they were, that he was with that godawful Phil – three stone heavier than when she last saw him all those years ago, dishevelled and already red-faced drunk – and two middle-aged Western women in short dresses. There was Johnny, in a neat suit.

The booming music briefly faded, and Phil started telling a joke to the two women, who offered a few forced laughs. Next to them was a stocky Chinese guy she'd never seen before, who was looking a bit worse for wear, the hand holding his cocktail threatening serious spillage any minute. Her own hand shook as she brought the thick, cold glass to her lips. This was crazy. What would her mother say? At least, she'd made sure she would fade into the background in such a crowded, dim room, and was dressed in a dull uniform of grey jeans and a loose, khaki top. Unlike Johnny, Felicity had aged (all those cigarettes) and, without make-up, was a muted, skinnier, hunched version of her younger self. Perhaps as a sort of armour, she also wore heavily rimmed, fake reading glasses as she tapped away at her phone, listening and waiting.

To her left, the familiar sounds of Melvis filtered into the room. *Christ*, Felicity thought. *How can I hear with that going on?*

A well-known Elvis impersonator, Melvis, was a local guy

who'd been performing with his guitar around town for years, playing for tips and warbling Elvis songs that had become more entertaining for their off-kilter tune than his melodious abilities. Felicity tried not to stare as he walked towards Johnny and Phil, but everyone else was.

Phil roared something to Melvis before singing along with "Blue Suede Shoes". Johnny handed Melvis a tip and he moved on, the music going with him, giving Felicity the chance to train her ears on what they were saying.

"Tell the story about that *other* night with Melvis," Johnny laughed, smacking Phil on the shoulder. Hearing him speak gave her shivers. "When the American tourist took offence."

Phil puffed up his chest. "Oh yes, sir! Of course, my lord!"

Johnny rolled his eyes at the mimicry. The stocky friend stood and started doing the same piss-take of Johnny, but everyone ignored him. He looked embarrassed and sat down, swiping a hanky over his sweaty forehead. The background music started up again and whatever they were saying was drowned out. Johnny had obviously had enough and was placing a few bills on the bar.

And Felicity? She'd realised the hair on her arms were standing on end. Had she really just heard that correctly? Could she trust herself with this, or was she going mad? Surely not. But it did seem like some kind of sign. *Impersonators. Two of them.*

It was then, Felicity realised, she needed to speak to someone. Fast.

CHAPTER SIX

Shek O Village, Eastern Hong Kong Island.

One week later.

Chen Wang had been asked to give a speech and was nervous as he hopped on the bus to Shau Kei Wan. So far, he'd managed to keep such a low profile that only two to three people knew he had any sympathy with the democracy groups, let alone that he was playing a pivotal role in the movement.

But then, he'd given that interview on Radio Television HK on the final day of the protests, more than two years ago now, and one thing led to another. He shouldn't have spoken to the interviewer. She was young and he felt sorry for her, doing battle with the CNNs and BBCs. But it gave him a public persona, one he didn't want just yet. Now he was afraid, even though he hadn't been questioned by the authorities, which was more than he could say about several of those he was working with.

Whatever fear he felt, however, always gave way to indignation and a powerful sense of believing he was doing the right thing, a character trait his parents instilled in him from the second he could understand the words.

In the 1990s, his family fled China for Hong Kong. His father was warned he could face arrest for an article he'd written for a US newspaper decrying the 1989 Tiananmen Square atrocities in Beijing.

A couple of years after arriving in Hong Kong, Wang's dad, an academic and journalist, took a job as a Beijing commentator for a daily newspaper, working there for twenty-five years. Many of his stories focused on Hong Kong's political stage since the British-Chinese Handover in 1997. But four years ago, he was asked to leave.

No one gave a good explanation as to why his father was asked to leave.

Eighteen months ago, his father had died of a massive stroke. Wang's mother was a shell of her former self.

* * *

Ironically, the room where Wang was about to speak was in a dingy basement flat in the New Territories, not far from where he grew up. It was sure to bring back memories. Not that he was particularly fond of the place – organised blocks of faceless high-rise buildings in pale, sickly shades of blue and pink. Underneath were the usual Wellcome supermarkets, ice-cold preschools and concrete bus stations fronting local eateries. Nothing had changed since he was ten, except the addition of a few new upmarket malls selling mid-range designer clothes. *Same shit, different name.*

Once seated, Wang pulled a copy of his speech from his backpack as the bus gently swayed along Shek O Road, the fishing village visible below as they ascended the steep, meandering country road. He looked to his left, the semi-circular blue of the surf beach, reminding him again of why he chose to live in that little slice of tropical paradise by the South China Sea.

After he'd delivered this speech, he reminded himself again, he'd simply go back to his normal life. He would be seen publicly as just another young guy who thought the protests were a good idea. He'd attend democracy party rallies still, to make his interest all above board, but to onlookers, he would simply be doing what he always did – surfing, hiking, running his graphic design portfolio from home and basically being a lucky bastard.

He put on his glasses and reread the speech, feeling a rise of trepidation.

Hong Kong: Behind the Façade

You are Hong Kongers. This is your home. But what do most people see when they visit the city? They see skyscrapers, rows and rows of them. They see countless thousands of rushing people. Bamboo surrounds modern structures being rebuilt, taller and bigger and shinier. They see five-star hotels, crowded restaurants, the food enticing and exotic. It is a fast-paced, efficient, money-making city crammed into a tiny tropical island at the geographical base of a giant power.

There is a reason for the energy we have here. People came to Hong Kong to escape, to work. They worked very, very hard and still do. The more money they could make, the freer they would be. Hong Kong was the escape route, the future.

Yet things are changing. And they continue to do so – because our freedom of speech is now under threat. The Umbrella Revolution in 2014 was testament to this concern.

We have always had the right to express discontent, to feel confident of a fair trial, our voices respected. If we want this to continue, why do we not finally break free? We don't need the English to help us. We need to help ourselves.

The beating heart of Hong Kong is real. Let's hold each other's hands and forcefully, but sensibly, refuse to back down. They say we can't face up to the might of a superpower and maybe, they're correct. But still, I refuse to give up. Maybe with the right tactics, we can realise our dream of glory to Hong Kong (PAUSE HERE!).

Did anyone in the world care about Hong Kong when so many places in the world were truly suffering? Probably not. But Hong Kong people – and his parents – did and, to Wang, that was all that mattered. Sure, he knew it disrupted business, even his own. But what did he have to lose? This was his home and he didn't want to one day give up the freedoms he had been born with. It was worth it, he'd decided some time ago. And he was determined.

Yes, we have democratic representatives, but if we don't fight fire with fire, these politicians will be forced to stay on the sidelines.

So now, we must take care of our Hong Kong. It is better than sitting back and watching others be silenced, naively thinking it won't happen to us. It is already happening to us now.

Wang ran his fingers through his long thick fringe and closed his eyes, just briefly. The plan was to stage the protest in early summer, before the high temperatures hit and hopefully before the typhoon season was in full swing. Wang knew his audience would lap it up and that was what he needed. More eager supporters, driven by emotion. He read the last sentence. *The storm is coming. Be ready.* He held the paper in his hands and noticed it was shaking.

* * *

The bus reached the terminus at Shau Kei Wan and the *po pos*, the grandmothers, were shuffling to the door, plastic shopping bags by their sides, shoulders rounded. Behind them, waiting patiently, was a group of hikers dressed for the part. No doubt they'd just walked the Dragon's Back Trail, a popular route for all ages but a particular favourite for Hong Kong's many super-fit retirees. *If they knew*, Wang thought, *what I am doing, what would they say?* You never knew. Not everyone wanted to pick a fight with Beijing. Many people in Hong Kong had business interests in China that ensured they kept their mouths shut. Others felt a historical loyalty to the "motherland", something Wang found incomprehensible. He suspected, however, many Hong Kongers of his generation at least were on his side.

To calm his nerves, Wang allowed himself a brief thought about his new neighbour, Alice; how he had recently taken her surfing. She was a beginner and her panicked squeals had brought even the lifeguards onto the shoreline to make sure she was okay. The first wave had upturned her into its wash, her limbs flailing about, a childlike grin glued to her face for nearly an hour afterwards as her beautiful red hair dried in the salty air. And she had, he was pleased to see, got straight back on the board. The memory of her determination triggered a warm flush to his cheeks.

Getting off the bus, Wang made the most of the rabble as people stood to leave and ripped his speech into small thin strips. After alighting, he balled it up and threw it into a bin on the far side of the road opposite the terminus. He had made no other copies and had handwritten it only. He'd have to remember it, but he wasn't worried. What was in your heart was in your head.

He half walked, half ran to the MTR train station, a little bit excited. "This is for you, Dad," he said aloud, smiling to himself as he descended the slippery steps into the station, making sure the hood of his sweater covered his face.

There was, as always, a small but fast-moving queue at the ticket turnstiles. Wang jiggled from one foot to the other, his smartcard ready to go. *Come on.* A family of tourists were fumbling with their paper tickets, unsure which way it faced. Wang could hear them discussing who was doing it right or wrong. He leaned forward to show the harried Americans what to do. He'd studied in the States for three years and felt a kinship with people from the US.

"Just tap it, like this," he told them, a small smile forming. They thanked him profusely. "Not at all. You're welcome."

He went to tap his card, but a presence near his left shoulder made him pause and turn. A heavy hand landed on his shoulder.

"Chen Wang?"

He felt something hard pressed against his ribs and before he could speak, his feet were pulled from under him.

CHAPTER SEVEN

Central, Hong Kong Island.

Two weeks later.

The party lights were always on in Hong Kong, but on Friday nights, the neon volume was blasted that bit more, its intensity matched only by the human frisson emanating from every street corner. Cigarette smoke hovered cloud-like under flashing colour. The laughter was as deafening as the steady beat of bass bouncing from the concrete walls that towered over the chaos. The steep, sometimes cobbled roads of Lan Kwai Fong and SoHo, south of Hollywood Road in Central, were slippery with spilled drinks. If you stood still and deeply inhaled, you'd smell garlic and onions fizzing in oil, the sting of cheap perfume, wafts of wet rice and exhaust fumes. Red Toyota taxis honked and private drivers stopped just about anywhere, their bosses, heads bowed, quickly slipping into darkened elevators. Backpackers clung to each other and the impatient strode confidently on the roads themselves.

If you bothered to stop and look up, you might see a faint yellow light illuminating a 350-square-foot apartment above, a few T-shirts drying on a makeshift line, sometimes – in late winter – a dangling red lantern left over from Chinese New Year celebrations, the shadow of a head bent over a book or a computer, steam from a pot on the hob. But below – in a respectable downtown area of this important global financial centre – Hong Kong was busy partying with the zealousness of a sex-crazed teenager, no matter age or background.

And no one loved a party as much as Bobby Ling.

In modern-day Hong Kong, Bobby had risen to social stardom like a psychedelic phoenix from the ashes of mediocrity. The only grandson of Mainland Chinese immigrants, Bobby was brought up with his sister and parents in a two-bedroom apartment near his parents' place of work, Taikoo Sugar, not far from Aberdeen. His father held the lofty expectation Bobby would become a lawyer or a doctor and was as flummoxed as he was furious with Bobby's imperfect grades.

By the time Bobby's schooling had finished, he couldn't stand the feeling of being trapped anymore, of lying to himself and others, and decided to do something about it. He took two jobs: one as a delivery driver, the other seating guests at a mammoth seafood restaurant. Then, after saving enough money for a flight and to eat for a week, he left Hong Kong for the UK. There, he slept on the sofa of an old family friend until he found work. Immediately, he took odd jobs in kitchens – a dishwasher, a cleaner, a delivery guy, a waiter in a big hotel, a front-of-desk, and finally, a restaurant manager of an up-and-coming Chinese restaurant, the kind where the waitresses looked like supermodels and everyone wore black. By day, Bobby perfected his English at language classes, befriending his shy teacher, a repressed homosexual who blushed and fidgeted whenever Bobby entered the room. The two often discussed Bobby's plans to start up his own restaurant business and his inability to come out to his family, or anyone for that matter, something they had in common; but how could he get out of service and into business?

For eighteen months, this went on. The skin on Bobby's fingers peeled painfully from his hands being constantly immersed in either leftover food or soapsuds.

One afternoon, the young English teacher told Bobby that he knew a guy who ran an events company, who was looking for someone to help out on the ground. Bobby made it clear he would jump at the chance. He had spent enough time watching and listening and learning and was ready to leave his service work. A month later, the teacher snared him an interview and, a week after that, he was offered a job as a personal assistant for an upmarket events company in London. It changed his life. But the biggest turnaround was that, away from the shackles of his conservative family for so long, he had finally come to terms with his own homosexuality and decided to run with it. Five years later, Bobby returned to Hong Kong with some savings, a suitcase of flamboyant outfits and a devil-may-care attitude about what others thought of him. Back then, he was thirty years old, his father had passed away and he was ready to get rich.

And he did.

But he had one major regret.

* * *

It was a balmy night. Scarlett had entered the downstairs reception of the Albemarle, carrying with her a waft of jasmine and an aura of skittish energy. In the lifts, she reached into her soft black leather evening bag, pulled out a small silver tin and, from that, plucked out a round white pill. She swallowed it. No water. Sometimes, she wasn't even sure if these pills did anything. She let out a big puff of air. "You can do this," she said out loud to the closed door.

The chatter and music hit her like slipstream from a speeding train.

"Dahling, dahling, dahling," Bobby called as she entered the bar area, perched at the top of the PMQ, a renovated building that had historically housed the colonial-era Police Married Quarters. The chef was Michelin-starred, the atmosphere relaxed refinery with a propensity to turn boisterous on a Friday evening.

Scarlett usually went to the Albemarle for the food. But

that night, she was there to speak with Bobby. It had taken her months to form their friendship and for him to find a night for just the two of them, and she had to work quickly with what little she'd been told.

"So glad you're here," she said into his ear.

Early diners were sipping cocktails and the atmosphere was as effervescent as Bobby's bright orange sports jacket. It was piped with navy blue and finished with a large gold pocket insignia in the shape of a serpent.

"I'm going out of my mind with boredom not working," Scarlett mewed.

Bobby gave her a sympathetic frown.

"Oh please, Bobby, don't show me pity. I hate being pitied." Scarlett gave a small, sideways smile. "It's been a tough time." She waved a hand in the air. "Long story."

"We all have *those*, dahling."

With the flair of the protagonist's first entrance on stage, Bobby guided her to his table by the window. Scarlett could see people dutifully turn to stare at Bobby, as well as snicker – or admire, depending on your taste – his dyed blond hair long down his back and tied with an orange ribbon in a single plait. He left his scalp bald and shiny. But they also glanced at her, she could see. In cream cashmere, grey velvet boots and a diamond brooch, she exuded a Romanov princess glow, as though minor European royalty was gracing the dining room. Bobby, they all assessed, wouldn't bother with just anyone. If only they knew.

"So, tell me," Bobby gushed as soon as they sat down, "I assume I have been asked here to hear about your new life as a wealthy lady of leisure, lounging all day in the luxe Peak mansion? Hmm?" Scarlett tried to laugh but found her lips wouldn't move.

"No. Come on, Bobby. It's dull. I hate it. I've always worked. It's kind of strange."

"I know. I can imagine. Having said that, it's only temporary. May as well enjoy it."

She shrugged. Their champagne arrived. The waiter made a big fuss of Bobby, ensuring the glass was placed just so, the silver bowls of olives and dips arranged with artistic neatness. Bobby tapped him on the arm and dramatically mouthed: "Thank you."

Scarlett leaned forward, trying to focus. The pill was having a little too much effect.

"I still don't get why Vivian felt the need to sack me," Scarlett said softly. "I had a few bad days, not twenty. I'd done so well up until then." She fiddled with the white napkin on her lap. "You know her well, Bobby. Don't you? I mean, you know what makes her tick?"

Bobby nodded.

"I *know*." They sipped at their drinks. Scarlett stayed silent. She knew he couldn't bear a long pause. "I met Vivian *years* ago. Stealth PR was just starting to do well then. She was always supportive of her staff. Always. She did the PR for my first bar, the Maestro. You weren't here then, but it was *the* place to be and Vivian made that happen. And you know what," he leaned forward to whisper, "I know she adores you. Thinks you're wonderful. What the fuck is she thinking, getting rid of you?" He noticed Scarlett's eyes begin to well. "Oh, stop it. Vivian's also known for her moods. Trust me. And anyway, rumour is she's gone a bit nutty lately. God knows why. But, rest assured, she ain't perfect. *Bitch.*" Bobby giggled.

"Nutty?"

Scarlett noticed his hand wobble a little as he brought the drink to his lips. He often had a long lunch on a Friday and Scarlett guessed he'd probably been drinking all afternoon. Scarlett and Bobby had briefly discussed their confusing childhoods since meeting through Vivian when Scarlett had first arrived in Hong Kong. Their mutual estrangement from both parents had helped them form an unlikely bond for two virtual strangers. But Bobby, unfortunately, dealt with his demons through embracing the bottle. Lately, it had escalated.

"Oh, you know, sacking people – like you, for example – snarling at people. Must be the…" he paused and covered his mouth with a cupped hand, "the men… o… *pause*." They both laughed a little. Scarlett felt grubby.

"Do you think…" she started, but then shook her head. "Do you think she has something to do with Johnny?"

"Oh, come on," he spat.

Scarlett threw back her head and took a big gulp.

"I mean, do you think that Johnny could be…"

"What? You don't mean…"

"Yes. I do. Could he be, you know, seeing Vivian and she sacked me because it was a conflict of interest for her?" Her hands went to her face. "I don't know. Maybe I'm going mad."

Bobby waved for a waiter and whispered something in his ear before turning back to Scarlett.

"Listen, babe," he said, an edge of seriousness to his voice. "Impossible. Vivian is shacked up with the gorgeous Tom Jamieson and not interested in the likes of Johnny." Scarlett's worried frown turned to the beginnings of a scowl. "Sorry," he winced. "You know what I mean."

"I know you don't like him," she huffed, "but he's my boyfriend." They finished their drinks as the waiter placed their ceviche entrée. "You know, you've never actually told me why you don't like him. I still don't really understand what it is about him you find unpleasant. Most people love him, but you…"

Bobby flicked his fingers to stop her from going on.

"Now come on. I never said I don't like him."

"But you… well, you seem disparaging of him. I can tell. I know I've asked you this before, but you never give me a straight answer."

Bobby hesitated. "I don't mean to be disparaging, dahling."

Scarlett looked across the restaurant to see if Alice had arrived. She was late, as always.

Bobby wiped at a little champagne dribble on the side of his mouth with a napkin.

"How did you meet Johnny anyway?" Was she pushing too hard?

"Oh God. Some party in the 1990s. Maybe '94? Wild times. Seriously fun times. Johnny and Phil and Viv. Everyone was on a roll, then. Nothing could stop us." Bobby's eyes sparkled at the memory. "But things change."

"How so?"

"*Age*. Underneath this jacket are a pair of serious bingo wings." He lifted up his right arm and flapped it around, killing himself laughing.

"The thing is," Scarlett continued, "Johnny's not *my* favourite person at the moment either. We're having some issues."

Bobby opened his mouth a little and then closed it. He frowned as he picked at his dish.

"How so?" Bobby finally replied.

"I'm simply suspicious."

"Of what?" Bobby didn't take his eyes off his plate.

"This and that. Mostly Phil, that slimy sidekick of his. He's not above board. I can tell."

Bobby nodded. "Whatever," he said with a barely susceptible eye roll. He scooped a morsel of fish into his mouth.

"I mean, what does he actually do at Berwick? Then Phil comes around to the house and I know there's drugs. I'm not a fool."

"Drugs. Yikes! Come on, Scarlett. Half the town is into them." Scarlett sat on her hands to stop them shaking. "As always, Phil is probably helping dig dirt on a potential deal with someone who may have a shady past," Bobby suggested.

"It's more than that."

"How so?"

Bobby rubbed at his eyes.

"Um. Well…" How would she word this? It was all so unfair on Bobby. "I found a drawer, hidden under Johnny's desk."

"No!" Bobby widened his eyes. "What do you mean, a drawer?"

"You know, one that's hidden under the desk itself. A *concealed drawer*, like you see in the movies." She fanned a napkin in front of her face. "God, this is crazy."

"Please. Go on," Bobby urged.

"Well. It has a code on the lock. I swim early most mornings, and Johnny knows it. Sometimes, he goes for a run. Before I left for the pool, I'd seen him fiddling about under the desk when I'd walked past. He'd been holed up in there with Phil for the previous two nights and when I'd asked him what they'd been talking about, he'd snapped and told me to leave him alone. He'd never spoken to me like that. He'd hardly been home for the previous two weeks – off in far-flung Chinese cities doing God knows what. And, well, yes, there it was. This drawer."

She was sweaty just thinking about how she'd watched him from behind a door, seen him go out and then snuck in and tried the code a few times, knowing full well he thought she was still swimming in the pool. She was also sweaty with the lie she had just told. Johnny had never been rude to her. Ever. Furthermore, she had never seen him do drugs. But she wasn't going to get anywhere telling the truth. And she was on to something, she needed to be believed.

"To be honest," she said, without meeting Bobby's eye, "I had tried to open the drawer once before. But this one morning, before my swim, I had spied on him from the edge of the hallway. Oh, I know, I feel like such a *sneak*." Another lie. She had tried to open the drawer about four times in the past few weeks. Every time it was locked and her attempts at breaking the code had failed. "But it's only because of the secrets he seemed to be keeping from me."

Bobby pushed a courgette flower around his plate.

"Then what happened?" he asked, without looking up. The waiter arrived with a bottle of red wine and Bobby stuck out his glass.

"I was going to ask him about it."

Bobby's hand flew to his mouth. He spilled red wine on his napkin and giggled.

"Oh, my God!"

Scarlett stole a quick glance at the table next to them. Two women. Tourists, taking photos of their hand-rolled gnocchi. She paused to nibble at some food.

Bobby waved a limp hand in the air, his polished fingernails opalescent in the mood lighting.

"Listen, darl," he hissed across the table, "don't go there. Okay?"

"Why? What could he be hiding? I've half a mind to leave him if he's so... secretive."

Bobby plastered a palm to his forehead, as though about to faint. He composed himself.

"Well, Scar, I always thought it was strange you were with him. I mean, you're this innocent flower and he's, well, he's not as pure as the driven snow, so they say." Scarlett reminded herself to be patient and kept her eyes trained on Bobby's, *searching*, she hoped the look said. He cocked his head to one side. "Now. If I tell you something, will you do me the biggest favour a friend can do and keep your mouth shut, dump the guy and move on?" She nodded. Her palm was damp when she lifted the wine glass to her lips. "I know you love Johnny, but I do know that... well, I do suspect that he may have connections to some people who aren't exactly reputable, if you know what I mean."

She shook her head.

"No. I'm sorry. I don't. He's a good, solid businessman. How can he have?" Bobby fiddled anxiously with a napkin. "Do you think, Bobby, you would have any idea of what this code could be?"

Bobby sucked a gust of air into his mouth and slammed two palms onto the table. The people around them jumped.

"God no, Scarlett. As *if*." He wiped at his brow. "Look, we all make mistakes," he stage-whispered. "God knows I have,

which is how I know about Johnny and Phil. *The boss*. Erg."
He sighed. "But Johnny has too. And maybe this is connected
to that mistake?"

Scarlett was speechless. "The boss?"

Bobby wagged his index finger. "Forget I said that. *Gawd*.
A hundred years ago now."

"Shall I talk to Johnny, Bobby? Tell him I'll go to the
police?"

Bobby placed both palms on either side of his pink cheeks.
"Oh God no! No, no, no! Jesus. And tell them what?"

She let out a puff of pent-up air.

"All I'm saying," Bobby had lowered his voice, "is that
you should walk away. Nicely, of course. Or don't ask him
anything else. Ever."

She nodded.

"Really?"

"Really."

He very slowly crossed his arms.

"You know, I do know one more thing. One more thing
that might convince you to ditch the guy. I can't help myself."
He gently held her forearm. "*Madeline Chung*." He shivered
theatrically. "Go on. Do a search. From the 1990s. Where
there's smoke… and by the way, stop sneaking into his study.
I'm sure there's not much to find and, knowing Johnny, he's
got his back covered."

"I'm so confused." Her mouth was dry and her voice
caught in her throat. She reached for the water jug as Bobby
frowned into his glass.

"Whatever," he snapped.

To her left, a well-dressed elderly couple sat down slowly.
The silver-haired woman, resplendent in diamonds and pearls,
glanced over at Bobby. She smiled at him and mouthed hello
before Bobby turned back to Scarlett.

Bobby blinked, rapidly, as though realising where he was,
then closed and opened his eyes, very slowly.

"Oh, I've gone on too much. I have no idea if Johnny's

involved in *anything*, other than legit deals. I mean, I have only *heard* things." He turned a crimson shade that matched his fruity-hued jacket. "Please. Stop me now. It was just a thought, having known Johnny for so long."

"And as you have known him so long, you obviously know about his 'other' side and believe I should dump him? And that there is some guy called, 'the boss'?"

Bobby shook his head vigorously. The plait down his back swung back and forth. Scarlett was reminded of a squat Palomino pony she had once ridden at the Easter Show.

"I know nothing. I am only guessing, based on idle gossip and the fact that…" He gulped his wine and again wiped his moist brow, "In the old days here, we all did things we shouldn't have. People try to get ahead. It really is nothing. Pretend you never talked to me. Please, darl."

Scarlett looked sulky. "I hate that Johnny may be involved in something illegal," she said softly. "And what's this about a Madeline Chung?"

Bobby did the index finger wag again. Scarlett was reminded of her high-school religious education teacher.

"Oh, forget it, hon. I am now going to zip my lip."

She was itching to ask more.

"Okay."

"End it with Johnny and go find yourself a bronzed Bondi lifesaver. Now that'd be something I'd like to talk about." He fanned his cheeks with his palms.

Scarlett tried to laugh but it came out hollow.

"And, by the way, just to confuse you more, I'm drunk, I'm getting old. I'm a silly old fag who gossips. So ignore me." She took his soft white hand. "Oh look. There's Ally!" He raised himself, dropping Scarlett's hand and slowly stood to wave to Alice. "Over here, hon!"

Alice, as always, looked cool and calm. The three of them kissed and Alice made small talk with Bobby about the weekend ahead.

After a few minutes, Bobby staggered to his feet.

"I'm off, ladies," he said, glass in hand. "Got a party over at The Lee. It's gonna be *huge*."

Scarlett watched as Bobby sauntered through the tables, waving to people as he struggled to stay in a straight line.

She sighed as she poured Alice's glass.

"Poor guy," Alice half-whispered. "Although I hate to say it, I hope he doesn't change. He's too much fun."

Scarlet nodded her agreement.

"He just told me the strangest thing."

Alice raised her glass as if to say cheers. "Go on."

"I'm…"

Alice raised one brow. "You're…?"

"Oh nothing." Alice raised one brow. Scarlett leant forward conspiratorially. "I'm thinking I might end it with Johnny. Soon. I can't keep it up, wondering who he really is."

"Whatever you think is best."

"Let's see," Scarlett almost whispered.

Alice laughed.

"Only a couple of months ago, you were loving every minute with Johnny, or so it seemed."

Scarlett scowled and, for a second, felt her gaze give away a cool bitterness.

As she realised it, she replaced her look with an inexpressive softness.

"I know. But it's got complicated."

Alice placed her glass down. "I already did my bit," Alice sighed. "You know that. And I've told you all I could, despite wishing I hadn't. But do we have to talk about Johnny again? It was more fun when you actually liked him. And, to be honest, he's clean. Well, clean-ish. Don't worry. I detest Phil, which makes me wonder about Johnny. But, other than that, I can't enlighten you any more right now. Please, Scarlett, can we just have a laugh?"

Scarlett almost winced.

"Okay. Sure. I'm sorry. I do go on. But just so you know, if I disappear from town, I'm okay."

"Sure," Alice smiled. "If you ever need to stay at mine, feel free. Okay?"

A waiter appeared.

"The gentleman at the table to your far right has sent this bottle of champagne to you," he said, staring at Scarlett.

"Happens every time." Alice beamed. "But only when I'm out with you. Oh, well. Might as well drink it."

* * *

A week later, in a quiet Italian restaurant at the end of a rat-infested, pot-holed alleyway in a darkened corner of downtown Wan Chai, an unlikely pair in the form of psychologist Carolyn and self-anointed PI Felicity sat huddled over a pile of documents, a candle flickering and light jazz music tinkling. An enthusiastic waiter brought a large plate of slippery *vongole* and refilled their wine glasses. They'd met a couple of weeks ago and had formed a fast – potentially unethical – bond. But, as Carolyn reminded herself, this was a social occasion, not a counselling session. Well, that's how she framed it.

"*Bon appetit*," Carolyn said, taking a hearty spoonful.

She couldn't help but think how refreshing it was being at a dinner for two with a woman, and not some guy from a questionable dating site. She could drip tomato sauce all over her chin and not give a hoot. She could guzzle a glass of wine and not monitor if she was going too hard. Carolyn had been on her fair share of disastrous dates recently; boring being their most common trait. She wanted someone who made her laugh, someone with stories. Hanging out with Felicity was so far removed from those recent dull encounters, she'd take it. And anyway, after her dinners with Felicity (something she masked as therapy sessions), Carolyn could go home alone, chat to her kids and sleep in her own bed, arms and legs spread, no second-guessing about what she should have said or didn't say and not have to listen to some blowhard snore until 3am. For her to invite any of her recent dates home, he'd have to be George Clooney – ten years ago.

She and Felicity had only met up a few times but it already it felt like they'd known each other for years. Felicity was a straight-talker, as was Carolyn. They didn't shy away from unsavoury subjects either, having each experienced quite a few upheavals in life. Furthermore, they'd both travelled far and wide and shared a love of food and wine, finished off with a cynical distaste for most men in their age bracket.

"That's why I go for girls. Thirty per cent of the time, anyway." Felicity shrugged as a late-fifties businessman ambled past with a woman young enough to be his daughter perched on his arm.

"That's an interesting stat," Carolyn smiled sarcastically. "If you get to thirty-five per cent female, what do you do? Backtrack and have two men over the course of a weekend to make up for it?"

"Exactly. How'd you know? Fancy joining me?"

"Oh, *please*."

They ate for a few brief, comfortable seconds.

"I suppose I don't go for anyone anymore… *at all*." Carolyn sniffed.

Felicity laughed and leaned forward over the table.

"Remember. No man is better than a bad man."

Carolyn nodded. She knew Felicity had been through the revolving door of psychs and therefore such sentiments were sage, if depressing, advice.

"Now," Felicity clapped her hands together, "let's get back to business."

Carolyn looked at her dining companion. Felicity had what you'd describe as an interesting face. She was wearing a bomber jacket and, underneath, a simple white T-shirt. There was a green cotton scarf tied loosely around her neck. No jewellery, no make-up, save for a lick of mascara. Her eyes were Asian, a piercing intensity burning away behind two dark brown orbs. But her face heart-shaped – Western – her skin pale and freckled on the cheeks but with a marble smoothness, as though she'd never seen the sun. She wore her dark brown hair in a loose low ponytail. Paler brown wisps hung across her forehead. Her lips turned down slightly at the sides, but every few minutes, she'd curl one side of her lip into a snarl. She rarely smiled, although when she did, her teeth were small and perfectly aligned, like a preschooler's. Almost annoyingly, Felicity gesticulated wildly as she talked, constantly verging on knocking over the wine, the water jug, the candles.

Carolyn kept one hand on her glass as she forked at her pasta.

"We definitely look like a couple," Felicity was saying to her.

"What? Sorry? A couple?" Carolyn looked around the room at the other tables of two, all seated under moody lighting. "I'm too busy enjoying the food."

Felicity shrugged. "Just saying."

Carolyn put down her fork.

"I thought you said let's get back to business?"

* * *

They'd first met the day after Johnny had visited Carolyn's office.

Minutes before Felicity had walked in, Carolyn had been reading a copy of an old newspaper article she'd tracked down at the Hong Kong Library just that morning, one detailing the claims Madeline Chung – or the girl she now knew as Felicity, and whom was sitting across the table from her – had made against Johnny all those years ago. Just by going to the library, Carolyn knew she was being that little bit too curious – nosy, really – considering Johnny was a client. But his name had been on her mind more than it should have been and she knew that if she could just find out why, then she'd relax. It was kind of like scratching a very large, very irritating itch.

And then, *bang*, what had seemed like some divine

intervention, Koffee was knocking at the door and claiming a Felicity Cussler was waiting outside.

"*Who's* here to see me again?" Carolyn had squinted at Koffee.

"I told you! Felicity Cussler. Says she is a private detective." Koffee had snorted. Carolyn was still squinting as her assistant turned to shuffle down the hall. Koffee had muttered under her breath.

Carolyn knew very little Cantonese and whatever Koffee had said went over her head. But Felicity spoke the language perfectly and, standing in Carolyn's doorway, replied to Koffee, "I'm not so sure she is, you know."

Koffee had disappeared down the hall.

By the time Felicity had sat down on Carolyn's velvet easy chair, legs askew and the leather of her jacket squeaking as she rolled her shoulders back and down, Carolyn knew she was hooked.

"I'm being paid to follow Johnny Humphries," were the first words Felicity uttered. "By his girlfriend. We met at a café in Kowloon a couple of days ago." Carolyn placed a hand over the newspaper article on her desk. "And I saw him come in here the other day." She paused and jiggled her left leg a little. "I don't expect you to tell me what he told you, but I've just realised that you might be able to help me. I too need a shrink. I thought I could go without it, but I think I will need someone to talk to until the day I die. So how about it?"

Carolyn had looked at her watch. One hour and fifteen minutes to go until her next client. Felicity, holding an unlit cigarette in one hand and eyeballing Carolyn, started talking. Carolyn pushed back her chair.

"It *is* a conflict of interest. I think you know that." Carolyn felt she needed to say it for the record. "If I am treating Johnny and you are spying on him."

Felicity had glanced around the room.

"It's only unprofessional if you tell me what he tells you. Other than that, I'm just coming to you as a client."

Carolyn had paced the back of the room a bit, her stockinged feet slippery on the parquet floor. She'd briefly watched a few daredevil construction workers scaling the bamboo scaffolding on a nearby building.

Felicity started talking again.

Carolyn didn't stop her.

Felicity explained she had one more day to go before her contract with Scarlett was satisfied. She'd found that Johnny was not having an affair. Job done. Yet, she'd realised that she wasn't done with her own issues with him and her past. She told Carolyn this was a personal problem, one that had reared its head after years of managing to avoid it. So much time had passed that she was getting confused about the details and she needed someone to talk with. Someone new to her.

Carolyn had squirmed in her seat. What was this woman trying to tell her? Felicity then unveiled some minor details of having grown up in Hong Kong, her father in hotels, her mother American.

And then, just as Carolyn had brought a cup of tea to her lips, Felicity hit her with the big one. Carolyn had paused, steam from the tea clouding her glasses.

"I am Madeline Chung," Felicity had said quietly. Carolyn guiltily glanced down at the newspaper article on her desk. "And you're the only person I can trust right now."

* * *

Carolyn instantly knew it would be problematic, possibly unethical, to be involved in interconnected clients' lives, and could hear her mother: *You've always been much too intrigued by other people's business.* Her mother would thwack Carolyn with a tea towel when she arrived home late for dinner from long sojourns to the library. How many other mothers would complain of such a thing to be doing after school? Hers did, for sure. Then again, she would have complained if the sky was blue, if the sun was shining, if no one died that day. *No wonder I became a psychologist*, Carolyn wanted to say to her in more recent years. She couldn't. Her mother was long gone. Emphysema at sixty. That's what two packs a day will do to you.

On that day they'd met, Carolyn did all she could to assuage her guilt for taking Felicity on.

"Why me?" Carolyn pressed Felicity before they said their goodbyes on that first meeting. "Why tell me your real identity when you've gone so far to hide it from everyone else?"

Felicity took a candy from the bowl on Carolyn's desk and slowly popped it in her mouth, biting into its hard shell, the crunch as loud as the strange ringing in Carolyn's ears, a sensation she often noticed when excited.

"Right woman, right place. That's all. I mean, if Johnny hadn't come to you, I wouldn't have found you. It felt… fitting. To have a psychologist at a time like this and one I can use as a sidekick while I kick that bastard's butt."

Carolyn winced.

"I'm not sure that should be my role."

Felicity nodded. "Hey, I know. Okay. Let me put it this way. There's a few things I need to clear up. It was a long time ago, my memory of it all is kind of challenged right now – something I saw and heard in a bar has added to that – and I'm sure I can get to the bottom of it all if I have some clarity. Well…" she crossed her arms.

"If he is a bastard, of course."

"See? You're already making me more cautious."

"I assume you did research on me?"

Felicity had nodded.

"All above board, except the jaywalking incident in Causeway Bay in 2010."

Carolyn barely remembered it.

"Yet aren't you suspicious about Scarlett? I mean, why did she come to you? Is it possible she knows you're Madeline Chung?"

Felicity tugged on her left earlobe, as she weighed things up.

"Possibly. But I doubt it. Who would tell her? No one except my mother knows I am here. I assume governments don't reveal one's former identity to just any old person and, as Scarlett is a housebound former PR girl, I doubt she has inside contacts who would give her sensitive and highly personal information."

Felicity had shot Carolyn a steady glare. "No. No one knows my identity. Only you and me. Having said that, I don't know why I've become so secretive about it. It seemed like a good idea and, to be honest, it's been quite liberating. But—"

"And?"

"It was so long ago. I don't know if I trust myself as much. But, at the same time, I'm truly motivated to keep going."

"Post-traumatic stress?"

Felicity offered a half-smile. "No. Post-traumatic revenge."

* * *

The problem with Felicity, however, was that Carolyn found she went from psychologist to friend very quickly and against her better judgement. *I'll be careful*, she almost said out loud after they spoke, remembering that not so long ago she had been a busy mother and a wife with an active social life. Now she had little time for friends, being both mother and father to her children. She knew it was loneliness she was feeling. Loneliness and that sinking feeling that her life had become routine and predictable. So, in a way, Felicity's arrival suited her just fine.

* * *

It was getting late, the *vongole* nearly gone, and Carolyn needed to get home to see her youngest before bedtime. She'd promised she'd make it home by ten and it was already nine. He was only eleven years old, but on Friday nights, he could stay up late with the nanny and play violent video games that he assured her were not violent and *just about combat techniques and, you know, using my initiative, like you tell me to do.*

She gulped her last glass and slid the crusty bread around her empty bowl.

"You okay to go ahead with this?" Felicity asked.

Carolyn paused to think. Was she? Yes. She was. But she was also a little confused. She lowered her voice.

"I know how I can help you as a client, but as far as playing your co-researcher on this, I'm sorry to say, that would be a step too far." *There. She'd said it.*

Felicity didn't even blink. She was confident, Carolyn had to hand her that.

"Doing research into Johnny and discussing it with you is as much about friendship as it is emotional assistance." She shrugged and neatly put down her glass. The eager waiter bent over their table to take away the vestiges of their dinner. "With someone who has a brain and not a dick."

The waiter fumbled and noisily clanged a glass with a fork. Carolyn smiled. Felicity continued. "I don't have any close friends here and no one knows who I am. I know you'll keep quiet. You've taken the oath. And, furthermore, I already know you don't have a shady side, unlike so many other people I tend to meet in my line of work."

A few seconds of quiet contemplation passed. Carolyn worried how their "research" would affect Felicity, as her client. The woman had major issues with this guy and if he really wasn't guilty, as the law had found him not to be years before, what then? Carolyn figured she'd be there to help and would offer her services. Either way, Felicity was on a roll and didn't want to let it go, and Carolyn easily convinced herself Felicity would be doing this with or without her.

So far, it'd been kind of fun. As Felicity had explained over dinner, her PI job had connected her to reliable police and legal contacts. They had allowed her to locate reports relating to the case about Johnny, reports her parents had no doubt seen and kept away from her at the time. In these, it correctly said Felicity believed he may have been involved in her kidnapping and ordering they cut off her finger.

Yet Johnny had an alibi; he was at a dinner with a major client in Beijing – a former employee of Felicity's father, no less – and had flown from Hong Kong the day before. Felicity had always known what day it was during her captivity in that dark, dank room, because she could hear the radio from the kitchen. Through the walls, her captors had discussed the weather and horse racing. Killing time.

Felicity realised most of them were not much older than she was. She could smell the cigarette smoke and hear the hiss of beer cans being opened, but most importantly, she always heard the news, the time and the date. *Thursday, twenty-fifth of March.*

"Why would a young British banker, one who was no doubt already successful, get involved in something like that?" Carolyn was saying – again – as they paid the bill. "Sure. Money. I get it. But he was a young banker. He was going to get paid very well as the years progressed. Why start by breaking the law?"

Felicity didn't have the answer, but that didn't change her desire to find out.

"He loved Johnny," she said of her father. "He was impressed with Johnny's upper-class Britishness and education. Johnny was eager and intelligent and super hard-working. I first met Johnny at a Christmas function at the Hong Kong Club, although I had noticed him twice before in Dad's office. But you can imagine, I was halfway through being nineteen when this function was happening and two sips of champagne had gone to my head. And there he was, just twenty-two, a centrepiece under a chandelier, holding a flute of vintage Krug and wearing a tuxedo. I mean, he was the Eurasian James Bond, and he worked for *my father*. Dressed in some flouncy silk shirt with puffy sleeves, I stared at him all night. He barely registered my presence. I cried all the way home."

* * *

Over the course of a year, Felicity had found any excuse to appear when Johnny was around. She'd turn up at her father's office, invite herself to company events, run into Johnny on the street near his office and follow him to a restaurant or café, blushing and fumbling as he smiled with a smug approval of all the attention. Without fail, Johnny brought with him a fragrant waft that sent Felicity into a kind of trance. It was, as Johnny had explained, a bespoke fragrance, one he had made at a French *parfumerie* in the Central Building. A touch of fruit, a hint of jasmine and a musky spice that – combined – smelled romantic and exotic.

As always, his friend and colleague Phil was there with him, like a limpet, mirroring Johnny, mimicking his – and everyone else's – voice and gestures, which Johnny laughed about, Phil also trying to take over every conversation with a put-down designed to move the conversation to him.

"I don't think so, mate! Pull the other one! You need your head checked! Now, what's the plan for Friday?" And so on. Phil would steer Johnny this way and that, to ensure he was facing him; that Felicity was sidelined. Phil was jealous of Felicity's presence. He wanted Johnny all to himself. But so did she. Phil knew what he was doing. In a way, Felicity suspected Johnny enjoyed the competition.

Anyway, Phil was fired and, a few months later, Johnny left, or was asked to leave, after some kind of altercation with her father. Phil and Johnny then set up their own business. She understood. Some people couldn't stand her father's hard-line approach. But, naturally, her overprotective father told her to keep away from Johnny. He was deeply disappointed that they'd fallen out. As is common with young love – let's face it – lust, Felicity's (though she was Madeline then) feverish infatuation for Johnny had quickly died.

Nearly a year later, a big part of her died, too.

* * *

Grey skies, no breeze and a thick humidity that hinted at a long, sticky summer. Looking back, it was ominous. But everything's clearer in retrospect.

Felicity was studying a law degree at University of Hong Kong – well, pretending to study. She had no intention of being a lawyer, but she was doing the right thing in her parents' eyes and most days, when classes were done, she'd shun offers from the family driver and, instead, walk the winding, steep streets towards Sai Ying Pun, often finding herself at her favourite teahouse off Ki Ling Lane. *Same, same.* Except that week, she spotted Johnny. Twice. The first time, she'd seen him just as she left the teahouse, egg tart in her hand. A vague glance upwards and there he was, head half-turned so she knew it was him instantly. He was in a dark suit, midway up a flight of narrow stairs at the end of the lane. He walked to the top and turned left without a backwards glance. The second time was two days later. Felicity was smoking a cigarette at the far end of the lane, contemplating tackling those same stairs, when, to her right and down the hill, there was Johnny, alone, head bent walking, unaware of her presence. She mentioned it to her best friend, and she'd teased her for still stalking Johnny. Felicity left it, cringing at the memories. And, as her best friend stressed, it was hardly unusual, seeing him on a Hong Kong street. *He lives here, you know.* She assumed she'd never entertain a thought about Johnny ever again.

A couple of days later was a Friday. Felicity finished class and, as usual, undertook her concrete amble, past the elaborate lanterns of the temple, past the traditional Chinese medicine stores and the pungent odour of dried seafood, a detour to glance in the window of a storage room that housed rows of lacquered cabinets and canopy beds, along the avenue of hardware stores with jumbles of plastic bottles and laundry baskets dangling from the ceilings, stumbling to avoid construction sites at the top of a darkened row of dirty steps and – pausing to take her breath – watching the retirees carrying small birds in wooden cages. She was happy. Walking like this cleared her mind. She was dressed in jeans and a loose pink shirt, her heavy backpack wobbling left and right as she got to the top of a narrow road, completely out of breath. She'd turned and took her usual shortcut down a lane fronted by low-rise warehouse-style buildings. At the end was the teahouse.

It was quiet when a grey van came careering around the corner behind her. She'd tripped over the kerb in the urgency to get off the road and righted herself in time to press up against an iron door. She had no chance, really. The men jumped from the rear of the van and, before she knew it, Felicity was in the back, face down.

'No one said a word during what seemed like a lifetime of a journey, then, seconds after the van stopped, they covered her eyes. She was walked to a room where they threw her on a thin bed that smelled rotten from damp. It took her a long time to open her eyes, as in, *really* open them. She didn't want to see it. Her brain couldn't take any more.

Days passed in a haze of tears and fitful sleep. Her head throbbed, she couldn't stomach the vile slippery rice they left at her door. The stench of fried onions, garlic, nicotine and sweat permeated her every waking moment. There was no lamp, but slits of sunlight would slice across the far wall in the afternoon, enough for her to see the filth of her surrounds. Only one of the kidnappers showed his face when he came in with water once a day. On the third day, in a fury, she kicked at him. In return, he simply spat on her and called her a dog.

And then came the day, twenty-fifth of March. By then, she had to admit, she was feverish, no doubt from the stress of her ordeal. Or perhaps the cockroaches and the rats.

Naturally, she was also tired and thirsty, but still, she later told police she was sure of one thing – she awoke on this day to hear whispering between a man speaking English and one of the kidnappers. And that's when she smelled it, clear as day: Johnny's distinctive, bespoke fragrance. It was his personal identifier. Anyone who knew Johnny knew that he carried this fragrance waft wherever he went. Felicity had lived and breathed it when she had been infatuated with him. And then there was that voice, a man's voice. Johnny's? Possibly. Just three words, but enough to know it was British. Well-spoken. "Do it, now!" he'd finally said. Of course, Felicity's memories of that voice are hazy, but at the time, she was convinced it was familiar. Or was it? Who knows? But either way, the smell, the sightings of Johnny on her walks, his and Phil's distaste for her father... The puzzle pieces were not that hard to put together.

Minutes later, she was dragged into the kitchen and they held her down with one hand placed on a timber cutting board. She can't even remember the pain, or if she screamed. It came back in jolts of memory that her brain filed away in little dark boxes, broken down to minimise the trauma.

A witness later told investigators that one of the kidnappers, still unsure if the ransom would actually be paid, so wanting to keep her alive, had gone into his shop looking for gauze and disinfectant. Felicity, however, had no recollection of being treated by them. Mercifully, she'd drifted in and out of consciousness, no memory of the physical pain, just flashes of weak light, radio static, sweat. She later read somewhere that the brain will do that when in shock; it has no time for fear or agony. Only survival.

* * *

Carolyn put down her fork and made a mental note to never order that dish again.

Felicity looked around the restaurant before speaking.

92

Police investigations showed Johnny to be squeaky clean, she said. Felicity asked them to see what Phil, his business partner, had been up to that day, but they told her he also had an alibi – he'd been at the office in Central. His assistant – whom Felicity never saw during the court proceedings – provided that for him. And Johnny, the police said, was a young, up-and-coming businessman and, for goodness' sake, he did not have crime connections. Phil was a former cop who would never be taken seriously by local criminals. Felicity couldn't think of anyone else to point the police towards. She knew, she just *knew*, in her gut, that all roads led to Johnny.

As for the kidnappers, they were arrested soon after. All local guys with good enough English. Young and desperate – no doubt also very afraid – they had let her go the day after the attack, about ten minutes after they knew the money had arrived safely. One of them had gone down the road to a phone box and called whoever was in charge and raced back to tell the others. She could hear them celebrating before they covered her eyes and dragged her down a long hallway, doors slamming, whispers and heavy footfall. The guy holding her then let go and told her to stay still. It was quiet, too quiet. After about ten minutes, she had no choice but to stumble a few feet ahead of her, finally emerging into what felt like morning sun. Felicity smelled car exhaust and heard the thunder of double-decker buses. She'd stood wobbling for a few minutes, her hand wrapped tightly in a bloodied T-shirt that served as a bandage, before someone touched her arm and a woman's voice spoke to her kindly. She'd collapsed into her arms.

Later, as the police reminded her, the kidnappers were seen in that part of Kowloon that day and known in the area for criminal activity. All things Johnny was most definitely not. They had acted alone.

So no one believed Felicity. Johnny's fragrance, seeing him twice near the kidnapping site in the days beforehand, and the man speaking English, were considered the ramblings of a silly girl. Her parents couldn't even believe the police bothered looking into Johnny and Phil.

Felicity sat back, and Carolyn tried not to, but she also found it hard not to think Felicity may have been delusional, considering such trauma. But Felicity remained adamant. And the fact she had never been believed seemed to be motivating her even more.

"So, once more, I have to know, who was this guy speaking English that gave the order?" Felicity continued, as they finished their pasta.

"I don't know," Carolyn said, reaching out to squeeze Felicity's good hand. "But thanks for sharing that story with me. You are very strong."

Felicity pulled her hand away.

"I was told by my parents to give up on the idea. They said I could have imagined the entire thing. Most likely, a doctor told them, the trauma had affected my senses."

"Did they ever try to, um, reattach the finger?" Carolyn half-whispered.

"It was too late by then." Carolyn closed her eyes as Felicity paused. "The pain afterwards, in that disgusting room, has been mercifully wiped from my memory. They say this can happen. A natural response."

Carolyn let it all sink in. Fast-forward twenty years, and now, Felicity found herself going through it all over again, delving into his private life, hoping to catch Johnny out for anything at all.

And it was all thanks to Scarlett, Felicity explained, who had come out of nowhere and was apparently jobless since failing to impress the perfectionist nature of Vivian Ma. Scarlett, she said, was just a small part of the puzzle, likely to be gone any day.

"I've heard Vivian's a firecracker," Carolyn said, glad to have some insight into the characters involved. She read the social pages' gossip a few times. "Tough nut. Does a brilliant job, but you wouldn't want to cross her."

"Scarlett is too frail for that kind of boss," Felicity explained. "I've met with Scarlett, as you know, and she always looks and sounds like she's about to cry."

Carolyn shook her head. "No comment. What Johnny has told me remains between us."

Felicity shrugged.

"One more wine?"

Carolyn looked at her watch.

She was feeling the effects enough as it was. The waiter sidled over, smiling. The other diners had energised a little, their voices rising and falling alongside more tinny 1980s' tunes. From the kitchen, another waiter emerged holding an oversized cake lit up like it was the Fourth of July. *How nice*, Carolyn thought. The last time she had been spoiled by Captain Loser (as she had come to call Greg, her ex), was her thirty-ninth birthday, ten years ago now. They had gone to the Island Shangri-La and had oysters, Carolyn hoping that, finally, he had changed. Carolyn later found out he'd snuck off that very night to have a little tête-à-tête with his new girlfriend when he was meant to be visiting the restroom. *Oh well. You live and you learn.*

"Come on," Felicity urged.

"My son."

"It's 9.30. And you have help at home!"

"Fine."

"Just one."

"Right."

"So," Felicity said, fresh glass of red in hand. "What's our next step?"

"You're a freelance writer, aren't you?" Carolyn replied.

"Yes. I write about how to cope with party-loving teenagers lying about their whereabouts, dealing with nursing care staff whom you suspect are mistreating your elderly parent, or," she waved one arm in the air, "knowing when to hire a PI to spy on your cheating spouse. Or something along those lines. You know, cases I've had. I could write a book."

Carolyn grabbed her arm.

"So. There you have it." She sipped her wine and sat back, briefly wondering if she was out of her mind getting so excited about this Enid Blyton adventure she was having. If she were truly honest, it was better than watching *The Housewives of Orange County*, which is what her school-mother friends would be doing, despite protestations to the contrary. "You're writing a book," Carolyn continued.

Felicity blanched.

"Am I?"

"Yes. You're Faye Win, your freelance alias, remember? On the side, you're writing a book about old Hong Kong crimes. You know, a non-fiction insight into the dark underbelly of the city's crime history. People love that kind of thing. And if I am not mistaken," she briefly stopped as a businessman passed by that little too slowly, "you can email the client in Beijing who Johnny was dining with the evening your finger was severed and ask him for his, you know, his comments. *Dear Mr Blah. I would like some personality and colour in my book and I would very much appreciate hearing the recollections of your meeting with Mr Humphries on the night of the twenty-fifth of March, 1995.*"

"I doubt he'll go for it," Felicity scoffed. "He'd be worried about it all coming back to bite him."

Carolyn shook her head. "No. People love to talk about their past. This guy was just having dinner with Johnny."

"And all he is going to say is that."

"That's the part you don't know. What if he says the date was wrong, that Johnny hadn't met him that evening?"

Felicity hung her head back.

"The date was not wrong. I heard it on the radio. Every day. They turned it on like clockwork, basically to hear about themselves, the kidnapping. How much money they were going to make. *Idiots.*" Felicity tapped the cigarette-she-rarely-smoked on the table.

"It was a long time ago, Felicity. What if… what if,

somehow, Johnny or his accomplices paid the guy he was having dinner with to lie?"

"You mean, why would the guy tell me the truth now?"

"Guilt? Maybe he won't. Maybe he will. You have nothing to lose. Seems that if you still hold this strong suspicion, then you should go for it. I mean, Felicity, some English-speaking man, most likely British, as you've said, who carried with him the odour of someone you knew well, ordered a kidnapper to cut off your finger and he never went to jail for it."

Felicity shuddered.

"It's worth a shot."

Carolyn was smiling.

"Ask the guy, in an email, in a way that sounds writerly. You're intrigued, not trying to implicate him to dig up old dirt. What was it like, being named in the papers after the event? How did Johnny seem? Do you think he was innocent? He'll be quoted in a very nice, very intelligent non-fiction book in English. He won't be able to resist. He'll give more than he has to."

"How do you know?"

"Years have passed. I bet he's retired. Secure. Didn't they say in those old reports that he was about fifty back then? It's his history and some reporter wants to put his name in a book. It'll give him something new to think about when he's pruning his bonsai plants. Most people probably never ask him a thing. They see an old man and they assume he's nearly dead or just plain old boring."

Felicity smiled her small-toothed smile. They were so rare that Carolyn felt a huge sense of accomplishment.

"See?" Felicity said as she finished her glass. "That's why I need you."

Damn it, Carolyn mused, *I should have been a detective.*

As they had done since their first meeting, they eventually said their goodbyes inside and left the restaurant within a few minutes of each other. Carolyn felt a thrilling chill every time, despite knowing it was childish.

Back out on the streets of Wan Chai on a Friday night, she inhaled, closed her eyes and listened. Car engines, music, laughter, children crying, trucks rambling, a ship's horn, a light breeze in her ears. She smelled the usual wet rice and exhaust and, for a split second, a waft of jasmine. She'd been in that city for twenty or so years and she'd never felt more a part of it than at that moment. Funny how the smallest change to your routine could bring you back to earth. She made a mental note to advise her clients to do the same. But at the same time, *Do not help a PI dig dirt on a client.* She laughed into the breeze as she raised a hand at a passing taxi.

* * *

Felicity was agitated and couldn't sleep. Her bed faced the window and she'd left the curtains open to let in the moonlight, hoping its soft glow would be comforting as it floated across her bedcovers. She sipped at some water, made a sandwich, sat on her balcony and let the crisp night air sting her bare arms. She walked in circles around her pitifully small living room and sang songs from *The Sound of Music.*

Felicity's only niggling doubt was Phil. From that night not long ago, when she'd been tracking Johnny at the Tequila Bar. At one stage, she'd been seated close enough to hear them, Phil was telling jokes, he'd just been singing with Melvis and then did an impressive impersonation of Johnny. Phil was a performer, with a bit of a chip on his shoulder too. Could it have been him who made the order to hurt her? It didn't sound like Phil, but maybe he was putting on that voice. It was possible. But then again, Phil had an alibi. And also, there was that smell: Johnny's smell. No matter what, Felicity surmised, they would have *had* to have been in it together. Johnny and Phil. Phil and Johnny. Just who was pulling all the strings? Felicity would have to deal with that issue after she got on to the guy in Beijing.

Eventually, she cracked open a beer. She waited fifteen

minutes, but nothing had worked. She was awake. She turned on her laptop, called up the newspaper archives and started digging.

Two hours later, Felicity had her man – the client dining with Johnny that night. His name was Simon Gu. How in God's name did she not remember that? Probably deliberately. It was a frightening realisation, though. Maybe her memories of the events were flawed after all. "Simon Gu," she said out loud, "Faye Win is coming to get you."

CHAPTER EIGHT

East London, 1980s.

He was handsome, even as a young boy. His mother told him so. All the time. If he caught his reflection in a shop window, he would look, surreptitiously, just to make sure she was right; that all those mothers in the park were right. *What a lovely boy.* His mother would pat his head and agree.

He liked to wear his hair slicked back, his shoes polished. Every morning, he took the time to smooth his ironed shirts that little bit more, brush and floss and check for loose buttons. The other kids around their parts were slobs, so his mother had told him, all long hair, exposed flesh. And the British girls. *Aiyahh!* She reserved most of her scorn for their ilk. Once, his mother not only scowled at a girl passing by in low-slung jeans and a crop top, she then hissed the word *slut* as the girl ambled by. The girl had given his mother the finger and – chewing gum – had winked at him. He was only eight years old, but God he fancied her after that. Blonde, petite, tanned. She was trouble, his mother said. *Exactly*, Johnny thought to himself.

Johnny knew he had a father from the minute he had a memory, but he'd only met him once, aged five, a brief and uneventful encounter which included a 3p Curly Wurly and a weak handshake. His father smelled of cigars and Johnny remembered very little except fanning at his nose after the man left the room.

His mother told him his father was a no-good bastard who left them broke. She said he had disowned them, had a wife and two other children and lived the high life, while she worked in Marshes' dry-cleaners, a place Johnny actually loved. It was always warm, the chubby owner gave him packets of Spangles and he got to watch cartoons on the old black-and-white TV in the back office, which was really a storage room. His mother said the Marshes were lazy people, fat and ugly and didn't work hard enough. Johnny didn't argue with her, but he loved Mrs Marsh's soft hugs and her husband's cosy inactivity, the boiled kettles and tea caddies. Oh, well. His mother was his mother. What could he do? She loved him and cared for him. She doted on him and gave him whatever she could – decent clothes and shoes, a warm bed, as many schoolbooks as he needed.

"We suffer," she had repeated daily, "while he stays at the Dorchester. You hear me, Johnny? That man, he forgot you. He forgot you, me and how hard I work. One day, you make him pay. Okay? You *make… him… pay!*"

Johnny had slunk away to his squat, colourless bedroom and counted his matchbox cars. He would make voices, pretending to be the people driving the cars. *I say, do move out of the way, old boy. Of course, my good man. But before I depart, please come for tea tomorrow. And the children too. Lovely. Must run. Rrrrrrrrrrrrr. Oh, dear! I've lost control! Whatever will happen!*

He'd seen people talk like that on TV. But not in real life on Grundy Street.

* * *

One afternoon, everything was a little different. He came home from school and – as always – washed his hands and used a little water to slick back his hair. He admired his reflection and gave himself a flirty grin in the narrow, cracked mirror. Back in the yellow-stained hallway, it was quiet. Normally, his mother would be watching soap operas, screeching angrily at the screen in Cantonese and interspersing it with English swear words as she washed the dishes or prepared his supper. *You're stupid!* Chuk sang dou but yu*! You're worse than the animals.*

But this day, all he could hear was the ticking of the clock on the kitchen wall. Then he smelled it. Cigars.

"Jarney," his mother gushed, as he placed one foot slowly in front of the other. She was sitting on her favourite easy chair, facing the TV.

"Mummy," he said, a little accusingly, swiftly turning his head to the corner of the room, the part hidden by the doorway, the space that reeked of Cubans.

The man stood and stuck out a hand. Johnny followed suit. His father was tall, more than six foot, and Johnny craned his head to take in his thick silver head of hair and billowy pink cheeks. His shirt buttons strained but he stood ramrod straight and put one hand on a hip.

"Mother tells me you're doing well at school," his father said. Johnny's mouth opened and shut. He blushed. He felt his mother prod him in the back and he swatted at her hand. "Tells me you're a hard worker, a good help around the house too."

He nodded.

"Jarney," his mother said in a cloying voice he had only heard her use once – it was the time she didn't have enough money for the heating one bitter winter and managed to get an extension on the payment. "Tell your father what you got for maths. And science. Okay? Tell him."

Johnny recited his high marks in a girly whisper. He hated his little voice against his father's commanding baritone and pressed his skinny thighs together, worried he might wet his pants.

"How old are you now? Ten?"

"Uh, yes," he said, his voice cracking a little at the end. He heard the clink of his mother's teacup as she placed it down. It was the good tea set they never used, given to her by an old boss when she left a cleaning job at the biscuit factory. Only three of the six cups were chip-free.

"A man!" his father boomed. "When I was nine, I was sent to board at Bramar Hall and saw my mother twice a year! Silly old bat she was anyway. Well…"

His mother giggled. Johnny wanted to throw up. For a split second, he thought of Brian Feathers, his best friend, in fact, his only friend, the only one who understood his unusual situation, being in a rather dire one himself. Brian the Brain. Brian with the big ideas.

* * *

They'd met walking home from school two years before and had become inseparable. Johnny had dropped a penny down a drain and was on his knees, peering into the filthy muck below. Brian stopped. *I can see it*, Johnny told him. Brian got down on his knees and, with his pin-like freckled arms, helped Johnny yank the grate open. He had held on to Johnny's ankles as Johnny reached down and fetched the coin. Johnny had smiled. Brian had smiled. That was all it took.

Brian was a mechanical whizz with oversized eyes and a slight droop to the left side of his face. They made a curious pair: one the scrawny ginger son of an out-of-work abusive drunk with a lopsided face, the other the particularly attractive son of a Chinese cleaner and an absent British father. The local ladies hanging out the washing or serving tea at the café couldn't take their eyes off the two of them as they scurried along the high street, heads pressed together like conjoined non-identical twins. Brian's father was particularly unhappy with their tight union, reminding Brian regularly that "No son of mine should be best mates with a chink!" Johnny and Brian ignored the sniggers and Brian's father's disapproval. They were busy planning to build their own car from old parts they'd scavenged around town. Brian's uncle was a mechanic and he could show them how to do it. They'd talked about it for weeks when walking home from school.

"It really isn't that hard," Brian had said. "We can use a motorcycle engine and use its wiring for the spark and ignition control." Johnny had nodded excitedly. After they'd built it, they were going to horde all the tinned food they could find, take off and never look back. *Maybe go as far away as Oxford.*

* * *

One afternoon, the two found themselves ambling closer to Brian's home. It was a cool evening; a biting wind gripped their skinny ankles as they kicked a football. Muddy water from puddles splashed their crumpled school socks.

"Over here!" Johnny called. Brian kicked the ball on an angle. Johnny chased it.

"Oi! Not there!" Brian yelled back. "Leave it. I'll get it!"

"Why?" Too late. Johnny had already retrieved the ball and was kicking it to his mate.

That was when Johnny heard classical music. A faint rising and falling being carried on the breeze. Brian stopped. The football rolled past his feet and Brian didn't even notice.

"What are you doing?" Johnny huffed as he raced to his friend's side.

"My house is just… there," Brian said quietly.

"Yeah? So?"

"Well, it's best you don't come…"

The music was turned up louder. It wafted towards their ears and rooted Brian to the spot.

"Wonder who's playing that?" Johnny asked, bending down to pick up the ball.

"No one. Let's go." He pulled on Johnny's sleeve.

A door slammed hard. A man grumbled. The music soared. As Johnny started to walk away, a burly man, red-cheeked and wild-eyed, stumbled towards them. It was Brian's father. Johnny had seen him a few times on the high street, dragging

Brian's long-suffering mum behind him. But he looked different this time. Crazed.

Brian didn't move. Johnny frowned.

"I've told you, boy!" the man roared at Brian, grabbing for his collar. "No son of mine is friends with a Chinaman!"

Johnny could smell something strong and tangy. Perhaps because Brian's father was drunk, Johnny somehow wrestled out of his grip and ran away.

"Run, Johnny!" Brian cried.

For a few seconds, Johnny couldn't move. But then, just as the violins reached a crescendo, he ran – but not away from the man. Instead, he ran straight into the side of Brian's father, a wall of flesh that was as hard as it was soft. The man made an *ooof* sound, as though winded. Johnny kicked and thwacked and shut his eyes so tightly he saw stars.

"Bloody hell." Johnny opened his eyes to see Brian's father shuttling away towards a gate, towards the music, towards his misery. He saw Brian's father wipe spit from the corner of his mouth, or was it vomit? "I'm goin' to get you, boy," Brian's father gurgled over a hunched shoulder. Johnny, bent forward huffing and puffing, couldn't tell if the threat was directed at him or Brian.

He turned.

Brian was standing there, head hanging a little.

"You shouldn't have done that, Johnny. It's Tchaikovsky's Fifth," Brian whispered. "It makes him maudlin, Mother says." He pumped his tiny shoulders a few times before reaching out a hand to Johnny. "Come on. Let's go."

Back at Johnny's house, the two sat quietly on Johnny's bed.

"I hate this," Brian said. "Let's not be sad. It's dead boring."

Johnny nodded.

"Got any ideas?"

"Got a chess set?"

Brian taught him all the tactics. It was a game Johnny instantly understood.

From then on, they played it every afternoon in Johnny's

darkened room until suppertime, Brian squinting at the pieces as Johnny tapped his fingers impatiently on the metal frame of his bed. "Strategy," Brian stressed. "This is the kind of strategic practice we need to utilise for our eventual escape in the car. This is what we need to get out of here one day and be happy."

But Brian always won. He was like that.

* * *

At that very moment, with Sir Robert Humphries' pink fleshy lips half-open like a trout on a hook, Johnny wanted that home-made car like nothing else.

"Must run," his father finally said, placing down the teacup from which he hadn't sipped. "Duty calls." His mother nodded and fussed and Johnny noticed she had applied bright red lipstick. He felt sad.

As Johnny's father left the house, head bent, his wrinkled eyes slightly watery, he handed his mother an envelope and patted her hand. Johnny's mother looked up at his father and batted her eyelashes, hopefully, like a child. His father recoiled. Johnny hated him more at that very moment than ever before.

"Well done," his father said to his mother, while throwing Johnny a passing glance. "Much better than I ever could have imagined. Must be my father's genes." His father had snickered a little as he put on his hat and emerged into a weak afternoon sun. Johnny's mother closed the door and her smile morphed into a dramatic grimace. She began counting the money, clenching her jaw and frowning. Just like the baddy in a comic book, Johnny thought.

For weeks, his mother rang his father. Johnny could hear her yelling into the phone. The calls were brief but bitter. "It's not enough! You made a promise for Johnny. Do you want me to tell your new girl? I could ruin your life too!"

"Mum!" Johnny snapped one morning, jolting her from the gloomy after-effects of an emotional outburst on the phone.

"We are fine! You and I are fine! I'm happy here, with you. With us. Please leave it. Leave him. We don't need him. Soon, I can work and take care of you!"

"No, my darling boy," she'd sighed. "You are going to be a doctor or a lawyer or a famous scientist. Marry a beautiful girl and have babies together. Not like, not like…" She'd burst into tears and slumped to the floor. She was tiny. Frail. *An injured bird*, he thought.

* * *

Not long after, a letter arrived. At age eleven, he would go to Bramar Hall. It was to all be paid for by his father. Johnny was to stay hush-hush at all times about his parentage. *Or else there could be repercussions*, the letter had stressed.

"You keep your mouth shut." His mother had poked him in the chest. "Tell them your father's dead. May as well be."

She had hugged him and he could feel her wide lips smiling against his skin. That night, after dinner, she drank one glass of sherry and passed out on the sofa.

Johnny thought Brian would be upset he'd be leaving soon, but Brian had slapped Johnny on the shoulder with his tiny palm and told Johnny he was pleased for him. *Good old Brian.* He'd never had such a genuine friend and doubted he ever would.

* * *

A week later, Brian went missing. Johnny ran all around town for three days: the sweet shop, the grocers, the café, his uncle's mechanic yard. He was nowhere. He told his mother. She pulled him close and said not to worry, but Johnny could tell she knew something.

"What is it?" he whimpered.

"Nothing. I don't know. He'll be back at school soon, I'm sure."

Brian wasn't at school the next day. Johnny was bereft. Even one of the teachers frowned into his paperwork when Johnny asked for Brian's whereabouts. "Johnny, I tell you what, take this document to the headmaster's office, there's a good boy."

Johnny tried to call Brian's home phone, but it was cut off. He asked his mother again if she knew anything, but she was too busy at the laundry and told him not to worry, which made him worry more. Finally, when he couldn't take it any longer, Johnny dared to visit Brian's house.

It was down a lane and behind a red brick wall, not like a house but an add-on at the back of a bigger home owned by Brian's aunt. Brian told Johnny it had three rooms and a small bathroom. But Brian had never let Johnny go further than the front gate. If his dad was home, Brian had said, you just never knew. Johnny knocked, even though the gate was slightly open. No one came. He called out. No one answered. A dog barked next door and he jumped, as he pushed at the gate. Someone kicked a can in the lane behind him and, for a second, he froze. *It was only a can*, he told himself, thinking of what Brian would logically advise.

"Brian?" he called, opening the rickety timber gate, the metal handle rattling as it closed behind him. "Brian? It's me. Johnny." Nothing.

Inside, it smelled damp and sour, a combination Johnny couldn't quite place – old vegetables, off milk, onions sweaty and hot in a pan. Disinfectant? In one corner was a small orange sofa, faded and, curled up on it, a fat moggy cat, sleeping soundly. A pot of tea sat alongside a small jug – no cups – on a metal tray in front of the sofa. There was a low bookshelf, a table on the far side dressed with a white tablecloth and, in the middle, an empty butter dish. A small grimy window let in enough light for Johnny to see an open newspaper on the table and a red Formica chair placed at the far end. Johnny walked over, thumbed at the paper and breathed a little sigh of relief. Everything looked relatively normal.

"Brian," he dared to utter.

Something shuffled, somewhere to his left.

Johnny walked towards the sound. There was a door, half-open. It led to a narrow room, oblong-shaped, grey and airless. Johnny turned to his right and there was Brian, lying face up on a perfectly made bed, the brown bedcovers tucked neatly into the sides of a timber frame.

"Brian! You're meant to be at school. The teachers are angry! If you've been working on the car without me… What the hell are you…?" As he got closer, Johnny could see more clearly, Brian's small, pale face, swollen, bruised and cut, a couple of hastily applied bandages placed over his blackened right cheek. Dried blood stuck to the skin around the lopsided skin near his eyes. He smiled at Johnny.

"I think I lost a tooth," Brian said. His voice was hoarse. Johnny sat on the edge of the bed. Up closer, Johnny could see Brian's left eye was weeping, the bruise on his friend's cheekbone a purple lump with a deep laceration in the middle of it.

He cradled Brian's head in his arms and cried without making a sound.

"I promise you, mate. I promise you. That arsehole will never touch you again. Ever." Brian tried to speak, but a little gurgle came out. Johnny stroked his friend's head. "Whatever you need, whatever it takes, I will help you. I promise. You won't be alone. Okay?"

Finally, Brian took a deep breath.

"You and me, Johnny. It's just you and me. For ever."

"For ever," Johnny muttered, his eyes overflowing with angry, vengeful tears. "Anything you need, I'll do whatever it takes."

* * *

Three months later, Johnny set off for boarding school. Brian the Brain stood on the corner of the street and waved a racing-car flag. Johnny watched until Brian was a shimmering black-and-white dot in the late summer sun.

By the end of the first term, Johnny was given the news that his mother had died.

CHAPTER NINE

Shek O Village, Hong Kong Island.

Wang was standing at Alice's door, dishevelled, a small Band-Aid over the bridge of his nose and a half-healed scratch on his right cheek. Alice gasped. She wanted to be angry, but she couldn't hide her relief and concern.

"I've been calling, for days and… Are you okay?"

"Sorry," he smiled and shuffled his feet. "Work."

"Two weeks?"

She wasn't going to let him in. They'd had three fantastic dates and he'd called after all of them to tell her what a great time he'd had. They'd kissed. Alice didn't want to jump into bed with him too soon. She'd been there, done that. With Wang, she'd basically followed Dating 101 by the book and then… nothing. This was also the first time she'd ever even considered a local guy. Her type was British, witty, middle- to upper-middle-class professionals. Men her mother would have told her had promising prospects. But Wang was different. He had a youthful energy, a finesse about him, a kindness she was ready for. *No more egomaniacs.*

And then, he'd disappeared. After a few days of not hearing a word, she'd finally texted him. No reply. Alice was seething. She was embarrassed. She was sure she'd run into him in the village and, when she didn't, asked the guy who owned the local café if he'd seen him around. The answer was a shrug. Alice decided Wang was a waste of space, a waste of time and a waste of her energy. He was just like the rest of them. She buried herself in work and walking her dog and reading non-fiction books. She had an entire wall lined with biographies of Bob Dylan, Barbra Streisand, Nelson Mandela, Keith Richards. She decided to move on from thoughts of romance. Being alone was better than waiting for the phone to ring, like some 1970s' ABBA song. *Fuck you, Wang.*

"Are you angry?" He said it with a smile, a slight upward turn of his – Alice couldn't deny it – generous lips.

"Yes," she spat. "I assume you got my texts? And where have you been anyway? You look exhausted. What happened to your nose?"

"Um. It's a difficult one. Sorry." He hung his head a little and Alice felt a pang of inexplicable pity. "I know it's all a bit weird."

He ran a hand through messy hair and glanced over his shoulder. Behind him was the narrow, bougainvillea-lined alleyway that led to Alice's bright-blue village house. As always, the alleyway had again been washed down by their neighbour, Mrs Lam, who ran the local grocery store. It always smelled faintly of Pine O Cleen, but the waft of clogged drains usually won out. Often, when Alice arrived home after a long day at work, Mrs Lam would be sitting out the front on a folding chair, legs akimbo in her printed pyjama suit, just watching everyone come and go. She was elderly, had lived in the village since she was five years old, and spying on the villagers was her pastime. As Wang set his pleading eyes on Alice, Mrs Lam's front door slammed shut. Wang smiled at Alice knowingly.

Alice couldn't help but smile back.

"That's it. The whole village will know I came over now," he whispered.

"I'll put a stop to that rumour," she snapped.

He looked straight at her. "Listen. It's hard to explain. Do you mind if I come in?"

"For five minutes," she replied curtly. She opened the door

slightly. They walked up an airless flight of white interior stone stairs to reach another door that took them into Alice's upstairs apartment.

Alice noticed he was walking a little gingerly, but he stood taller when he saw her register.

"Coffee?"

"Thanks."

She pointed to the sofa.

"Nice place."

"Small."

"We all have small places in this village." Instead of sitting down, he walked towards the terrace to his right. "But if we're lucky, we have that view." Wang unlatched the terrace door and in raced a medium-sized, caramel-coloured mutt with long ears and little legs.

"Nice dog!" he called.

From the kitchen, Alice clanked at some pans. "Wang, meet Turbo, the only reason why I go walking in the summer heat."

Wang sat down on the sofa and Turbo followed him. On the table, Wang noticed a pile of hardcovered books – one on art history, another a biography of Charlie Chaplin.

"Sugar?" she called.

"Yes. Two."

Above him were old fisherman's baskets Alice had hung as light fixtures. The walls behind him were painted a light red. The net curtains fanning the bamboo chairs near the window were aqua. Every inch of wall was covered in a riot of colours. Alice could see him from the kitchen, taking it all in around him.

"You paint?" he said, as she walked in holding two bottles of Tsingtao beer.

"Oh God no," she laughed, plonking herself next to him. "No creative bones in my body. I work. Then I work some more. And sometimes, I get drunk, hike with the dog or swim at the beach. In the shallows."

"I thought we were having coffee."

"Too bad." She slugged at her beer.

Wang studied her thick red hair as it hung loose and wavy around her shoulders. He cleared his throat and sipped at the beer.

"So," she said, shifting away from him a little, "are you going to finally tell me where you've been?"

He put the bottle down, slowly. He shook his head and scratched at his right cheek. Alice braced herself.

"If I tell you," he said, sitting back into soft neon-hued cushions, "that there is something about my... my life that I can't reveal just yet. It's nothing to do with another woman or anything. If I tell you that I can't explain it in full, not yet anyway, and that it has to do with doing what's right for my mother, for my father's legacy, would you... would you respect that? Please?"

Alice looked sceptical.

"You know, I used to be an idiot when it came to men," she said. Wang reached for his drink again. "I'd believe any old rubbish they threw at me. And then, I grew up."

"And?"

"And so now, I want honesty, about everything. I don't want to know what colour your shit is, but I do want to know why you disappeared for two weeks and didn't call me."

Wang laughed so hard he had to place the beer bottle back on the table to stop it from spilling.

"The colour of my shit? Did you just say that?"

"Yes." She crossed one pale angular leg over the other. Her toenails were painted bright green.

Wang shrugged. His lips were parted but the words wouldn't come out. Outside the window, Alice could hear a couple arguing loudly in Cantonese, something about one of them forgetting to bring the beach towels.

"Weather's warming up," he finally mumbled. "The crowds will be coming to the village soon. I prefer winter here."

Alice stood. "Me too. But still, answer the question."

Wang stood and walked to the terrace. The sea was bubbling nicely.

"I've got an idea," he said chirpily.

She stopped walking towards the kitchen and placed a hand on one hip. She was only wearing a long T-shirt, grey with a V-neck.

"I'm listening," she said quietly.

"The wind. It's perfect today." He waved a hand towards the window.

"The wind is perfect for telling the truth?"

Wang took a few paces and opened the iron-rimmed terrace doors. They rattled noisily and a flock of yellow-beaked miner birds scattered from the railing.

"It's perfect for a catamaran," he said loudly.

"I don't sail." Alice was now in the kitchen.

"You're crazy. It's the best day out. It'll be ideal. We could make it to Po Toi in forty minutes. Have lunch at the restaurant, a few beers. You'll love it."

Alice pointed at his nose.

"What about your injury? And you seem to be a little sore when you're walking?"

He shook his head. "No, honestly. It's nothing. Sailing is the one thing that I probably *can* do right now. I'm a natural out there."

He pointed over the terrace, south, across the sea to Po Toi island, a small, hilly rock of weathered granite, the top of which was shrouded in morning mist. She'd been to it, of course, on a large seafaring boat sailed by a professional. Po Toi featured a few old temples, a walking track, an ageing population of only about two hundred people and a famous seafood restaurant, on stilts and backed by a rancid public toilet. It overlooked a bay and was a popular weekend getaway location for families, large junk boat parties and avid sailors.

Alice said nothing but walked back into the room, wiping wet hands onto her T-shirt.

"No way. I'll be terrified. I can't sail. I'd need a life jacket just to sit on a catamaran that wasn't even in the water."

Wang turned and walked towards her. He took her in his arms. She could tell he wanted her, was holding himself back. She watched as he closed his eyes, breathing her in.

"Steady on." She made a lame attempt at pushing him away. "I barely know you. I thought I did and then…"

He let go, just a little bit. She refused to meet his eye.

"Okay. I'll explain, but not now. I can't. Please just take my word on this. But come sailing with me. I'm a very safe, very *caring* instructor."

Alice hesitated.

"Sailing, open sea… I don't know. I'm British!"

He kissed her softly on the cheek and whispered into her ear.

"And I'm Chinese. What could possibly go wrong?"

* * *

Alice screamed. The water was freezing. Wang shook his head and smiled at the rising sail.

"Come on. Get on!" he called.

She hopped onto the catamaran and huddled her legs into her chest.

"It's tropical water," Wang said, secretly enjoying her dramatic reaction. "Even at the end of winter it's only about twenty-two degrees. That's pretty warm."

"I don't want to do this."

"You'll love it."

He knew she would. It had been terrifying his first time, too, the day his dad took him out to sea when he was fourteen and he could barely swim. But as soon as the wind took the sail, and all other people, all cars, buses, all man-made sounds, disappeared with the green hills behind them, he had changed. After he and his father had landed back at St Stephen's Bay, a small sandy beach near the tourist hotspot of Stanley, his father had told him to take off his life jacket. Wang had done so. Within a second of Wang removing it, his dad pushed him overboard.

"Swim!" his dad had called as Wang splashed about, doggy paddle, which was all he knew. Wang swam to shore, furious.

The weekend after, Wang jumped overboard himself. The weekend after that, he was swimming in a relatively normal fashion, arm over arm – without any skill or style. His dad bought him swimming lessons for his fifteenth birthday and, at sixteen, he got his diving licence.

"The sea is freedom. It is space. It is something we fear but should not avoid, like love, like dreams," his father had said, salt spray dotting his cheeks as they'd cruised towards Repulse Bay one summer. "If you can't swim, you live in fear of the sea. If you avoid love, you live in fear of being hurt. What is the point of being afraid? You only miss out. And then you die with no adventure in your heart."

Wang wouldn't repeat such cheesy sentiments to Alice. Not yet.

* * *

He grinned stupidly as Alice turned to watch the Saturday-morning fracas that was the norm at Stanley's renowned market stalls, bayside cafés and bars. By then, the seaside boardwalk was just a series of red-and-blue specks in the distance.

"It's a quick trip!" he called to her. "Don't throw yourself overboard, will you?"

She was holding tightly to the mast and for the first time since he'd set up the vessel, she honoured him with a half-smile.

"I'm okay," she called back, hair plastered across her face. "It feels quite nice, really, cutting through the water like this. It's not that windy, is it?"

"Not here!"

She grimaced.

"Are there sharks? I mean, I know they're around sometimes, but at this time of year, are there… more of them?"

"Only once we get further out."

She mouthed "Fuck you", turned away, still smiling.

After this, he still didn't think he'd tell her about what had just happened. It was too risky. He'd have to keep putting her off the scent. Maybe he'd never tell her, or he'd be dead soon anyway. He shuddered against a rising wind.

Further out to sea, it seemed Alice dared to help him with a few ropes, her brow furrowed in concerned concentration.

"Perfect," he called as they tacked southwards to the island. "Close enough now to see the boats in the bay."

Wang called out a few instructions. Alice yanked at some ropes. It was calm, the water and wind perfectly aligned for an easy sail.

"I can't believe I did that," she said, wiping seawater from her lips. "I pulled it, the boat moved and then…"

"You're a natural."

The village where they both lived, Shek O, came into view as they approached Po Toi.

"I can see the terrace of my house!" Alice cried. "The blue! And the Headland. You can tell by the pine trees. My God… I've never seen it like this. It's so, so colourful, so quaint. So picturesque."

Wang nodded, sagely. He'd had the same thrill when he first saw it too, his home by the sea, no high-rises, no chain stores. Just one road in and then one road out. He hoped it would stay that way.

"See the house with the orange walls to the right of the beach café?"

She nodded.

"That's the old lady with the dogs, the one who has a walker. Not sure of her real name. Lived in Shek O her entire life. She's in her late nineties now. You probably see her sitting on the beach wall all afternoon, feeding the birds."

"Oh, yes," Alice said. "She tries to give Turbo leftover rice. He loves her. Never misses a chance to race over."

"During World War Two, when the Japanese invaded and took control, the story goes that a group of soldiers came to Shek O and gathered as many people as they could, rounded them up on the Back Beach and shot them dead. Po Po – let's call her – and her sisters had run away and were watching from the bushes on the hill above, the one in front of the Shek O Country Club. They hid for days afterwards but eventually, they had to return. Many people died. Po Po lost two brothers and an uncle. But I'm not sure if it's true. That village is filled with rumour and folklore."

He sensed a change in Alice. He could tell something had lifted. As though she was trying not to smile too much. She was happy. He had made her happy. And he knew it.

* * *

The catamaran slid peacefully into the bay. A few junks, a couple of sailing boats and a fishing boat were moored in its calm, brown-tinged waters.

"See? How do you feel?"

"I loved it," she told him honestly, as he helped her on to the wooden jetty. "I mean it. It felt so, so…"

"Exhilarating?"

"No. I've gone out of my comfort zone, for once. I feel brave. Embarrassingly. For me. Listen," she stopped walking, looking straight into Wang's eyes, "I know you'll tell me when you're ready. I trust you, I do. But don't do it again." She smiled, lightly smacking his arm.

He kissed her, slowly. At the seaside entrance to the restaurant, a large group of sunburnt *gweilos* sat with three ice buckets full of champagne atop their plastic dining table. Macklemore's "Downtown" boomed from a speaker attached to a mobile phone. As Alice emerged from Wang's embrace, the group clapped and cheered. Wang bowed before taking her hand.

"You were very brave," he said as they sat down as far from the large expat group as possible. The word *brave* sat heavy and ominous on his tongue. He had to say something else; remove it. "Now. Thirsty sailors need sustenance." Alice had to agree, she was famished.

A waiter threw two plastic-covered menus on the table – they decided on clams, beef and noodles.

"I'm trying not to think about work," Alice said out of the blue. "It's starting to get me down."

Wang was pleased to change the subject. He listened as Alice complained about her micromanager boss, the sterile environment, how she wanted a change of scene.

"What about you? What did you study?" she asked.

"English literature. Later, I did a graphic design course. Now I'm a freelance designer. I've got some loyal clients, so it works."

"Why English literature?"

"My mother, she had an English nanny. She came from a wealthy family in Shanghai. We read English language books, all day, all night. She loved P.G. Wodehouse. I'd hear her laugh out loud from the living room when I was little. She never let us watch TV, even when we were teenagers." They laughed.

"I watched plenty of it," Alice said. "But often I was by myself."

* * *

Wang smiled, but still, he felt a small lump settle in his throat. He wished he hadn't said that word. *Brave.* He felt anything but. He needed to enjoy the moment. Forget about those men. *Brave.* He allowed himself to think it once more and then shook his head vigorously.

"You okay?" Alice asked, holding his forearm with a tenderness he hadn't seen before.

"Couldn't be better."

In a way, he meant it. In another way, it was a complete lie.

* * *

On that day at the MTR station turnstile two weeks ago, he'd barely had time to register what was going on, a stalled thought process that stopped him from fighting back. Wang was not used to rough treatment. He had a strong mind but had never encountered aggression, save for schoolboy scuffling. Although he was physically strong, he found the men's threatening shoves and heavy grip on his arms to be much more distressing than he imagined when watching such scenes in a movie. As his legs started moving – and not of their own accord – he was embarrassed to recall he was voiceless. Why didn't he call out? Scream he was being taken? Surely someone would have done something. But he froze.

Within the space of a couple of minutes, two burly men had frogmarched him back up the stairs, oblivious commuters saying nothing and doing nothing. They reached the street and then swiftly entered a door and up more stairs.

They stopped, breathing heavily, bathed in sweat and swearing intermittently.

Wang could see they were now in a darkened corner of a two-storey car park. One of the men had held Wang's head down as they'd entered the building, but he'd managed to raise it enough to see that they had walked past a few parked vehicles in the middle section. The back corner where they were was half closed off by a crumbling wall, creating a kind of hidden car port. Wang tried to lift his eyes to look at the men, but the same guy pushed harder on his skull. He had no idea if they spoke Cantonese, English, Mandarin. One of them had said his name when they'd found him, but that was it. And even then, Wang couldn't clearly remember how it sounded. Deep, yes. Accent was hard to tell.

Seconds later, a third man appeared, stopped, then walked

away. Wang only knew because he heard heavy footsteps and a new pair of shiny black shoes enter into the circle, as he and the other two continued to huff and puff. What were they going to do to him? It seemed they were waiting for the third man to come back. No one spoke. At all. Behind him, he heard something being unzipped and realised they were opening up his backpack, searching his things. He heard the ping of his phone turning on.

Strangely, Wang didn't think about death or pain. He thought about his mother. If she were alive now, she would be coming home from her job as a teaching assistant in a local high school. She'd be preparing dinner, chopping the garlic and the onions. She would be watching the news, maybe she'd call her sister in Taiwan, the one who was an important doctor in Taipei. She would fry the chicken in oil, tell her sister stories of her students, of Wang, how proud she was of his design business; but would he ever get married? Give her grandchildren? So far, only short-term girls, ones she never even met. Then, his father would have come home, tired and complaining of a bad back. He would pour iced tea and sit on the stool in front of their tiny kitchen with the U-shaped breakfast bar painted in a sickly green and tease her about her cooking. "You don't like the helper's food?" he'd say. "Not good enough for someone as fancy as you? How did you ever marry such a lowly man as me – not rich, not sophisticated? What did you see in me?" His mother would tell him to go away, to have a shower. She would laugh. "I loved you for some unknown reason and now I'm stuck." Wang wanted to call his dad on some imaginary phone line to the dead, a childlike fantasy in which he could wallow, as he faced what he believed was a fate that made him want it all to end anyway. He wanted to apologise to his parents for no doubt having his name splashed across the newspapers. Maybe his dad would be proud. Or would he instead call him a blind fool? Either way, all Wang could do was breathe slowly through his nose to stop from breaking down.

From then on, the only sounds he heard were his own terrified groans, a fist making contact with his nose and the restrained grunts of his near-silent attackers. Thankfully, the memory of it came in short bursts of motion-picture sequences, like a scene from an old silent movie. The blessing? He had no memory of the pain during the attack. It seemed his brain shut that out. He comforted himself with the notion that this was some kind of gift from his father. The only way he could protect him now that he was gone.

When the car park attendant found him nearly an hour later, Wang had started to rouse and was attempting to sit up. He had a bloodied, broken nose and was badly concussed. The bruises on his thighs and back were extensive, his muscles swollen and pink, on the verge of turning purple, but he could stand and walk. He was lucky, the doctor told him. No breaks, save for the nose. When would he go to the police?

Just a stupid disagreement with an old colleague, Wang said without meeting the doctor's eye.

An hour after that, as he eased himself onto one of the colourful fabric seats of the Number 9 bus, he decided now was a good time to do nothing. Tobias and Tommy would know, seeing as he hadn't turned up to the speech, that something had gone wrong. They would lay low. He'd get a message through to them eventually. Somehow.

Wang had never been so happy to arrive in Shek O. Avoiding the suspicious glares of Mrs Lam at the Fook Lee store, he bought himself a Coke and a Mars bar and sat in a park that faced the beach and watched the children play in the sand, his head throbbing but their squeals of delight calming his whirring brain. He would go home and stay at home, sleep, eat and think. He would not talk to anyone. Not for at least a week. Not even Alice.

* * *

"Wang? Do you want the chilli prawns?" It was Alice. She was waving a menu under his nose. "And beer? What kind?"

He rubbed his eyes and let out a gust of pent-up air.

"Whatever. Tsingtao for me. And yes, clams. Prawns too. Rice. The lot. Let's go for it."

"You were frowning," she said, as the waiter walked away. "Lost in thought."

"Ahh, it's nothing," he said. "I was just thinking about my dad. I miss him."

"Your dad? Where is he?"

Wang told her the story, cutting out the bit about him being fired and dying of a broken heart. For now, the less Alice knew, the better.

* * *

That night, ensconced on Alice's sofa, watching a movie, drowsy and content, Wang felt the anger rise. *How dare they? What kind of place did he live in that such men could control him, control his future and that of the city he loved?* He extricated himself from Alice's embrace and told her he was getting out for some air.

"I'll take the dog," he said, "and buy some more tea. You're all out."

"Fine," she'd nodded and yawned.

In seconds, he had reached the store, a ramshackle corner shop that sat under a pressed-tin roof and was dimly lit with plastic red lamps. Wang tied the dog to a pole and lazily scrambled about the dusty shelves for the teabags. Lipton, Dilmah, Bushells. They had the lot. Which one would Alice prefer? He had enjoyed the most perfect day with her, the kind you knew was special when you were in the midst of it and then didn't want it to end for fear of breaking the spell. At the counter, Mr Lam was now in charge, seated on a plastic stool watching horse racing and sucking on a toothpick. He'd ask him if he knew which kind of tea Alice bought. The

Lams knew everyone, especially the *gweilos*. They brought in Western food and wine just for them, charging double what they'd pay in Central. "Convenience," he'd told Wang, nodding knowingly. Behind him, in the corner of one eye, Wang saw a man in a white shirt enter the shop. As Wang reached the counter, the man stood next to him, rattling a few coins in his fist. Wang turned, feeling a coldness wash over him. Wang looked up. The man smiled.

"We know all about Alice," he said through a gold-toothed smile. He backed out and, seconds later, a taxi pulled up and whisked the man away.

On Mr Lam's TV, the horse racing commentator was in a frenzy as the race ended with a neck-to-neck finish. Wang's head buzzed as he handed over the money.

"You still owe!" Mr Lam barked as he went to leave.

"Sorry?"

"For the champagne. Last night. Your friend. He bought it and put it on your account. HK$700. Mrs Lam will get angry if you don't pay now." He jerked his head towards a darkened back room, where Mrs Lam was known to snooze and make dumplings.

Wang hadn't bought any champagne.

He took out his wallet again, handed over the cash and found himself back on the brightly lit street corner. He walked to Alice's front gate, opened it and let the dog in. Wang closed the gate as quietly as possible and turned his back on Alice's apartment.

On the brief walk back to his own place, he didn't hear laughter tinkling from open windows, the waves crashing on the beach, nor the distant thud of party music from the barbecue pits. All he could hear was a deafening ringing in his ears. He double-locked his front door and, from his bedroom window, kept his eyes trained on the lane that led to Alice's front door. He wouldn't sleep that night.

CHAPTER TEN

Hong Kong Yacht Club, Causeway Bay.

One week later.

Johnny held Scarlett's hand on his lap. For a brief moment, he felt as though they were meeting for the first time, that this was something good, not tainted. She had called him and said she wanted to talk. He was hoping that, finally, he could get through to her.

"I'm confused, that's all," Scarlett was saying. She was tired, she'd said, but still, to Johnny, she looked perfect. Scarlett made him feel he was looking at a dream, the elusive lover from a Victorian-era romance, the kind of woman he admired as a young boy, those fleeting glimpses of golden-haired unearthliness. She talked with a lilting voice and walked with fluidity. Her features were petite and her round pale green-grey eyes, earnest.

As a boy, he would have been enthralled by a woman like Scarlett. A woman who was accidentally sultry, oblivious to her attractiveness. He knew his mother would have approved.

Despite her recent bizarre behaviour, it somehow drew him closer to her, all that neediness followed by a moody distance. He never knew what he was going to get and it drove him crazy; in a good way. He wanted to fix her, care for her. He guessed he was like that with those kinds of people, like the way he had been with Brian. The thought made him smile. *Brian.*

On the surface, he and Scarlett made an intriguing pairing, a bit like he and Brian once were. When people saw them together, they commented that she was as pale and celestial as he was dark and robust. Johnny felt proud of such comments. Scarlett appeared irritated.

At that very moment, a small boy ran past, dragging a plastic toy that scraped noisily on the stone floor. Johnny wondered how Brian was doing. He held such admiration for his old friend, despite the challenges he'd faced to get there.

Johnny smiled at Scarlett. "You're confused?" he chimed. "I'm the one confused here." He laughed a little and shrugged, not wanting to show her how upset he was.

"Well, I… I don't like Phil. There. I've said it. And you never tell me anything about yourself. It's been a really fun six months or so, but…"

"What does Phil have to do with you and I?"

Scarlett scowled. She was sick of scowling.

"I don't trust him."

Johnny was pleased. If it was just some kind of trust thing to do with Phil, he could work on that.

"It's work, Scarlett. That's life in Hong Kong. I make good money with Phil, which is why I live in that gargantuan house over there and you get to live in it, even without a job."

"Well, I would like a job, Johnny, but that Vivian sacked me, didn't she?"

"*That* Vivian," he sighed, "tried to help you, but you kept taking days off, behaving strangely in meetings, you said so yourself."

"That's not…"

"Look, I don't care if you don't work."

Scarlett rubbed at her eyes. She had small, delicate fingers, narrow with pointed pale-pink fingernails. Johnny wanted to take her, right there and then.

She shot him a direct, angry glare. She sipped at her wine, its icy coldness seeming to jolt her into action.

"I don't think this is working," she whispered.

They were seated on cane loungers at the harbourside bar of the exclusive Royal Hong Kong Yacht Club in Causeway Bay. The white, nautical-inspired building was perched on Kellett Island but – since the land in between the island and Causeway Bay was reclaimed – it was no longer separated by water. Johnny sailed once, a long time ago. He'd given up now. Now, he only went there for drinks.

It was quiet, only 4pm on a Tuesday. There was no one else on the upstairs terrace, furnished in a tropical, Colonial Club fashion. In the distance, container ships and ferries vied for space on the choppy waters. Cars inching their way through a nearby cross-harbour tunnel created a constant background hum of engines.

It was warm; early summer and the heavy dampness of humidity had meshed with the thick polluted atmosphere. Scarlett, however, hugged a pale-blue shawl around her shoulders. Johnny could see goosebumps on her forearms.

No one had ever dumped Johnny, he wanted to say.

He was sure she could sense his mood change from caring to mild anger and she seemed to prepare herself for the onslaught.

A waiter appeared. "Finished?" he said, picking up their wine glasses. Johnny must have nodded. Scarlett was still watching a helicopter race to the harbour's edge, no doubt just over from Macau.

"What's happened?" Johnny tugged at her shawl. He noticed she flinched a little. *I'd never hurt you*, he wanted to say.

"I need to have my own life, somewhere else. It's not that you're a bad guy." Johnny fell silent. She turned back to face him. His face was ashen, his lips in a straight thin line. She touched his hand and he pulled away. "We're not married, we've only been seeing each other for a few months. I moved in on a whim and you've looked after me. But it's just not the life I thought I'd have. So…" She tried to slow down. "If you come home one night and I'm not there, don't worry. I mean, don't go looking for me."

Johnny tried to smile to lighten her mood, but it came out like a grimace. A couple of young guys dressed in shorts and T-shirts, their hair wet from being on the water, strolled past and smiled at them. Well, at her.

"Okay." His voice was suddenly a whisper. "But still, I think we can make this work, if you…"

"No." She bit at a fingernail, her head on an angle. "I ask you about your friends and you say nothing. I mean, your childhood is off limits. I feel I can't get to know you, really know you."

How would he handle this? He fell silent for a while, to think. He was quite sure Carolyn would advise him to at least try.

He would tell her, just enough. Then that would be it. He'd be more open with her and see how it went. After all, he never talked about himself with his girlfriends. There were too many difficult things to explain. But maybe, if he did, she'd agree to talk to Carolyn. After all, if *he* could, so could she. So far, he had been too wary of her reaction to bring it up. He weighed up the idea of telling her something, anything, to bring her closer. But no, he would do it. He inhaled.

"Scarlett." Her head shot up, eyes wide and eager for information. "The thing is, when I first arrived here, in this city, I was young and naïve. Many of us are. We come here, full of drive and ambition and we *can* get caught up with people or things that seem exciting but can be a bit, you know, careless. And Phil, well, let's just say Phil was even more stupid then than he is now. Don't get me wrong, he's a fantastic… assistant. But…"

He tried to smile. Scarlett smiled back. He was going to tell her something.

"So, Phil did something really foolish one day and I had to help him out the only way I could."

"What did he do?"

Johnny glanced around him and leaned closer.

"He was with a girl, a girl in a bar. She was young and pretty. This is a long, long, long time ago. Phil and I had been discussing starting up Berwick. We had big plans and there he was, gallivanting in Wan Chai."

"I can imagine. I suppose he still is," Scarlett replied, somewhat cynically for her, Johnny thought.

"Well, one night, he calls in a panic. Seems he'd been super stressed and one of the girls… Oh, I don't know… She displeased him. He was drunk and he got a bit rough with her."

"A bit rough? I see." Scarlett pursed her lips.

"Well, whether you like it or not, that's the truth." Saying this made Johnny's skin crawl. He was furious with Phil at the time and bringing it all up now made him realise he still was. "So he calls me and when I get there, this poor woman has her face smashed in. I took her to the hospital, explained I'd found her in the street. She backed up the story. I spent some time with her, making sure she was okay. She lied for Phil and I looked after her. Turned out she had some heavy debts to a few nasty people and I did her a favour because she'd done us a favour. Phil a favour. That's all."

"How did you look after her?"

"I can't tell you any more than that."

"Yes, you can." Johnny looked at Scarlett. Her lips were slightly apart, her gaze fixed on his. She wanted more and he couldn't give it.

"Part of the deal, Scarlett, was that I would never tell anyone how we met and she would never expose Phil. Phil was married then. Not only that, I was about to move into a new job and take him with me. If he was arrested for battery, then all hell would've broken loose."

Scarlett raised her eyes to the sky and sat back against the striped blue cushions. A waiter passed and she waved him down and ordered two coffees.

"How could you go into business with a man like that?"

"Well…"

How could he explain this? That Phil needed him? That he owed Phil? That without Phil's dirty deeds, he couldn't have done what he did to finally free himself from the past?

No. He couldn't tell her that. There was only one person he could talk to about all that and that was enough.

"In some ways," Johnny finally said, "I'd like to, you know, get Phil out of the business. But I can't find the right way. I thought that if you and I had a life together, we could make some changes. Go away for a while. Start a new kind of life. Maybe New York?"

Scarlett let out a harsh bark that took him by surprise.

"Why do you care so much about Phil?" Johnny winced his frustration at her attack. "If Phil is that bad, then what does that make you? And does Phil get involved in illegal activity anymore? Do you?"

Johnny stiffened.

"I explained, Scarlett, he has his uses in business circles. Yes, he's flawed in many ways as a man, but as a business partner, we have been very successful together. And, as I said, I would prefer it, honestly, if I could walk away from him at this stage of my life. But I can't. I will soon. But don't pass judgement on my character in the meantime. I'm not the bad guy here." She opened her mouth to speak, obviously thought better of it, then hung her head in her hands.

They sat still and silently for a while. Scarlett looked deflated. Her tears came easily and naturally.

"I suffered a terrible loss about six, seven months ago," she started. Johnny moved slightly closer to her. "I can't explain it all now. But I didn't deal with it well and, to top it off, my family life was strange. My mother had postnatal depression and my father hid her away, too ashamed to tell anyone." Johnny was taken aback. The insight into

Scarlett's life came spewing out, volcanic. "He eventually put her in a home. I barely saw her. It was terrible. No one helped her and I was too young to understand. Now I've lost my job and all I want is to be calm and stable, but all I see are nasty people, troubled people, dead people." She crumpled upon herself, overcome with rasping sobs. "I just don't understand it."

Johnny reached over and placed a comforting arm around her shoulders. She wept.

"Hey. Come on. There's always a way to make things better."

"How do you know?" she whined. Johnny bit down on his bottom lip as he placed his hand over hers. "You've had a great life!"

He shook his head. "That's what you think. I've never told you anything, I suppose."

"Well," Scarlet huffed, "if you want me to stay in your life, I think it's only fair I know who you really are. I've opened up, so should you."

I've never done that before, Johnny wanted to say. He grappled with this dilemma. Scarlett was right. With other women, he kept them as a trophy until he tired of them making demands for commitment. Yet here he was, growing weary of his life, Phil, the business. Fuck it, he was even a little sick of Hong Kong at times. If he were honest, it wasn't just Scarlett that had prompted him to see Carolyn. It was the start of a kind of emotional breakdown.

He watched a kite soar under low grey clouds and clasped his hands together.

"Scarlett. I know that things get better after a… a dilemma, because I've experienced death and violence and fear," he whispered. Scarlett's head shot up. There were a few tendrils of white hair plastered to her wet cheeks. "Yes. I know. It's hard to say out loud. But I have."

"When? Who?"

He blinked a few times.

"My father. His name was Sir Robert Humphries. I barely knew him. He's dead now." The left side of Johnny's lip appeared to rise into a half-smile. He inhaled deeply. "My mother brought me up in East London, before I was sent to Bramar Hall. And then…"

Scarlett sat very, very still.

"Well, my best friend. He didn't die. He was badly hurt. Brian. That's his name. I think you asked about him. He's in the photo in our room. I don't like to talk to people about him. In fact, I've never talked to anyone about him."

"Why?"

"It's nothing. He doesn't live here."

"Do you see each other?"

Johnny cleared his throat.

"Not really. We went to China together in the mid-1990s. A bit of an adventure. But he doesn't really like airplanes, so he never came back this way. Suffers from bad anxiety when he's in enclosed spaces."

"What happened to him?"

Johnny pictured Brian, the stench of disinfectant, the bleeding cut on his lopsided little cheek.

"His own father would beat him." Johnny clenched his left fist, gritted his teeth and then came to his senses. He relaxed into the chair. "It was terrible. He nearly lost an eye. It's so badly damaged he can't really see out of it. It appears glassy and empty."

"What about now?" Scarlett seemed fascinated. Genuinely.

"He struggled with life. I had to help him a bit. His mum finally got away from Brian's dad. Brian helped with that, setting her up in a house after a bit of a… a bit of a windfall. Long story." He lowered his eyes to his shoes. "He had a few stints in hospitals – PTSD you see – but he managed to get an accounting degree and works for a small firm in Essex somewhere. But he could've done so much more. He has brains, there is no doubt about that. Brilliant at languages, mechanics, mathematical equations. You name it. His old bastard of a father couldn't knock that out of him."

Scarlett had a thought and it showed as she sat upright and wiped at her eyes, trying to smile a little.

"So, just to be sure, Brian is the guy in the photo in our room?"

Johnny nodded. "Yes. I said that." He grasped her hand that little bit more. "The short guy. We're outside his house. Lillian Street. 25B. I'll never forget it." He smiled and laughed a little, as though enjoying a private joke. "Sometimes, I take the photo away. It can make me angry. Other times, I need it there, to remind me of…"

"Of what?"

"Now," Johnny said, loosening his tie a little, "let's talk about something happier. How about dinner tonight? Or shall we plan a Phuket weekend? I've got that beachside villa available, the one I bid for at that deadly dull auction last month. Come on. Say yes."

She blew her nose, loudly. "Can we get the bill please, Johnny?"

He pulled her towards him and kissed her cheeks. She let him.

"You're so lovely to me," she sputtered, "and I'm so horrible to you."

He beamed. It felt so good to have her in his arms. The coffee arrived.

Johnny noisily stirred three sugars into his cup. Scarlett watched in silence, letting the question he could see she was about to ask swirl around her head a little.

"Alice," Scarlett almost whispered. "Why does she hate Phil so much? Why is she so… wary of you? And Bobby. He told me you made some mistakes. He mentioned Madeline Chung. I mean, I have since read about it. But Bobby was intimating you were not… you were not what you appear to be."

Johnny's face fell. This was not what he was hoping she'd

ask. That fucking Madeline Chung story had haunted him for decades now. And bloody Bobby Ling, he would never get off his case if he kept up the boozing. They thought Bobby would leave it, but the drink had got the better of him.

"Well, let's start with Phil. I assume Alice isn't into him for the same reason you don't like him. As for me, I don't really care whether she dislikes me or not. Having said that, she was sweetness and light not long ago at the Captain's Bar when I ran into her. But I'm too old to worry about such nonsense. And Bobby? He's on death's door and is a pathetic drunk who gossips. Satisfied?"

Johnny would definitely suggest Scarlett see Carolyn tomorrow. They could have lunch and he'd take her hand and calmly ask her to make an appointment. He was sure she would understand. After all, her own mother had failed to get help. Surely, she would be able to see that her emotional state was a direct relation to her mother's own problems. Then, once she was happy again, he could make her want him more and more and then? Johnny thought of marriage and, for once, he didn't go into a white-hot panic.

The two of them walked arm-in-arm to the car park, where Johnny's driver waited patiently in a white Lexus, washed and polished to showroom specifications.

Johnny tapped on the car's roof. "Take her home safely," he said, the driver jumping to attention.

Johnny bent forward and kissed her, lightly, both lost in their private concerns. Once inside, Scarlett lowered a tinted window and gave Johnny a withering smile.

Johnny jiggled from foot to foot at the taxi stand, a strange feeling of discomfort settling in his belly. As he looked up at the sparkling windows of the surrounding skyscrapers, reflected in a sharp afternoon sun, he was jolted by a sudden desire to rid himself of a few ghosts of the past. He was sick of it all coming back to haunt him when he'd only ever done anything to help, not hinder. And he had the power. Why not use it?

Johnny watched the Lexus turn right at the exit gates. His hands were clammy from the humidity as he pulled out an old Nokia phone from his briefcase. He fished around for a new SIM card, inserted it into the phone and dialled.

"Can you talk?" he said. "Okay. Just one minute." He paused. One of the city's famously efficient red taxicabs arrived and Johnny hopped in, barking his office address in Cantonese.

He spoke into the phone again. "Someone's become a bit of a liability," he said in a hushed tone. "Yeah. Him. You're right. I was hoping it wouldn't happen, especially after all this time, but I suppose there was always the risk." He nodded a few times and sighed. "Yeah. I hear you. Let's get him on to it now."

* * *

As a child, it wasn't easy for Phil. He was the fat kid, the beach ball, too slow to win a race, the one the other kids picked on, laughed at, ridiculed in the changing rooms after football. He was an easy target, lacking street smarts, his shorts too tight, his T-shirts the wrong shape.

It was the late 70s and early 80s in East London and no one gave a flying fig about bullying. There were no posters in the school corridors extolling the virtues of self-love, mutual respect and communication. Even the teachers would have scoffed at such self-indulgent sentiment. Boys would be boys and all that.

Phil's only release was movies. He watched them every week at the local cinema, always the side-back-left row with a packet of Spangles. His mother, the manager at a Budgens supermarket, paid him a few quid if he helped her with the laundry and cooking most days; his chubby hands wringing the sheets or peeling the potatoes.

Privately, he became obsessed with *Monty Python* and the *Pink Panther* and knew every line from both. It was no wonder. He'd listened to and watched every episode and film three times.

* * *

One steaming mid-summer afternoon – lost in comedic thoughts as he sweated along a British Rail pathway shadowed with scraggly bushes – Phil was set upon by the main school bully, a scrappy kid called Mickey.

Mickey was not much taller than Phil but with the languorous gait of someone who held himself in very high esteem. Furthermore, he was talented at football, which gave him an overinflated sense of importance and a loyal following of wannabes.

Later in life, Phil often recalled this story in his head and to others. He would never forget it. Ever. He always made it sound hilarious, but at the time, it was torture.

"Give us the cash, or you're dead meat," Mickey crowed. He was surrounded by two other boys, one freckle-faced, the other sickly. Phil could now not remember their names but to himself, he called them Spot and Snot.

"What?" Phil had cried pitifully. "No luck today. Mum hasn't given me any money yet, lads."

Mickey snarled and grabbed his shirt.

"Listen. You lie once more and you'll do my head in. I'm fucking starving and you look like you've eaten enough pies for a week."

The other boys sniggered and shuffled their feet. Phil, who had two pounds stuffed in his school satchel, felt the fear rise. But in the back of his mind, *Monty Python* was hammering away at his head.

"You know I'm the man, right?" Mickey hissed. "And I am your boss. So come on, *pay*."

Phil looked. All he could think about was *The Holy Grail*. He'd seen it the day before and had been giggling to himself when Mickey had appeared. Before he knew it, he had put on a high-pitched voice.

"Well, *I* didn't vote for you!" Phil screeched. One of the other kids smiled curiously. Mickey shot his mate a cool glare.

"Eh?" Mickey said, and slapped Phil on the cheek.

"If I didn't vote for you, how'd you become king then?" Phil piped in a sing-song voice. Both Mickey's mates laughed.

Mickey let go of Phil's shirt, just a little.

"It's from *Monty Python*, you dumb shit," one of Mickey's friends said.

Phil felt a wash of relief.

"I fart in your general direction!" Phil yelled at Mickey. Mickey's friends bellowed at the line from the movie. Mickey retaliated by punching Phil in the gut. He doubled over. "Your mother was a hamster!" Phil managed to wheeze.

Mickey was angry. The other two boys were in fits.

"Leave him, mate," one of the kids said. "I'm off."

"Hey!" Mickey called to his pal, as he walked off, hands in pockets. The other kid paused, looked at Mickey's grimy cheeks and turned and left as well.

Phil straightened his shirt and walked away, never looking back. He was half-expecting Mickey to run at him, but when he finally did turn around, the path was empty.

Mickey never went near him again.

From then on, Phil used humour to defuse every situation. Over time, it became his redeeming feature, one he used to great advantage as he turned into a spotty teenager. If he could make the kids laugh with razor-sharp movie mimicry, they'd go easy on him. This gave him some respite from the bullying, and over time he settled into relatively comfortable teenage years, followed by a rollicking good time in his early twenties, new to the police force and moving up the ranks, thanks to his ability to sniff out a bad egg when he saw one.

"Takes one to know one," he often joked at station meetings.

It was his wife, Karen, who took them both to Hong Kong. Phil had married Karen for no specific reason. She was five years older than him and looked it. She was a property developer and worked like a demon, making a mint in the process. She'd been dumped at the altar the week before she met Phil and until the day they divorced about ten years ago, Phil was convinced he was just the rebound. He was the one silly enough to fall for her mature-woman ways in the sack, confusing it with love. *Ah, well.* The marriage brought him to his adopted home and he was now as happy as a pig in shit. *Sort of.*

* * *

He was meeting Shania, his new girlfriend, at the Peak Café for lunch. It was mild already – summer nearly in full swing – and as Phil hopped off the Peak Tram, he walked with a jauntiness that surprised even him. Shania was only thirty-two and, already, Phil was tired. Not tired of her, as such, but tired of the demands, both physically and emotionally. He'd got into the devil's dust big time not long after arriving in the city – the cop shop was full of it in those days – and had never really been able to wean himself off it. Johnny had tried. Put him into rehab several times. But Phil always went back to it. He found life overwhelmingly dull without it and terribly sad with it, but either way, he never lasted on the wagon. He knew it was why he lost that lucrative job as head of security with Albert Chung all those years ago, but Johnny had saved his butt. Johnny had it in for Chung too, kind of. Chung had lost his rag at Johnny one day in front of an entire boardroom of horrified staff; told him to get out and never come back. The names Chung had called him, and all because Johnny hadn't placed one phone call to some property developer Chung was trying to cosy up with. Johnny told Phil that he never forgot it, no matter how hard Chung tried to absolve himself afterwards.

Now Phil had the boss to keep him in cash and ensure

he had top-notch medical in case his ticker couldn't take his lifestyle anymore.

Phil fingered a piece of paper in his jacket pocket. The boss has asked him to call later that day. Phil knew he was still paying the price for various past mistakes, but what could he do? The day before, he'd got a text message on that damn annoying Nokia phone that the boss wanted him to contact him, *ASAP*, something about Bobby talking about Madeline. *Ancient history, mate*, Phil wanted to yell. Of course, he didn't. His only income had come from the boss and it did the job. Still, Phil didn't really want to take on anything unsavoury right there and then. He was enjoying his life, dining with Shania, helping at the office. He pulled out the old Nokia and the SIM card he'd bought earlier, inserted it into the phone and sucked air through his teeth, a bit like Shania's gobbing mother was prone to doing.

He stopped outside the tourist haven of the Peak Mall, trying to get out of the way of the tour groups being shunted from buses to tacky trinket stores selling magnets and T-shirts.

He turned on the phone and waited for the signal to beep. He dialled the number the boss had given him and tapped his foot on the tiled forecourt as it rang. Strangely, he'd never even met "the boss". Wouldn't know him from Adam. He could be a Buddhist monk, a retired bookkeeper in Calgary, maybe even a Saudi prince for all Phil knew. But the boss and Johnny were connected and that's how Phil got into it all.

The phone rang and rang and a second before he was about to press the end button, the boss's voice came on the line.

"All quiet here," Phil replied to his greeting, in as relaxed a manner as he could muster. "Anything going on your end?" Phil listened, nodded and sighed with relief when it was over. "Can do. Will do. ASAP. Righty-ho. Thanks." He hung up.

A minute later, he was striding boldly into the cool, colonial environs of the Peak Café, the green hills of Aberdeen rolling like waves on a deep ocean below, as he weaved his way past wrought-iron tables and platters of antipasti. A Bloody Mary was shoved into his hand and as he kissed Shania, the sickly scent of her designer perfume filling his nostrils. He completely forgot all about the phone in his pocket.

CHAPTER ELEVEN

Central.

Scarlett was now all out of fresh ideas. She was confident their meeting at the yacht club had finally resulted in some of what she wanted, and soon she'd have more, if all went to plan. But would it all come together? Plus, her tears had been genuine. She was exhausted with the life she had been leading. It had nearly broken her. She hoped to God it had been worth it.

Later that evening, Scarlett had made a decision. If her instincts were correct, she'd give it one more day and then move out while Johnny was at work. Disappear. She'd get on a plane soon after and be done with it. If she had got it wrong, she'd think about leaving anyway, jack it all in. She'd almost had enough.

To think her plan through more clearly, she went to Hong Kong Park, sat on a timber bench and drank weak tea from a polystyrene cup. It was a shady spot and rare that she could even get a seat most days, but with the night sky just starting to crowd out a weak, hazy sun, she had the place to herself. It overlooked a small waterfall and Scarlett watched the terrapins slowly edge each other off the rounded rocks jutting from the shallows. From the corner of her eye, she spotted a yellow-crested cockatoo shoot out from a tree overlooking the nearby aviary. She breathed, made a list of all that she knew already: *Johnny had been publicly named in a kidnapping case many years before. Johnny was in business with the evil Phil. Johnny's name was whispered to her nearly a year before as the man who knew everything. Yet Johnny was, from what Scarlett had seen up close, relatively hard to fault and unfortunately – or fortunately – in love with her.*

Scarlett had gone to the park in a bid to garner a sense of peace, but her mental lists and bird-spotting could not shake the tension.

She grappled with the reality. She had done her best to see his good side in a bid to find his bad. He'd taken her on countless hikes, boat trips, dinners to exotic locales. She admired the way he took pride in their home, entertained friends generously and – when she was feeling particularly generous – the two often shared a few laughs. The entire time, she watched and listened. Mostly, she was riddled with confusion – she hated him, but then she began to doubt herself and the information she had been given, hence the moods.

Still, she would try one more thing. She looked at the sky. No stars. A plane in the distance.

As of late, it was the knowledge he could never really please her that kept him interested in her. She remained slightly aloof, even when living with him. Then, she'd turned. Gone crazy, although whether or not that was all an act was anyone's guess.

Living a lie was, of course, empty and a waste of her young life. It had also nearly sent her mad. It hadn't started out that way. When she'd met him and gone along with the romance – and he was terribly romantic in the wooing phase – there was an element of excitement, a dangerous thrill. But now, well, she couldn't really trust herself, especially with the pills on board. God, she was screwed up. Did knowing you were make it less of a fact? Scarlett doubted it.

Her phone buzzed in her bag. It was Felicity Cussler, the investigator. Felicity had promised to spend some more time watching Johnny. She'd hired Felicity to tail him some time ago now, just for a few days, but all she'd found was that Johnny dined with Phil, went to work, the gym and met clients. Scarlett, however, still wanted to utilise Felicity's professional skills while she was playing house and had kept her on a retainer, just to see what she could find. But so far, Felicity had found nothing and no doubt believed her job was done. Yet Scarlett hoped she was ringing back with something more.

Before answering, she felt the pressure rise. The lies were getting her down. She cleared her throat.

"Hello, Felicity."

Felicity got straight to it.

"I've found something you might be interested in." It was noisy in the background wherever Felicity was, rattling trucks passing, muting every second word. "Not sure if it has anything to do with what you're looking for. But anyway." The phone line crackled. "Photos," Scarlett heard. "His father. His best friend."

Scarlett made out enough words to understand that Felicity had found something important.

"Go on," she said.

Her hunch about Felicity had been right.

After about ten minutes, Scarlett hung up and pecked again at the keyboard of her phone. She sat back into the hard bench and crossed one leg over another as she waited for it to ring. A male passer-by turned to admire her bare calves. A teenager suffering from acne seated on a nearby bench glared jealously at her alabaster skin. Scarlett didn't notice. As the phone in her hand rang some more, she spotted a fork-tailed sunbird. Her first in months! She found herself smiling.

The person on the other line answered.

"Guess what?" Scarlett said. "Can you hear me? The line's bad." She paused. "Okay. I can hear you now. I wanted to let you know, I think I may have cracked the code."

144

CHAPTER TWELVE

Shek O Village, Hong Kong.

It was the boy racers – the teenagers speeding in their souped-up racing cars along Shek O Road late at night – that woke Alice from a deep slumber. A glance at her phone showed it was 4am. She had pins and needles in her right arm, pushed herself to a seated position and cast her eyes around the shadowy living room. No Wang. She stretched and walked to the bedroom. He wasn't in there either. She checked her phone. No message. Turbo was back, though. He'd let himself in through the dog door and was curled up in his bed by the refrigerator, his black-and-tan snout pressed deeply into the tartan blanket she'd bought the day she picked him up from the SPCA.

Where is Wang? She sent him a terse text, threw back a glass of cold water and hopped back into bed. By the time her eyes quivered shut, he still hadn't replied. Alice drifted into a dream about grey crashing waves and circling sharks, only coming to her senses upon waking at 7am that Wang's absence was strange. *Not again*, she thought cynically, as she dressed in trainers and leggings to take Turbo for his morning walk. If he'd disappeared this time with no explanation, then that'd be it. She couldn't stand a man of mystery. Stability, normalcy, comfort. That was what she was looking for. After the comings and goings of her mother's so-called love life, it was no wonder.

"Come on, Turbs," she called quietly, as she weaved through potted plants and children's bicycles pushed up against the back doors of the village houses, many of which were painted bright oranges, blues or yellows, like her own. The thrum of air-conditioning units was like a village incantation.

Two minutes later, she had reached the large metal gate that heralded the entrance to Wang's three-storey terrace house tucked behind a high bamboo fence resplendent with fuchsia bougainvillea. She pressed the buzzer. Waited. Felt a trickle of perspiration run down her breastbone.

***

Alice and Wang had first met walking down that very narrow alleyway, him in blue runner's shorts and a white singlet that clung to his chest, her in high heels and a pencil skirt coming home from work. He'd tripped over the shopping bag she'd placed next to her feet and he'd stopped to apologise. So did she.

"Are you new in the village?" he'd said, huffing a little from his jog. "Haven't seen you around. And I know everyone in this corner of the world. I'm Wang."

She'd introduced herself and explained she'd only moved in the week before.

"I can't live in a high-rise anymore," she said, for no apparent reason other than she liked his earnest, eager face. "I'd been in Mid-Levels since I got here and I'd had enough. I wanted a dog. I wanted some space. Shek O's close enough to Central that I can catch the bus and be at work in forty-five minutes." She'd looked back over her shoulder at the menagerie of her village house and realised she was blabbing. He kept staring at her. "And I just love this place. It has character. Don't you think? The whole village does. It's different. I needed that."

He was nodding his head. He wiped at his upper lip and pointed towards the beach.

"I suppose you surf?"

She'd burst out laughing. "Look at me. I'm a redhead and I have the looping arms of a chimpanzee. Surf? It's the name of a washing powder in my world."

That's when he'd asked her to go with him. He'd teach her. He said he'd buy her lunch at Cococabana, the only Western restaurant on the beachfront and one that served gourmet dishes instead of greasy chicken wings. She said no thank you and they said goodbye. After he'd walked away, she realised her heart was beating against her cotton shirt. Alice knew that sometimes a strange confluence of human quirks resulted in a package that lured you in, made you want to know more, despite there being no one factor that had any merit. *Substance*, she almost said out loud. Wang had *substance*.

The next morning, early on a Saturday, she'd been walking Turbo on the beach and within seconds of her feet sinking into the warm sand, there was Wang, running towards her in a wetsuit, his hair pushed back, wet and glossy.

They sat and talked for half an hour – the village, her job, their Hong Kong pastimes – before Wang disappeared to get coffees. He returned ten minutes later with a wetsuit in hand. Hot pink. "I borrowed it from my mate at the hire store near the car park," he'd explained.

"No," she'd said.

But somehow, he made her kneel on the board on the sand, showed her how to push herself up to standing, arms wide. Next thing she knew, he was zipping her into the wetsuit. Alice saw Mrs Lam from the shop giggling with her tea-sipping friends on the tiled steps at the top of the beach.

Alice hadn't managed to actually stand on the board, but she hadn't completely humiliated herself either. In fact, she had to admit she enjoyed the stomach-lurching thrill of being picked up by a surging wave and hurled towards the shoreline, that it proved much more invigorating than terrifying and by the time they were tucking into Dover sole at Cococabana, her cheeks ached from smiling. Wang was plumped up with self-pride that he had managed to get her in the water and, like a proud parent, glowed at her over his paella. Then, of course, he had managed to get her to sail. What was it about him? She found herself wanting to do whatever he asked.

* * *

She buzzed at his door again. This time, there was a rattle from his front door, followed by soft footfall on the timber decking that constituted his small garden.

"Wang?" He didn't answer. "It's me."

She heard him clear his throat.

Alice had been impressed with his apartment the first time she'd seen it after her unscheduled surfing lesson. He'd designed the renovation himself, knocking down all the poky interior walls on the ground floor to create an open-plan living room with wide windows and one wall lined with bookshelves. Upstairs was a bedroom, en suite and sitting room that opened onto a terrace with a clear view over the main beach, the sudden rise of the Dragon's Back Hills and the often murky, rubbish-strewn Back Beach, with its seaside bar and small sandy bay. He had hung a few simple watercolours of beach scenes, ones he said he had done himself over the years, and – forcing you to duck every few seconds – were dozens of indoor palms and ferns hanging from the ceiling, intermittently dripping small beads of water. It felt tropical and calm, an understated hideaway down a dark, damp alley, but one with a million-dollar view.

The gate opened and Wang stood, eyes red-rimmed.

"Alice," he said, his voice hoarse. "Come in."

He closed the gate behind them. Her stomach lurched. What had happened? She tried to stay calm.

"The last thing you said was that you were going to the shops with Turbo to buy teabags," she started as they stood across from each other on the terrace. "And then I woke up and…" He leaned towards her and hugged her. Very tightly. "What's going on?"

"It's hard to explain. Listen."

The dog yapped at Alice's feet.

"Can we talk and walk?" she said. "He needs to go."

"Sure," Wang said, "hold on."

The entire way through the village, Wang kept checking around him, behind him, even above him where neighbouring balconies hung low over the lane, blocking out an increasingly cloudy sky.

"Are you okay? Is there someone you're waiting for? Come on, Wang."

She stopped him and placed a hand over each of his slightly slumped shoulders. How different he seemed this morning. The man the day before was gregarious and lively. This Wang was lugging around a heavy weight.

"I'll explain. On the beach. Let's walk there. The inspectors aren't out until 9am. Turbo is free to run wild."

He grabbed her hand and squeezed it as they crossed the main road, at that time completely void of life. In seconds, they were shoeless on the sand. To their right, three elderly ladies were practising tai chi, moving fluidly in gentle unison – the white crane, parting the horse's mane, golden rooster stands on one leg. The usual stray dogs that barked with false ferocity at Turbo had edged their way out of the barbecue pits and, behind them, a trio of abseilers was preparing their kit for a rock climb up to the Headland. Outside the lifeguard post was Mr Chan, slumped against the wall, a can of beer in his hand and his chin resting on his chest.

"Big night for Mr Chan," Wang nudged Alice in the ribs. She giggled.

"It always is," Alice said. Mr Chan was infamous in the village for beer-swilling and raucous singing in the early hours of the morning. He was harmless to everyone but himself.

Wang managed to smile a little.

"Now that I have you looking relatively normal again,"

Alice said, "can you please tell me why you left me alone last night and didn't return my messages? I'm starting to get paranoid here."

His smile faded.

"Hold on. Two more minutes. When we're at the rocky end of the bay. Over there. Okay?"

"Are you really a spy?" she mocked. "A secret agent from China? Or are you a hitman? Now *that'd* be exciting."

He lowered his head and gently pulled her along the sand.

"Why did you come here, to Hong Kong?" he asked her with what seemed to Alice an unnecessary seriousness. "I mean, why this city, why stay here for more than twenty years, tolerate the pollution, the crowds, the lack of space? Why Hong Kong? What does it mean to you? Can you tell me that? Maybe then, when I know, I can explain. Because what I have to say is all about this place. Our *home*." He turned his head to take in the sea.

* * *

When Alice was twelve years old, her mother, Linda, took her away from her father and they moved to Devon. Alice had spent her life in London and she had been perfectly happy in their two-bedroom Fulham terrace (on the wrong end of Fulham, her mother often reminded them). It had a rectangular mossy back garden and stone pots of herbs to which her father lovingly tended. She often helped him plant new basil or rosemary and they'd talk as they got their hands dirty in the dark, wet soil. She'd tell stories of her day's happenings – the boys with dirty sticky hands and false bravado, the impatient teachers with their sarcastic comparisons, the playground taunts. In turn, he would recall his own childhood, the eggs he collected from the chicken coop as a boy, his mother's famous pies, the long walk to school through rain-soaked fields. He always smelled of pipe smoke and the wool wash from his cardigans.

Being taken from him, being removed for a reason she couldn't fathom, was heartbreaking.

"You'll understand one day," her mother had snapped in her raspy voice. "It's hard now, but one day, you'll realise this is for the best."

As they had driven away, her father at the roadside with both hands in his grey trouser pockets, eyes slightly averted, Alice had quietly wept in the back seat of the rusted Austin 100. The car's suspension causing great bouncing waves that made her stomach flutter as her mother soared carelessly over every bump. "See? Even when we leave him for good, he has no emotion. Stiff as a board," Linda groaned.

Alice sniffed from the back seat.

"Oh, I know he seems like Mister Perfect to you now, but he's certainly not. He's weak. I can't take it. I'm sorry, little one, but your father is not a good husband."

That shocking news had made Alice cry even more. She shared her father's red hair, his long limbs and pale skin. They shared the same lolloping gait, the same pointed eyebrows. He had taught her to read long before school lessons came along, giving her, she often stated, the greatest love of her life so far. To be told he was a bad man, a no-good husband, was akin to a scathing critique of her own character and while she loved her mother, at that moment, she wanted to scream, kick her until she upturned her frosted-pink, bitter lips and went home, where Alice belonged.

"Can I stay with him? Is it too late to go back?"

Linda had slammed her foot on the brakes. Alice's head jerked forwards then back. She could barely see through the tears.

"How dare you?" her mother hissed. A sharp waft of patchouli stung Alice's eyes, making them water even more. "The things I do for you. Every day. It's me, while he slumps like a geriatric in a lounge chair, reading dusty books and smoking a pipe. It's like living with my grandfather, although at least *he* had a sense of humour."

"He is not a geriatric!" Alice surprised herself with this outburst. She was a quiet, compliant child, primarily because her mother's bubbling temper was always close to the surface. Alice had learned to stay small, walk away and hide in the shadows if Linda was on the upswing of a bad outburst.

Linda slumped over the steering wheel and breathed deeply.

"Darling, darling, darling," she muttered into her hands, cheap silver rings that had turned black around the edges decorating all five fingers on her right hand. "I'm sorry, but Daddy can't look after you as well as I can. One day, you will see." She'd sat up, glanced back at Alice and reached around to touch her arm. "Come on. Get in the front. Let me give you a hug. It's not easy, I know."

Alice's mother was not all bad. She was ambitious, young, hungry for more. She'd been brought up by her grandparents with a wayward brother for company, a troubled, quiet young man who became a small-time drug dealer. Linda, by contrast, was pretty and bubbly and used this to her advantage, landing evening jobs in restaurants and hotels as she paid her way into a mid-level drama college. She hadn't meant to get pregnant to a part-time tutor in her final year of a degree in the dramatic arts. But being middle-class and sensible, he did the right thing and offered his hand in marriage. She married him, thinking his intelligence would be enough, that his brief but illustrious glory as a theatre director in the mid-1970s could sustain her interest and that together they would become a creative duo – she would tread the boards while he directed her with respectful adoration. But, sadly, he spent more time staring into the middle distance in a sombre sitting room, sipping tea and occasionally banking pitiful cheques from meagre royalties he'd secured from a gargantuan, yet deadly dull, historical novel he wrote in 1979. Linda found work in a bookshop two days a week and as a receptionist at an advertising agency three days. Sometimes, she auditioned for ads and, for several years running, she had major roles in local amateur productions of such plays as *Educating Rita*, *Abigail's Party* and *Pygmalion*. In fact, it was these acting gigs that brought Linda's true nature to light, to Alice anyway.

It was not long after the closing night of *Pygmalion* that Alice realised her "Uncle" Jim, their married neighbour – a charming accountant with long fingers and a toothy smile – was more than just a friend of her mother's. He had starred as Professor Henry Higgins alongside her mother's Eliza Doolittle in the play and would call around often, usually just before Alice's bedtime, "To rehearse, you see." The two would laugh heartily around the kitchen table while her father looked on, vague and wordless, as his wife and the jovial Jim reminisced over fluffed lines and imagined stage glories. Her mother touched Jim's arm as they spoke and every so often – as Alice noted in the way an observant, lonely child is prone to do – Jim's eyes had glinted. *I'm not stupid*, she felt like saying.

One night, after a long evening of Linda's so-called rehearsals with Uncle Jim, her mother produced a second bottle of cheap Bulgarian red wine and told Alice to hurry up and go to bed. Once Alice was under the covers, she found her suspicions were too much to bear and snuck out to sit on the top step, her ear turned to the voices wafting like smoke up the staircase.

"I think I'll go into the sitting room for a moment," she heard her father say in his slow, deliberate manner.

Her mother laughed, a little tinkle, before making a fussing noise, as though to calm a baby. "Goodnight, then, Bob," she'd slurred. Seconds later, Alice heard her father's slippers on the Peruvian runner in the hallway – the one Linda had been given as a goodbye gift from her boss at the Orchid Grand Hotel in Kensington, even though it had a faint brown stain in the middle – and seconds later, the murmur of a TV newsreader.

From the kitchen, Linda broke into song: "Poor... Professor Higgins." Uncle Jim joined in and the two sighed happily at the end of their kitchen-table performance. Alice waited. Nothing. She rested her head against the cool wall and wondered if she should sneak down and sit on her father's lap and tell him how much she loved him.

But then the voices came closer.

"Well, goodnight." It was Jim talking to her mother, his voice as clear as a bell from the entrance hall. "Coat, check. Glasses, check. Wallet, check."

"You're so forgetful," her mother cooed.

"Well, my mind is on greater things," he said with exaggerated vowels.

"I'm quite sure of that."

Alice craned her neck. She could smell her father's pipe smoke and the constant aroma of tropical incense her mother planted all over the house in a bid to rid the place of the whiff of tobacco.

There was a long silence, one that came with the faint sound of a raincoat being ruffled. Alice dared to sneak down two more steps and peer over the banister.

There they stood, engrossed in a warm embrace, not kissing, but hugging as though afraid to let go of each other. Alice widened her eyes and froze.

"Not now," her mother mumbled into Jim's shoulder.

"I know," he said. "I just…"

"Me too."

They pulled apart and her mother rested her forehead against his, like a cheesy movie poster. Jim gently lifted up Linda's chin and kissed her, slowly, on the lips. Her mother let him do it, then pulled away, wiping at her mouth.

"It's not fair on him. In the house. Tomorrow. Okay?" She whispered something else that Alice couldn't hear. Jim nodded, took his umbrella from the stand and walked out of the door. Alice watched as the circular bald patch atop his greying head ducked through the red doorway and into a cold and gloomy night. Her mother leaned against its closed timber frame and rubbed a hand through her long blonde hair, the bouncing waves she curled every morning having well and truly flattened out. Her eyes were damp and she bit her bottom lip before smoothing down her dress. Alice scurried back to her room, unseen, as angry as she was excited to have witnessed such an adult moment, an illicit, foreign sighting that turned her mother from a harried, angry, working parent into a romantically pained protagonist.

* * *

At first, Alice hated Devon. Well, that's not true. She just missed her father. She also missed the familiarity of London, her old teachers, the one friend she had made in the form of another quiet, bookish girl called Harriett who had small eyes that always seemed to be teary. Alice never saw Harriett again.

In Devon, however, her mother was much happier. She worked in a local art gallery as a guide and receptionist and found a social circle within the craft and "artistic community", as her mother called it. She took painting classes and, a month later, the teacher – a man eight years younger than her mother, who favoured leather motorbike jackets, surrealism and thin brown cigarettes – moved in. "His name's Pablo," her mother had told Alice, as Pablo stood eating a *jamón* sandwich in the breezy hallway of their poky terrace house tucked into a corner of a cul-de-sac. "He's from Spain. He's a brilliant artist. You two will have so much in common."

Of course, they didn't. Alice tried. Pablo had a vibrant, enthusiastic manner when he walked into a room – all hellos and whoops and positivity. He would ask her about her day and she found she opened up whenever he enquired about her new school or what she had learned. But once she had dutifully replied, Pablo nodded, went back to his canvas or his cigarettes and the conversation ended. He was not a child-minded person, not like her father was, with his sincere curiosity and calm presence. Understandably, really, Pablo didn't have any interest in walking with her, finding new nature trails or bookshops in nearby towns, even if she asked him to go with her. How could she have expected him to do such fatherly things, Linda asked. Alice had nodded sadly. She understood. Alice, by then halfway through being thirteen years old, had seen enough TV soaps when her mother was at work to know that Pablo was not to be around for long anyway.

Alice attended the local school. She found the lessons easy, but had difficulty making friends. She was annoyed at her own wariness yet unable to morph into something else – something more gregarious, funny, lively. It was easier to be reserved than risk rejection. So, for the first couple of years, she retreated into reading and walking, her socks always wet from stomping through long grass and seaside fields. The other kids avoided her. They didn't want to deal with her lowered eyes and tendency to hover in the shadows. It was shyness, but they saw it as being just plain boring.

She played the sport she was required to play, she did well academically, but she had become a loner, like her father. Her mother fretted about Alice's lack of social life and so did Alice. The solution, she decided, was to one day move back to London and live with her father. Over time, she might find a boyfriend, someone who worked in a library or a museum. They would grow their own herbs and tomatoes and read books and walk in the evenings and laugh their heads off at the rude bus driver, or saviour the delicious crêpes discovered in the new French patisserie just off Moore Park Road. Alice used writing as an outlet and – fingers tightly gripping a Hello Kitty pencil Pablo had brought back from a recent visit to Spain – wrote stories about her brilliant future in a series of notebooks, her brain awash with images of a tall man in a wool jumper, reading under a warm and yellowish glow from an antique lamp, at his feet an oriental rug and a red setter or an Irish wolfhound. And always, there were pots of steaming tea, warm embraces and adoring glances over reading glasses.

* * *

One afternoon, as Alice was heading home from trudging along the Exeter City Wall Trail, again imagining the medieval knights and their trusty steeds who had graced these ancient paths, everything changed.

Towards her, a boy was walking. He was tall, nearly a head taller than she, maybe a year or so older than her. He had a floppy dark fringe and legs that he flung in front of him, like elastic bands. Under the long fringe were two dark, rounded black eyes, boring a hole into her fragile exterior, too direct to be an accident.

"Sorry," he stuttered as they came into close contact. "I'm lost. I'm looking for a house. It says on this note it's number 30 Barnfield Close, but all I can find is Barnfield Road and so I'm wondering…" He held out a piece of paper with a map drawn in pencil. "It has to be close. Maybe, therefore, it is… close?" He laughed at his own joke and shuffled from side to side when Alice stayed mute and serious. Alice frowned as he spoke some more. It was his aunty's house, he said. Her name was Bethwyn Parkes. He was a boarder and on an *exeat* weekend. His parents lived in Hong Kong. They couldn't get to England to take him out so he was staying with Aunt Bethwyn.

"You don't happen to know her, do you? She has a daughter about your age."

She didn't, but she did know Barnfield Road. For the first time, Alice smiled. He smiled back. His cheeks were pink and dotted with angry spots. He scratched at one.

"Good stuff," he said, standing taller, and stuffed his hands in his pockets. "Let's go then, shall we?"

He was much posher than anyone Alice had ever met before. She sounded rough and brittle when her voice came out and she blushed as they walked the five hundred metres or so to his aunt's house.

Whenever Alice looked back on that first meeting with

Torquil, his aunt and his aunt's daughter, the equally fancy-named Cossima, she felt the same shiver of elation as she had when entering Bethwyn Parkes's home that day.

It was a large red-brick terrace with a narrow rectangular garden that had gone to ruin. Raggedy brown vines clung to the tall window frames and clumps of weeds grew sunwards from a small square of grass. A child's bicycle with a wheel missing lay on the front path, along with a rusted metal bucket and a spade.

"I hope someone's been planning on cleaning this place up," Torquil said, as Alice glanced at the spade. "Well. Thanks for your help. Take care." He stuck out a wide hand and she shook it weakly. He nearly crushed her tiny fingers and she winced. "Shit, sorry. Got into the habit. Now. Right. Where was I? Okay. Thanks and all that." Alice started to walk from the gate.

"Torquil!" A girl the same age and height as Alice suddenly leaped from the front door and ran into his outstretched arms. He dropped his rucksack on the ground and scooped her into his arms. "Finally! Mummy's been waiting. Sorry about the house. She's so lazy. And the hot water's gone too. Since Daddy left, it's been a shambles. She'll be so pleased to see you. So excited. We need a boy around here. I'm so sick of all these miserable adults. Oh do come inside, it's dire out here."

She shot Alice a look as Alice closed the front gate. "Hello? Who are you? Actually, I think I've seen you, walking around. In your school uniform, from the school round the corner? How do you go there? Looks *awful*. I should say that I might have to go there soon, too. Mummy says Daddy won't pay for Bramdean anymore."

"Will you shut up for once and make me some tea?" Torquil laughed.

"Bye, then!" the girl called to Alice. "Oh. Hold on. Why are you with Torquil anyway?"

"I was lost," Torquil chimed, as he pushed the girl towards the door. "She helped me, didn't you, Alice?"

The girl smiled and opened her mouth wide, as though in wondrous awe.

"Oh, that's *so* nice. Thank you, Alice. He is hopeless with directions. Aren't you, Torqs? Okay. Well, Alice, any time you see me around, come and say hello. If I go to the local, I'll need you. I'm going to be the odd one out. Don't you think, Torqs? Might need you to teach me how to fight."

"Right. You. Inside. Bye, Alice."

They bustled noisily to the door, jostling and giggling, like something from a a Famous Five novel. The door slammed shut. From a few metres down the road, Alice could still hear the girl's high-pitched babble coming from a side window at the back of the house.

Alice used their characters in a story that night. Torquil and his cousin, whom she called Jeanette. They went on trains to boarding school, rode horses and never saw their parents. They had trunks filled with mothballed woollies and visited Paris and Spain in the summer, for their "hols". In the story, Alice wrote that they came across an abandoned ship, in which they discovered a treasure chest filled with ancient gold coins. But then, they were being followed, by a shady figure in a long coat. Alice's heart beat fast as she wrote furiously in her notebook.

"Alice?" her mother called from downstairs. "Lights out! Early start tomorrow!" She heard Pablo's birdlike chattering and the Rolling Stones throb on the floorboards underneath her bed. "Come here, you devil," her mother cooed to Pablo.

She wondered what Torquil and his willowy cousin would be doing that night. Maybe they'd had tea by the fire, played charades. Maybe they'd quoted poetry and then fallen about laughing about how Prince Andrew was divorcing that freckle-faced Sarah Ferguson.

The next day, a spring Friday with the waft of briny ocean in the air, Alice tried to stop herself, but she couldn't. She had created these characters, she mused, so it was only fair she got to see them again.

As soon as the school bell chimed, her little feet trotted the long way home from school, finding her way back to Barnfield Road. She dawdled, watching Bethwyn Parkes's house to her right, as she scuffed the toe of her black leather shoes on the pavement. Looking back, she wasn't exactly sure why she chose to go back. Perhaps it was that Cossima – as Alice later found she was called – was the first girl in Exeter to ever really make an effort to talk to her. Perhaps it was that she looked up to their higher class, their ability to have nonchalant conversations in the way an adult normally did, without having to be asked to speak first.

Alice heard her before she saw her.

"You must. You *must*!" It was the girl and Torquil, walking along the path towards her. Alice tried to make it look as though she was moving with purpose, but she turned around enough to show her profile and the girl immediately called to her.

"Alice! Alice!" Alice turned. She took in the girl's beaming smile and hearty wave, the enthusiastic gait and her oversized windcheater. "Call me Cosy," the girl gushed. "Everyone does. Are you coming inside? Torqs bought these absolutely delish cakes. He's from the rich side of the family. Hong Kong. If you want to make a fortune, go East, so Mummy says. My parents are broke, you see. Well, we used to have money, but Daddy lost it all in the share market and now Mummy hates him because we have to live here."

"Don't tell tales, Cosy," Torquil admonished, and rubbed a fist over the top of her head.

"Owwwwweeee! Come on, Alice. Let's eat these cakes before he does. There's one with chocolate icing. Bags I that one. Now, Alice," Cosy stopped at the front door and looked over at Alice, standing slack-jawed behind her, the puppy waiting for a treat, "tell me about the school. I need to know everything. You can be my sidekick, my protector. You know, like in a prison."

"Oh, come *on*, Cosy," Torquil scoffed. "It's a local school, not a bloomin' jail! Stop taking the piss out of poor Alice."

Cosy giggled. "Only joking."

Inside the house, Alice smiled, inhaling dust, wet dog, fresh cake and the unmistakable scent of a heavy, musky perfume, like woodsmoke. *The Far East*, Alice imagined, as Cosy dragged her into a yellow kitchen with peeling paint and what Alice quickly realised was a large Degas on the far wall. Cosy saw her looking at it.

"Mummy's." Cosy shrugged. "She has only a few nice things left. She will never sell *that*."

Once inside the ramshackle, antiquated home of Cosy and Torquil Parkes, Alice never wanted to leave. For a long time, she didn't. Two months later, Pablo took off for a week in Spain to visit his family and never returned. Her mother was inconsolable. To escape the wailing and gnashing of teeth, Alice decamped to the Parkes house most days. There, she and Cosy lazed around in the overgrown back garden, wrote stories together, read books and ate endless honey sandwiches made with dry bread. When it was clear, they'd walk until their feet ached, making up tales of their glittering futures along the way, much of which were set in the unknown worlds of an exotic Asia. They would be beautiful and rich and accomplished and *never, ever be told by a man to do the washing up*, Cosy often stressed. Soon enough, Alice had started talking like Cosy, rounding her mouth, doing away with the verbal shorthand of her lower-middle-class London upbringing. It wasn't deliberate, but she was happy with it. Her mother never noticed. Linda had lost two stone and subsisted on crackers and watery soups. Alice comforted her, the two of them cuddled under a thin crocheted throw and watching *Blankety Blank* and *Blue Peter*. But doing so also made her resentful. Surely, her mother would have realised by now that her father had been a better option after all. Alice never said it out loud.

A dour figure with a rotund bottom that waddled like a zebra's, Mrs Parkes seemed to encourage Alice to stay close to her new friend at all times, maybe because she wasn't quite emotionally up to much herself. Conversely, Alice's mother seemed to barely notice her friendship with Cosy.

As such, the girls' mothers became hazy figures in the background, allowing the two girls to forge a bond they were convinced could never be broken.

Two months after Pablo left, Linda started spending several nights a week at the pub. Four months after Pablo failed to come home, Linda arrived at their front door with a new bloke, Garry, a stocky local estate agent with shiny new shoes and an expensive, well-stuffed leather wallet he pulled out and placed on the kitchen table. Alice grimaced at her mother. She knew, now aged fourteen, what this relationship was all about. "So tell me," her mother had said, placing her chin elegantly in the palm of her hand, elbow bent on the cheap pine table and pale, smooth flesh exposed right up to her bra strap, "where in France is your summer home?"

When June came around, her mother announced she was spending two weeks with Garry in Bergerac and could Alice please stay at Cosy's home? *Only for a fortnight, mind you.*

The two girls were ecstatic. Alice's mother sent her on her way with an overnight bag and a tray of peaches, fresh from the market. She must have got Garry to pay for them. For Alice, it was two weeks of bliss. When her mother returned, she went home with a heavy heart. Mrs Parkes didn't have schedules, you see, no dinner times or bath times. The girls ate bread and apples for supper and never polished their shoes or sat at the dining table, a space covered in old newspapers and piles of receipts anyway. Mrs Parkes didn't work. Most days, she was in her bedroom, the radio turned occasionally to BBC4 and the stench of Silk Cut hitting Alice's nostrils with such regularity that Alice found herself holding her breath as she reached the top step, the one that creaked in the middle. "Depression," Cosy had whispered and turned her eyes towards the far corner where her mother's pale-blue bedroom door was firmly closed.

Garry hung around Alice and Linda's home but didn't

move in, keeping Linda a little on edge. Several months later, Linda announced she wanted to travel to Las Vegas with Garry, who had a son working there on his gap year as a croupier. How could she resist? If she could get him to fall in love with her on the trip, she was in. Alice had rolled her eyes and left the room. "How dare you look down on me?" Linda had screeched, as Alice slowly ascended the stairs. "One day you'll see! Marrying a man with money is a career move!"

Yet there was a silver lining. Linda's holiday meant Alice could again move in with Cosy, despite it coinciding with Alice's fifteenth birthday. Cosy, however, outdid herself – a sponge cake with pink icing, Bethwyn's old copy of *Emma* (the one with the hard cover and a note on the inside from her mother's grandmother, dated from the Dark Ages) and a tape she'd made herself of all their favourite music. They lay on the thin brown carpet in Cosy's attic bedroom, the sun streaming through a tiled window above, lost in Madonna. At the end of the song, Alice felt a content, gentle smile cross her features.

"Let's play it again." She tapped Cosy on the shoulder. "Shall we?" But Cosy's eyes had filled with tears. "What's going on? Are you okay?"

Cosy covered her eyes with both hands.

"I miss my dad," Cosy sputtered.

Alice, too, felt tears form. She'd seen her father a few times in the past year – a quick Christmas visit to London, a few days over the Easter break. It was pleasant, but by then, they had grown apart. She wanted to be closer to him but the connection had been broken by distance and time. Whatever love she had held in her heart for her father had been replaced by her closeness to Cosy. This seemed to please Alice's mother no end.

"Where is he now?" Alice said softly. "Still in Brighton with the 'other woman'?" Alice sat up and rewound the tape.

Cosy shook her head. Her hair was mousy brown and pin-straight. It made her long, sunburnt face look even more protracted.

"Mother says he's broken up with her. Mother calls her

the 'prize cow'." Alice giggled. "No. He's not in Brighton."
Cosy gulped and grabbed Alice's hand a little too hard. "He's
in jail."

In shock, Alice's other hand slipped on the volume button
and Paula Abdul blasted her way unceremoniously into the
bedroom. Both girls jumped. It made them both chuckle a
little.

"Oh, shit. Oh, sorry. Hold on." Alice fiddled with the
knob and reached out to hold Cosy's hand, again noticing her
chewed fingernails, one all the way down to the quick. "Why?
What did he do? Are you worried?"

"Oh, he'll be out in six months. Fraud. It happens." She
shrugged and sucked at her bottom lip. "When he gets out,
Mother says she might let him stay here. I suppose. I don't
really get it. We have to go and visit him at Christmas, to pick
him up. Erg... Me. In prison."

"You'll be fine." Alice patted her hand, the way her own
mother did to her when she said goodbye before her romantic
jaunts with Garry. "Imagine having him home again."

Cosy pulled herself to her feet and, after taking a deep
inhale, did a little jig on the spot. She broke into Madonna's
'Express Yourself'. Alice joined in, four matchstick legs
bandying around the room like newborn giraffes.

"When we leave school," Cosy yelled over the music,
"let's go to Hong Kong together. To work. Do anything. Make
lots of money. Just the two of us. Promise?"

"Express yourself, nah nahnahnahnahnah, hey hey!" Alice
sang, off-key.

"Promise?"

Alice nodded. "I promise. I promise!"

A few months later, Cosy was sent to boarding school,
thanks to a fund that was finally released, one set up by her
paternal grandparents. Mrs Parkes had jiggled on the front
steps when delivering Cosy the news, her bottom thundering
from side to side, so much that Alice worried the entire stone
façade may crumble. The first thing Mrs Parkes had done when

the money came in was buy a new blue dress that hugged her girth. She also tore up the parched receipts from the dining-room table. The house smelled different. It smelled clean.

Alice stayed on at high school and regularly topped the year. The two girls stayed in touch by letter, reminding each other of their promise. When Cosy visited during the holidays, they walked and talked and read, and aged seventeen, drank vermouth mixed with gin on a clifftop and, again, made the same promise.

Just before their final exams, Alice's mother turned up at the school midway through ancient history. She had brushed her hair and pulled it into a severe ponytail. Her eyes were pink and she wore none of the heavy black liner she had favoured of late. Alice saw Linda's quivering lip and panicked, felt the rise of bile, as she walked towards her mother's outstretched arms.

That jittery Bethwyn Parkes. She was late getting Cosy back to school one evening at the end of an *exeat* weekend. The two of them had stayed with friends and spent the holiday preparing Cosy for her upcoming exams, heads bent over a kitchen table, drinking tea and endlessly revising. Bethwyn had lost track of time and – needing a Silk Cut to keep her calm as she raced around darkening country roads – had begun to reach down for her cigarettes; they'd fallen from her lap and were floating somewhere near the brake pedal. But a cyclist on a sharp corner caught her eye as she bent forward. She jolted the wheel to avoid hitting him and quickly lost control of the car. The old Rover went head-first into a large oak tree at top speed.

Cosy and her mother's necks were broken on impact.

* * *

By the time Alice and Wang had reached the far end of the beach, Alice could see he was shaking. She pulled him close.

"It's not even cold," she said.

"What?" He crossed his arms over his chest, as though freezing. "Your story, I suppose. Kind of a chilling end to it."

"I know. But don't worry. I've come to terms with it." Still, Alice could tell Wang's chills were not just to do with her tale. "Coming here helped. Doing what she and I planned to do. So now, it's your turn."

In her earlier life, Alice had loved complicated men. They reminded her of all the strays her mother picked up along the way. But in the past few years – as concerns increased that she may never have children – she'd taken a good long look at herself and realised she needed something real. She couldn't hide it any longer. She wanted a family, a proper one, the one she never had. And if there was one thing she'd lacked her entire childhood, it was stability. The result was that for most of her adult life, she had lacked an eye for what a good man looked like. She hoped with all her heart that Wang was complicated in a good way, not in a love-you-and-leave-you kind of way. She hoped his pressing dramas related to the fact he was, in fact, a man of substance, as she had suspected, and not one of unsteadiness. Her heart was not quite broken from the events of her past, but it was shattering from the beatings it had taken and one more could lead to permanent damage. She was dreading his news, but also eager to put her mind at rest.

Wang turned to her as they sat on a rock, waves lapping quietly at the shore. He touched her cheek and then pressed his against hers.

"I know we're only just getting to know each other, but I don't want to lose you, so there's a long story I have to tell. But once I have, you must promise to never breathe a word of it. And you have to listen to what I ask you to do and…"

Alice nodded. She felt a warm wash of something she assumed was love as he spoke, and pinched herself on the forearm to remind her to take it slowly.

"And what?"

Wang glanced over his shoulder, a gust of wind ruffling his fringe. "And be careful. Very careful."

CHAPTER THIRTEEN

Central Psychology. Hong Kong.

Carolyn had finished with her last client of the day, a forty-five-year-old businesswoman who had lost all her money in an online dating scam. It was depressing stuff and Carolyn was not in the mood for the thirty-minute train ride to Quarry Bay for dinner with Felicity. But Felicity – as was her way – had insisted. Furthermore, Carolyn could tell by Felicity's voice over the phone that she was on the upward swing of an excitable mood and, from experience, knew this could lead to bad choices. As her therapist, she felt it sensible to listen to what Felicity had to say.

They were to meet in a seafood restaurant on the street level of a winding lane at the top of a narrow road shadowed by a sharp rise of white stone. As she walked, Carolyn could see darkened hardware stores, plastic junk shops lit up like surgeries and a few car repair shops. The workers clanged their tools as they bellowed over revving engines and the waft of petrol caught in her throat. She felt a little dizzy. In the distance, she heard a ship sound its horn, a night of summer mist settling over the waterways. Above her, boxy air-conditioning units dripped water onto her cheeks and Carolyn, her feet sweaty and swollen, wiped her face with a skin-blotting cloth – the Japanese kind you found in mass-market beauty stores with names like BoBo and Pretty Pink Lemon. God, she hoped the food would be worth the trudge.

In the wet, humid air, Carolyn's hair had frizzed and she could feel it bounce as she strode hopefully towards the Golden Wing Seafood Palace.

As always, Felicity was waiting. She was never late. And also as always, she was tapping an unlit cigarette on the table, one leg crossed over the other as she swung back in her chair.

"Find it okay?" she asked Carolyn. Felicity looked cool and smug. She was eyeing a glass of white wine on the table in front of her.

"Sort of." Carolyn sat and poured herself a glass of water. "Was it a test of some kind?" Not for the first time, Carolyn wondered how she had befriended this strange woman, a child of immense wealth and privilege who was now a private investigator, hugging dark corners and wearing the same monochrome uniform every day. Having said that, Carolyn had occasionally taken on projects over the years. People like Felicity kept her guessing. She got bored otherwise. "I walked up and down the street three times before seeing the sign to the lane. Been here for more than twenty years and can confirm there are streets I will never ever walk down in this city, no matter how hard I try to explore."

"I was born here and I'm the same," Felicity smiled. "Now," she uncrossed her legs and picked up her chopsticks, "I've got something for you that will make your day. Here. Have a dumpling. Best in town."

Felicity pulled out her notebook. Carolyn briefly looked at her friend's stubby finger. Recently, Carolyn had stopped noticing it, but for some reason, that day, it caught her eye. She sipped at her wine and blanched. It tasted sickly-sweet and she placed it down without trying to hide her distaste from Felicity. A fly landed on the rim of the glass.

"I'll order you a beer instead," Felicity smiled.

Lately, the two of them had only been in telephone contact. Carolyn had been unusually busy and her youngest child unwell. She'd lost her earlier momentum in the search for Johnny Humphries's true character and, as such, Felicity had been out there alone, doing what she did best. Carolyn was curious, but she was also starting to wonder if Felicity was chasing a fantasy. Could Johnny have done what he did and – most importantly – why would he have done so? He had a glittering future, good looks, intelligence. Why work with violent underground criminals? Where was the motivation? Furthermore, she believed him when he told her about his girlfriend lashing out at him. Carolyn had a radar for the truth, a skill she had spent a long time honing and one she could now claim was mostly reliable. People gave little things away – their gaze shifted, their body language became defensive, they smiled furtively without meaning to. Or, they raised their voices steadily, as though speaking loudly would make it more believable. Furthermore, if Johnny were a complete low-life, why would he be seeking help from Carolyn when it came to his relationship? It was too unlikely for Carolyn to fathom.

Felicity was sifting through the pages of her notebook, regaling Carolyn with a story about an imminent rent hike. Carolyn let her talk. She didn't express her doubts about Johnny out loud. Carolyn knew Felicity's enthusiasm had not waned. In fact, it had picked up speed. Felicity, she told Carolyn, had barely slept in her quest, forgoing new clients to do so. Furthermore, she had stayed in contact with Scarlett, which made Carolyn even more uncomfortable, considering her own professional link to Johnny. Still, Carolyn was – as always – curious and this spurred her into taking the time to hear what Felicity had to say. If anything, knowing Felicity as well as she did now meant she could rationalise it was all in the name of support.

Finally, Felicity got to the point.

"We have a breakthrough and it will blow your mind," Felicity said excitedly, eyes glinting over the steam of a plate of garlicky noodles. Felicity put down her notebook and rested on her elbows. "Firstly, I received an email back from the wonderful Mr Gu, the businessman Johnny was, you know,

'having dinner' with in Beijing the day I heard his voice."
Carolyn went to speak. "But wait, even better. I have been
given something. Some photos and some documents. It was
like divine intervention." Felicity beamed at the memory.

"Okay. I'm ready to hear all about it," Carolyn said,
through a mouthful of diced chicken.

Mr Gu, it turned out, was more than happy to accommodate
Felicity's request as Faye Win, freelance writer working on a
book of Hong Kong's crime history. He replied some weeks
later, as he'd been in the US visiting his adult children, so
he'd explained.

*Luckily, I keep all my diaries from my working days, both
with Mr Chung's hotel company and in the years afterwards,
Mr Gu wrote. And after some time spent going through old
boxes, I discovered the diary and the entry from my meeting
with Mr Humphries. In your email, you asked if I had enjoyed
dinner with Mr Humphries. But according to my diary from
that date, I must report that I had dinner planned but then
it was cancelled at the last minute. The location was the
French Teahouse, then a new Western café. It was popular,
and I remember asking my secretary to book it regularly in
those days. According to my diary, Mr Humphries was due
to meet me at 7.30pm. I'm sorry to say that at the time, I
must have told the police I had eaten dinner with him... It
was my mistake. Time has erased my memory of such small
details, as you can imagine. At around the same time, I also
assisted with a large donation to an orphanage in Tianjin,
one that I was led to believe was on behalf of Mr Humphries
and his boss. A few months ago, I was contacted by the same
orphanage. The director was querying past donations and
potentially misappropriated funds. However, I have no further
information when it comes to this. Perhaps most importantly,
I would like to advise that I am not a well man. A few months
ago, I was diagnosed with lung cancer and will not make it to
Christmas. If you require any further information...*

A pot of jasmine tea arrived in a ceramic white teapot with

a clattering lid. Outside, there was a light rain. Felicity's face was flushed red. Carolyn let this information sink in.

"Did the police check if he flew to Beijing at the time? Did they get the flight records from the airline?"

Felicity chewed vigorously. Finally, she wiped at her mouth.

"They did. The airline confirmed he was in Beijing that day. He flew back to Hong Kong three days later. About ten years ago, when I was having a bit of a meltdown about it all – again – Dad reminded me of this fact. He was adamant. I suppose the police findings are etched in my brain. But now, now that I know he lied he was with Mr Gu, well, that changes everything."

Carolyn slumped her shoulders. "I know this may sound weird, but I can't help feeling that this is not a good revelation."

Carolyn watched a dollop of oyster sauce drip from Felicity's chopsticks and onto the white tablecloth. Her eyes were stinging in the arctic air-conditioning. *I'm tired*, she thought to herself. It'd been a long day, a long day of talking with the anxious, the depressed and the paranoid. Having dinner with someone who was potentially all three was not making things better.

"Why? I'm okay. Never been happier." Carolyn sensed this too was true. It seemed chasing Johnny gave Felicity a purpose, but one that could get her in trouble. "Food tastes better. I sleep well. Ever since that Gu email, I've bounced out of bed every morning and raced to the office with a smile on my face. I know it sounds crazy."

The same could not be said for Carolyn. She had hopped onto some kind of hormonal roller coaster, hot and flushed one day, aching bones the next.

"As long as you know that when it all ends – and it will end – that you have to let it go, no matter the outcome," Carolyn said, in her best counsellor's voice.

"I hear you," Felicity replied. "I'm not stupid." Carolyn curled her lip in apology. "Anyway, this story gets better."

Felicity took another mouthful. Carolyn fiddled impatiently with her old eternity ring. She wore it on her right hand now. She had chosen it herself all those years ago, spent hours in the jewellery store talking grades and carats and light and fractures and then dragged Greg into the store for him to see what she wanted. If she'd known then that when they divorced, she would have to pay him out and lose three-quarters of her assets, she might not have asked him to buy the damn thing. Whatever he brought into their marriage ended up being siphoned from her bank account anyway. Felicity finally finished her mouthful. "You are going to die," Felicity said.

"I hope not," Carolyn chortled.

Felicity ignored her.

"After Gu's email, I went to the library, to look through all the old newspaper articles about the kidnapping. Because of my work, I subscribe to a digital system that lets me search those older dates in certain libraries. For years, I'd stopped myself from doing just that, but now I had a reason, and I wanted to remind myself of the dates and times and reports, you know, just to be sure. God, it was weird, seeing photos of myself, so young. My mother." Felicity reached down and pulled a photocopy of an article from her bag. She spread it out carefully on the table. "She was beautiful, wasn't she?" Felicity's mother had been a model in the US. Texan, leggy, blonde, with a broad all-American smile. "She was famous, kind of like Jerry Hall," Felicity said wistfully. "But when she married my dad, she gave it all up. Dad travelled too much and she thought it wasn't fair on us kids to be left alone with the maid so often." She shrugged and wiped at one eye. "Oh, well."

Carolyn felt a little guilty. Felicity had been through a lot. So much so she lived under an assumed name. She trusted no one, except Carolyn, and this realisation jolted her a little and brought home the heavy weight of responsibility of being entrusted with such information.

"Sorry I haven't been so enthused by all this." Carolyn

rested a fist on her chin. "I've been kind of worried it was all in vain."

Felicity scooped more pork into her mouth. "Hey. I know. I can imagine it's hard for you, to, you know, believe everything I'm doing here. But this has been in the back of my mind my entire adult life. I can't leave it now. And then ever since Scarlett rang me that day, to see if Johnny was seeing someone else, this has been my new goal, my reason for getting up in the morning. It might be difficult for you to understand, but someone had my finger chopped off. Someone had me kidnapped. They spat on me. Verbally abused me. One of the men responsible never paid for it and I want him to. That's all."

"Could the police help further do you think?"

Felicity snorted. "No. Years ago, long after the kidnapping, I called them. Mum and Dad tried to stop me, but I was obsessed. The answer was the same. All the kidnappers had been punished. There were four of them. All local, young and a bit naïve. They went to jail. They did their time. The police said that whoever I heard that night talking in English either didn't exist – which is police code for saying I was crazy from the ordeal – or it was one of the kidnappers speaking in English, or one of their friends, maybe to hide their own identity. Either way, case closed. See how frustrating that is?"

Carolyn nodded. "Right. Got it. Yes. I understand. Now. Keep telling me the story."

Felicity explained she realised how little she knew about Johnny's past. She knew his mother was Chinese, his father English, but he had never named him. She knew, through information from Scarlett, that he had grown up in East London. With little else to do and a burning desire to scour every minor detail she could come up with, Felicity came to a dead end on anything else. But then her luck had changed.

"I rang Scarlett again," she said. "And wonders never cease."

"You said your work with Scarlett was done," Carolyn replied. "You've told her Johnny's not having an affair."

"Yes, but now she's on to something else. She wants me to help her. She said she was given some information recently and needed me to dig deeper for her. Having said that, I'm not sure why."

Carolyn tried not to look suspicious.

"Okay. Go on."

Felicity pulled out another photocopy of a newspaper article.

"Here. Take a look at this."

Tuesday, 5 September 1995. Sir Robert Humphries Shot Dead Outside London Pub

The former chairman of the Euroculture Group and celebrated philanthropist, Sir Robert Humphries, was found dead in an alleyway near the Rabbit and Hound pub in Fulham shortly after 23.00 Monday. He had suffered two gunshot wounds to the head. Police say he would have died instantly.

Early police reports state that Sir Robert had been toasting a close colleague's upcoming nuptials. He left alone and seconds later was killed at close range. There were no witnesses. A young man and a female companion walking home from a stage show had come across Sir Robert's body at about 23.20. Neither is a suspect in the shooting.

"We are not aware of any motivation for this cowardly attack on an elderly gentleman," Detective Sergeant Lance Philmore told the Daily Chronicle. *"We urge anyone with information to please come forward to assist police with our ongoing investigations."*

Police also stress that Sir Robert had no known enemies. His wife, Lady Arabella Humphries, told reporters last night that she and her husband were in a stable financial position and did not have any connections to business dealings that could have resulted in foul play.

"My husband is a victim of a callous and shocking crime

and my daughters and I will not rest until his killer is brought to justice," Lady Humphries said in a prepared statement through police media.

"We will continue to investigate all angles," said Detective Sergeant Philmore.

Felicity watched Carolyn as she read. Carolyn nodded, slowly.

"That was six months after my kidnapping," Felicity said, pointing at the paper.

"Right. Robert Humphries. So you – hold on, Scarlett – thinks this guy is Johnny's father? No mention of an illegitimate son. And, um, why does Scarlett care so much about his parentage if she's only interested in his loyalty to her?" Carolyn finally voiced.

Felicity frowned. "Don't you think it's interesting? Scarlett says for sure this was his father. She looked it all up. He was shot in the head. For no reason."

"How does she know he's his father for sure?"

"He told her. He also told her he grew up in East London with his mother and then went to Bramar Hall. I mean, all these years, and I never really looked into Johnny's distant past, just his Hong Kong life. I never thought it'd be important in relation to what happened to me."

"Is it strange that Scarlett is telling you this?"

Felicity rubbed at her nose, buying time.

"Yes. Probably. But—"

"But you enjoy this? The digging around into Johnny?"

"Yep."

Carolyn shook her head and raised both palms in surrender.

"I wonder if the police heard about Johnny's existence after Sir Humphries' murder and tried to track him down? I mean, people talk. Johnny can't have been completely under the radar as far as gossip went."

Felicity scratched the side of her head. "I don't know. He seems to have managed to keep his true parentage quiet. I mean, my father never mentioned he knew anything. And I've tried my police contacts here and in the UK, but there's no mention of Johnny in relation to Sir Humphries. It's only Scarlett who seems to have been given this information."

The waiter appeared and took away the plates. He asked if they would like any drinks.

"Glass of wine?" Felicity smiled at Carolyn.

"No."

"Really?"

"Yes. Okay. Just one. A nicer one, though."

"Knew it."

Felicity had gone to town with further research. She'd never dug so deep, she explained, primarily because every counsellor she'd ever spoken to was focused on getting her mind off Johnny Humphries, not further into his life.

Except me, Carolyn thought, a little guiltily.

Felicity continued. She had contacted Bramar Hall via email, which assisted her with the timeline of his academic career there. She used her Faye Win account and said she was writing profiles for the *South China Mail* newspaper on important Hong Kong business figures – how they got there and where they were from. Felicity asked if the archivist could tell her where Johnny had lived in London when he first attended Bramar Hall, as she was requiring more colour to tell his history in fine detail. In a stroke of luck, the woman finally came back, offering more information than Felicity expected – 32 Desmond Street, Hackney. ("However, his father died not long after and a temporary postal address nearby – 25B Lillian Street – was then registered until he finished his studies. I do hope to read this intriguing book soon," the school archivist had gushed.) The day after, the same archivist rang to say she was new to the job and had made a mistake; that she was not meant to provide such information to reporters. To anyone, really. Felicity could hear her embarrassment as she fumbled her words over the phone. She assured her she had definitely been "in touch" with Mr Humphries himself and would not publish those addresses. *Not in the newspaper anyway*. Felicity then created an account on the gov.uk website and searched for the name of the title deeds of the house at 32 Desmond Street between 1969 and the late 1980s, using her Faye Win name again to avoid any links to who she really was. The site only had information back to 1993, but thinking it was worth a try, she searched the address and found the house was then still owned by Camilla Humphries.

"Sir Robert's daughter?"

"I'd say so." Felicity looked very pleased with herself. "She would have been a young child back then. Earlier, he must have put the ownership in her name and then hid Johnny and Johnny's mother out there while he assumed his normal life. Camilla still unwittingly owned it in 1993."

"I'm going to start calling you Faye." Carolyn noticed her glass was already half empty.

"I signed up for the British Newspaper Archives database. I knew it existed, but I've never used it for my cases in Hong Kong, naturally. I had a lot of information to go through, and it took ages, but—" she spread her arms wide, "I did an international news search on the address and the year Johnny would have lived there, before he went to Bramar Hall, expecting nothing. And guess what?"

"What?" Carolyn replied, noticing Felicity's obsession over this was fuelling a manic thrill – she barely blinked.

"At the age of eleven, when Johnny had only just gone to school, the local newspaper ran small newsy items of the week. Unfortunately, it was reported that a Tammy Lim, originally from Nanjing Province, was found dead at 32 Desmond Street, having fallen down the stairs and broken her neck. Residents remembered her as a hard-working employee of a local laundry-cum-dry-cleaner and a dedicated mother to a young boy; father unknown."

Carolyn stopped sipping her wine. "He had a happy start in life, then," Carolyn snorted.

"Yeah. Well," Felicity guzzled her wine and placed the

glass carefully back on the table. She ran a finger around the stem. "Know what I think?"

"Is it—"

"I think Johnny thought his father had killed his mother, to get rid of her. He knew his father would be worried his kids would find out he had another son living in relative poverty and his 'public' wife and kids would find out. I don't know, but maybe Johnny's mother had forced Sir Robert to send Johnny to a good school and once Johnny was safely ensconced at Bramar Hall, Sir Humphries had her killed? Wouldn't be hard. Lonely woman, you knock on the door under the cover of night, shove her down the stairs?"

Carolyn sat back and groaned. "But where does this leave you, Felicity? Seriously. Does this lead you to finding out who ordered your finger to be cut off?"

"Don't you get it, Carolyn? Johnny would have had to pay – a lot – to have Sir Robert killed. Where would a young banker get thousands and thousands of pounds from?" Felicity nodded to herself. Carolyn wondered if Felicity was on the verge of a breakdown. "He would have had to kidnap someone. That is, someone like me. Take the ransom. Make a quick buck, have his father killed."

Carolyn placed her hand on the table between them, as if to beg for mercy.

"So they took a ransom? How?" Carolyn knew a little bit about this, having read the stories herself, but she wanted to hear Felicity's side of the story, too.

"The police said not to, but once the finger arrived via the post at my father's office, he naturally caved. He did what they asked. From the court case, I recall the money was wired somewhere. I mean, I've blocked minor details out, when it comes to my," she waved her missing pinkie, "to be honest."

Carolyn softened her features.

"Maybe it wasn't that expensive to have him shot. I'm not in the assassin business, obviously, but…"

What was she doing listening to this?

"Anyway, listen, Felicity. I need to go home. I'm pleased you're enjoying finding all this out, but to be honest, I can't see the benefits of it to your mental health anymore." She leaned forward. "I'm worried about you. You're talking about two deaths in London, a long time ago. Yes, both were Johnny's parents, but these things happen. What if… what if he hadn't been there that night when your finger was cut off? What then? Who will you obsess about then?"

Felicity called the waiter over and handed him her credit card.

"No one," Felicity said firmly. "That's the whole point."

"Right. Well, I better run. I think we need to talk about you, the effect this is having on you. Can you make an appointment with Koffee?" Carolyn reached for her bag, remembering with a sinking heart that Koffee had only given notice the day before that she was about to start her own journey to being a psych. She'd have to find someone new.

"Wait." Felicity took her friend by the wrist. "There's this, too."

She scrolled through her phone to find a black-and-white photograph. Two young men on a street corner. One of the men had an eyepatch. The other was, unmistakably, a very young and even more dashing Johnny. He was wearing a suit without a tie.

Behind them, the house number is just visible. *25B*. Johnny's temporary address after his mother died? Behind them is a burnt-out house. The second photo she showed her was handwritten words.

"This was written on the back of the photo," Felicity explained. "*August 1995. Brian and Me. Free at Last.*"

"Oh," Carolyn said. "That's Johnny."

"Yep." Felicity sighed.

"And who's the guy with the eyepatch?"

"That's Brian, obviously. Scarlett sent me this."

"And who is *he*? And why do you care?"

"Just wait. Okay. So, I did another exhaustive search and

found a small news item about a deadly fire at Lillian Street, in August 1995. The only person home was a man, John Feathers, father of two. His wife and son were not at home. He died of smoke inhalation. It quoted a neighbour as saying the man was a regular drinker and was long-term unemployed. What kind of kid wants that for a father? Not the eyepatch guy, whom we now know could possibly be Brian."

Carolyn let the information roll around in her mind. Johnny and his best friend are free at last – from their fathers? Is that what Felicity was saying?

Carolyn had to admit the photograph and the news reports did give the story some legs, as wobbly as they might be.

"But hold on," Carolyn said. "The Scarlett angle. Again. Why is she finding all this out and then telling you?"

Felicity paused, which was unusual. "I don't really know. I suppose she was trying to work out who Johnny really is, you know, to bust him for doing the dirty. She wants me to keep looking for her. For more."

"Okay. Well, sorry to tell the PI how to do her job, but I think it's time you did just that." Carolyn stood to go.

"That's fair," Felicity sighed, as she too stood to leave. "It is all a bit… coincidental. The Scarlett thing."

"And I assume you don't believe in coincidences?"

"I suppose she's just been doing some spying of her own. Seems she's sure he's up to no good in the world of business. I mean, as long as she's helping me out, what do I care?"

Carolyn decided to refuse to counsel Johnny if he came back to her. She knew too much. It was not fair on anyone to maintain her innocence if he continued to have a client relationship with her.

"Why would Scarlett be interested in this photo, though? Why doesn't she just leave him?"

Felicity opened the door for Carolyn to pass through.

"I think you're right. It's time I found out."

Just a couple of weeks before, Simon Gu had placed down the diamond-tipped Montblanc pen he had always used to write important letters, a special item he utilised significantly more often in the golden days, before the internet ruined proper communication for good. He had just replied to Faye Win's message, realising her email was probably a fake and dealing with that problem accordingly. Impending death had a way of making the big decisions quite simple. The thought made Simon smile, something he had not done for some time.

Another letter on the desk in front of him was addressed to his two adult children, neatly folded in an envelope. He'd had it in his drawer for a month, waiting for the right time when his children were away at university. He had just sent the maid down the road with a third letter, this one addressed to a Hong Kong Central office building. In it, he'd really put Johnny and Phil in the shit, big time. Yes, it may have been a cheap parting shot. Gu knew that Johnny and Phil had nothing to do with child trafficking. Johnny had simply asked him to transfer a massive donation years ago; some kind of guilt money, possibly? But Gu wasn't stupid. That money must have come from the Chung kidnapping. And now, Gu was atoning for his sins, too, by passing on Johnny's name to finally – hopefully – get someone to nail him, even if he himself had been a part of it all. *Not anymore.*

No doubt, his maid would be back any minute. Knowing her, she would sort everything out before the kids came home.

He reached for a tissue and let out a hearty cough. His lungs rattled like a bag of chains. A large spot of blood seeped into the tissue and he balled it up before reaching down to place it in the bin under his desk. He took one last look at the photograph of his now deceased wife and himself, smiling broadly on their wedding day in Shanghai all those years ago. What a fool he had been. A greedy fool, like so many of his contemporaries. Hopefully what he had since done would go some way to helping those who had suffered, which is what his beloved wife would have wanted.

He took a deep breath, opened a draw and pulled out a handgun. Without a second of hesitation, he placed the barrel in his mouth and pulled the trigger.

* * *

It was a Thursday. There was a brisk wind in the air and the harbour water crashed over itself in small raging waves as the Star Ferry ambled from Tsim Sha Tsui to the grand new terminal that fronted Central. Bobby loved the Star Ferry, its antiquated bottle-green hull and polished timber seats. He always had. As a child, he had occasionally sailed on it with his grandmother, who always ensured he never leaned too far over the side. Her Kowloon visits were to check on his great-aunt, a cantankerous woman bent double with rickets. Her apartment contained one red lamp, a small side table and a wok on top of a single-burner stove. His grandmother and aunt would talk so fast over each other that Bobby would cover his ears. His grandmother would scold him and thwack him on the back of the head for being disrespectful. The women talked about their wayward sons – all young adult men they worried had become involved in gangs. Once or twice, these "boys" (whom Bobby quite liked the look of) came to the apartment, took money from a tin and winked conspiratorially at Bobby. They were Bobby's second or third cousins, he was told, but he vowed then and there he would never live in such a shitty apartment when he grew up. If those cousins of his were planning some kind of heist, he could understand why.

After they left the great-aunt's shit box, the skin on his grandmother's hand callous and dry against the chubby softness of his palm, Bobby would admire the glamorous handbag and perfume billboards that soared above the new hotels and dreamed of riches beyond belief.

* * *

This Friday, as always, Bobby had enjoyed a long lunch with a variety of friends atop the Grand Hyatt in Kowloon, napped for thirty minutes in his office and then headed to the Long March Bar in the China Club for some champagne with an aged socialite from the UK. Her teeth were too big and her bright red lips flopped loosely as she spoke. But how these women loved to say they'd met with Bobby Ling. He endured her tedious conversation with a cheeky grin, for the sake of all the social connections he would have when he would visit London later that year, and drank heavily to compensate for the boredom.

Two hours after the socialite was whisked away in her car (a little wobbly on her feet), Bobby walked unsteadily the twenty metres or so to where his driver was waiting on Bank Street.

The Mercedes roared into life as soon as Bobby tapped on the window.

"The Club, thanks, Danny," Bobby slurred, settling himself into the back seat.

"No problem, sir."

Bobby grunted as he fiddled around with the seat belt, unable to slot it into place. Red-faced, he then jerked his head at the sound of a friendly tap on the window.

Bobby wound it down, his drunken half-smile quickly fading when he saw who it was. He instinctively sat back as the man peering through the open window bared a set of tombstone-grey teeth.

"Fancy giving me a lift?" the man said cheerily. Bobby did as he was told. "Big night, Bob? Mind if I tag along?"

Bobby sat back and bit his lip. The man jumped into the car.

"It's okay. Drive on, Dans," Bobby whispered to the front seat.

* * *

On Saturdays, Scarlett had taken to walking Johnny's dog, a Weimaraner, and was halfway along Lugard Road, admiring the splendour of Victoria Harbour and the sea of skyscrapers below, shrouded in an early-morning mist.

There was not a soul around, only trill birdsong resounding off the surrounding cliffs. Was it a swallow, a Himalayan swiftlet? Maybe a dollarbird? As she strode purposefully, Scarlett listed the names of Hong Kong birds in her heads. She liked to read about the world around her. It was how she had kept herself occupied as a lonely child. Her father's library was extensive, accessible. As such, she had become not only an avid reader, but a list-maker, the kind of person who needed structure and order for her to relax, both of which lacked greatly at the moment.

Her phone rang. *Alice.*

Alice never woke early on the weekends and the second before Scarlett answered, a sudden and inexplicable thud of dread settled in her stomach. She pressed the green button.

"Is this really you? I've never known you to..." Scarlett started.

Alice sniffed. "Scarlett," she said, sounding like she'd been crying.

"Yes. You called, me, Al. Who else would it be?"

"You haven't heard?"

"Is everything okay?" She was slightly out of breath and rested her arms on a cool metal railing.

"It's Bobby," Alice said with more clarity. "He's... he's dead. He fell down some stairs. There's more details but I—"

* * *

The house in which Scarlett spent most of her childhood and early adult life had the appearance of a luxury estate and the atmosphere of a mausoleum. It sat high and imposing on Wentworth Road in Vaucluse, Sydney's pre-eminent eastern suburb. Designed with a French provincial flair, it had harbour views, a cellar, a four-car garage, separate guest quarters and a grand *parterre* designed by a celebrated landscape architect from Paris. Scarlett's school was a short walk away – a school for girls, first built in 1887. She ambled along the sunny pavement every day, head bowed under a straw hat and covered in a tent-like array of the cotton and light wool that made up her unassuming uniform. She had bought it two sizes too big. That way, she could hide.

Her father, Don Shaw, was incredibly rich and incredibly intelligent. He was a history professor who – through his geologist brother – had lucked out on a mining interest in Western Australia in the early 1980s. He'd made millions overnight. More money than most people thought was possible in a country not yet used to significant personal wealth, save for a few established families. As such, their academic friends didn't trust his stellar rise to riches. They thought he must have done something illegal. He hadn't, but that didn't stop the naysayers.

Her parents quickly lost the bond they had once shared with their learned friends and soon after returning from a three-month tour of Europe, made the decision to escape the envious jibes and move from their humble brick-and-tile bungalow in Waverley to the refined locale of Vaucluse.

For Scarlett, an only child, the new life, at first, was overwhelming. Her parents had been mildly scholastic types in cardigans and sensible shoes and were now multi-millionaires with BMWs and a house in the country. Even more fortuitous (for Don anyway) was that he had invested much of his sudden wealth more wisely than the bitter onlookers thought was possible and soon, he was the toast of the town.

Handsome, educated, charming, he filled his new shoes with ease, as though born to it. For his much younger wife, Jill, a softly-spoken former English literature teacher with a slight widow's hump, the change of life was – as she told her therapist – as though her body and mind had been inhabited by an alien being; she needed an exorcism. The therapist declined. Jill stumbled through, following the domineering Don with a dazed smile and the blinking eyes of someone who hadn't quite woken up from a long slumber. Luckily – and not deliberately – Jill exuded a natural beauty that shone when she bothered to dress up and wear lipstick and the social pages were kind, gushing over the lavish charity events her husband hoisted upon her, despite her nervous disposition and propensity for dark moods. As such, society painted the family as a kind of suburban royalty, an Australian success story, immune to the struggles and pitfalls of everyday life, as they swanned about the marble and glass of their palatial abode.

As is often the case, the reality was starkly different.

For years, all Scarlett wanted was to go back to Waverley. Jill – when she was at home and not on one of her "stays" – was lost in thought, always tired and unable to stay focused for long on whatever Scarlett's day-to-day issues may have been. If a parent needed to go to the school for a function, it was her father who graced the halls.

Scarlett had worked out her mother was depressed and that when she "went away" for a while, it was to a place Scarlett assumed was starkly white with echoing hallways. There, her mother had mysterious treatments and returned with more colour in her cheeks, but that was about it.

While she was away, Scarlett was cared for by a series of faceless nannies while Don wined and dined and guffawed his way through dinners where everyone kowtowed to his beliefs and his likes and dislikes. To say Scarlett was close to her mother was a lie, but she wanted to be. She found solace in swimming, books, movies and birdwatching on the heritage trail that wound from Rose Bay to Nielsen Park, the white sails of the Opera House gleaming in the afternoon sunshine, dwarfed by the high-rises of Sydney's central business district. She studied hard and sometimes played netball, through which she made a few half-hearted friends. Her father watched her as though she were a pretty pet in the background. He ensured she was fed and went to school. He made sure the bills were paid and her school holidays were filled with educational camps. He took her to dinner sometimes – a little pizza place in Bondi that the teenagers favoured – and they sat largely in silence munching away, comforted by the fact the rabble around them meant their inability to converse could largely be ignored. In fact, silence was her most normal state. Speaking freely felt foreign and almost scary. In class, she answered questions quietly – monosyllabically – and when she had to make a speech for an assignment, she barely raised her voice above a whisper.

Once, one of her English teachers spoke to her father about it. He was called in. Within two minutes, the teacher had agreed with Don that Scarlett was such a good student that it was no great worry and to look at the girl as a whole, not the sum of her speeches.

As Scarlett and Don were being escorted from the school office, Don turned to the teacher and lowered his voice: "Her mother had postnatal depression and has never really come out of it. Maybe you already know this. It's been… a challenge. Scarlett has suffered, however. Her mother is on medications that make her somewhat vague."

The earnest female teacher patted his arm. Don gave her a flirtatious grin. "We donate generously to the school fund. The new Charterhouse wing is named after my company in fact, which I'm sure you're aware of. Well. Thank you."

The teacher stuttered a few goodbyes as they departed. Don, reaching for the car door to let Scarlett in the passenger side, placed a firm hand on her shoulder.

"People won't always understand your mother," he said. "I know it's been hard on you, but I am doing my best." Scarlett met his eye. She couldn't even force herself to smile back. It seemed being largely absent, rarely conversing and never showing interest in her emotional state was *doing his best*. Even at fifteen, Scarlett was making plans to escape and find her own way in a world in which she was tired of merely existing, of being a ghostlike presence, even to herself.

Later that night, she wondered if she, too, were depressed. Did it rub off or was it in the genes? In the murky early hours of a Tuesday morning, Scarlett had her first panic attack, her broken heart pounding so hard in her chest she thought it would explode underneath her cotton nightdress. Unable to control a sudden surge in fear, she felt herself float out of her own body, as though watching herself on the brink of death. Her head felt tight and full, the skull too small for the shell around it. But she didn't die, despite thinking she must have done. Even hours later, she simply couldn't move. The nanny found her there, at 9.45am, eyes wide and staring at the ceiling. Her father, summoned by phone, appeared an hour or so later.

"Not her too," she heard him mutter as he left the room, the echo of his leather soles on the marble staircase hammering at her temples long after he'd left the house.

* * *

As soon as school was done with, Scarlett planned to move as far away as possible. She graduated with top marks in all subjects and could have been accepted into any university in the country. Instead, she chose to study economics at the University of Western Australia, thousands of miles away in Perth, the furthest city in the furthest state from Sydney she could find in the entire country. She knew no one and no one knew her. It was perfect.

Her mother was fresh from a stint at some fancy rural retreat and flew to Perth with her, a rare occasion indeed. As they parted on Scarlett's first day in her new campus accommodation, her mother squeezed her hand, the glassy look in her eye still there but a single tear streaking her made-up face, a mask, hiding the imaginary dangers her mother constantly faced.

"Mum," Scarlett started as they stood awkwardly outside her bedroom door, "was it me? Was it my fault?"

Her mother looked blank and then, realising Scarlett was waiting for a real answer, started vigorously shaking her head.

"One day you might understand," her mother said. "I've been trapped. Trapped in this mind for decades."

"Mum. I, uh," Scarlett whispered, "I love you." Her mother let out a little whimper.

"I love you, too. I'm so sorry."

"It's fine. Please. Just… just go."

Her mother nodded. The two hugged each other gingerly.

"Be strong," she told Scarlett. "You don't need a man. But if you find real love, cherish it and don't let anyone get in the way of it."

It was the most personal statement her mother had ever uttered. Scarlett had no words, but for a split second, she recalled a time when she was a small child. She and her mother had been in the local playground near Waverley Library, the squeaky metal swings a sound of joy and freedom to little Scarlett's ears. She remembered that her mother had then laughed and whooped as they chased each other down the slide and back around to the ladder, over and over again.

"What happened, Mum?" Scarlett searched her mother's unfocused eyes for some kind of truth.

Her mother scratched an imaginary itch on her forearm.

"I don't know," she shrugged. "It's inside me. I can't get it out."

"Was it Dad? Did he do something wrong? Was it…" Scarlett leaned in to whisper, "was it that woman, the one with the dark curly hair?"

When Scarlett's mother was in various hospitals over the years, the woman often appeared at dinners by her father's side. He had introduced her to Scarlett as his assistant. But there was something about the way she moved next to Don, as though they shared a secret, their bodies invisibly intertwined.

Behind her, Scarlett could feel the presence of another

person approaching; the soft footfall of trainers heralded their space was soon to be invaded. Her mother looked over her daughter's shoulder and forced a false smile.

"Here's the other girl," her mother said. "Your roommate. She looks nice."

That was that.

Strangely enough, away from the emotional starkness of her family home and in a city where no one cared about her family name and all it conjured, Scarlett began to thrive, both socially and academically. After more than a decade of wondering where she had gone, she found herself and, subsequently, she found her voice, particularly at the many social gatherings on campus and in local pubs, and wondered occasionally if she was more like her father than she had earlier believed. With this new-found confidence, she cut her hair short and wore more revealing outfits. She got a tan and smiled when people passed instead of hanging her head. She joined a surf life-saving club and ran along the pristine white sand of Cottesloe Beach most mornings, never once wishing she was back in Sydney, or with her father as he strode along the marble corridors. Concerns of her own propensity for depression went out the window and for the first time in her life, Scarlett began to comprehend the healing wonder of allowing yourself to laugh out loud without worrying about how it might feel or sound to others. It was like a drug, this sudden desire for hilarity, and a steady stream of male students were soon knocking down the door to ask her out with alarming regularity.

"That blond one's been here again," her roommate groaned, as Scarlett arrived home one evening, a pile of books under her arm and a takeaway coffee in the other. "You've got to say yes to him. He's just adorable." Her roommate glanced towards the grimy window wistfully. "You know, looked like a Viking, maybe. God knows; I wish he'd pillage my village."

"What was his name?"

"Um. Can't remember. Let me think. There's been so many."

Scarlett had lain spread-eagled on the covers of her single bed.

"Looks like a Viking? I don't think I know anyone that exciting to be honest, and even if I did, all I want is to sleep tonight. I had to write thousands of words for that leadership essay. Finished it in the nick of time. It was due this evening."

Her roommate spun around on her swivel chair and winked.

"Now I remember his name. Nick. His name was Nick."

As Scarlett walked to class the next day, she again marvelled at the ghostly white gums lining the sandy path – like sentries – as she approached the flat greenery of the nearby university. She breathed in the now familiar smell of eucalyptus leaves and the brackish earthiness from the nearby Swan River and smiled as a soft morning sun prickled at her forearms. *Calm*. She felt calm. It was a new concept and one she was embracing. The mere thought that she had created a carefree life for herself away from the constant stench of depression and emotional abandonment sent a warm rush of pleasure through her body, and by the time Nick came thundering along the path behind her, she was still smiling.

"Thought I'd find you here," he huffed.

She tried to unsmile her lips, but it was too late. It looked, she realised, as though she had been expecting him.

That evening, Nick picked Scarlett up at eight and they walked to a local pizzeria. Scarlett ordered a Hawaiian, which Nick found repellent. He ordered a meat lover, which she said was ghastly. They drank a bottle of cheap Chianti and then, afterwards, walked along the river foreshore towards the moored boats and timber jetties of Matilda Bay. That night, it was protected from the wind and they sat huddled on a weedy patch of seagrass watching the night boats come and go, lights flashing and music bouncing off the calm, broad river water in front of them.

Nick began to talk, about his life, his family, his study. He was doing international relations and planned to move to China eventually. He would make enough money working in finance for a large corporation, so that one day he could take a couple of years off and work for a charity, maybe an orphanage. He felt strongly about children living in poverty or being abused in care, having been adopted himself, although not unhappily.

"I had the most perfect adoptive parents," he told her. In the moonlight, his hair glowed, a halo over his shadowed cheeks. "I can't fault them at all. They were loving, kind, generous, understanding. I want to find families just like mine for all those kids out there, suffering."

His mother had told him how they'd adopted him from Romania after travelling the world searching for the right kind of adoption agency. They'd been devastated by what they had seen and when they stumbled across a baby Nick, they had to bring him back to Australia. It took six months, but it was all done by the time he was eighteen months old. He also had a Chinese sister.

"Mum and Dad went to Beijing to see their baby and when they got there, they were told she had gone, or been moved. They were devastated. They brought in the agency representatives and, after a few days, Lana suddenly appeared, unharmed and healthy. They'd had to pay to get her back. She was only two years old. She hadn't, luckily, left the country yet. Some babies are actually stolen by criminal gangs from their parents to be taken to orphanages. Adoption is a lucrative business. Can you believe it?"

Scarlett shook her head. Nick was flustered with the emotion of the memory.

"Sorry. I'm boring you with all my personal stories, all at once. *Slow down, Nick. You'll scare her off.*" He sat on his hands a little.

"No. No you won't. I like it. Seriously. I mean, my story is pretty boring in comparison."

"Bet it's not."

A group of first-year students walked noisily past, pushing and shoving and swearing. They were holding bottles of beer and smoking cigarettes. One of them was carrying a stuffed sheep, another a boom box, Pink's 'Get the Party Started' bouncing off the water. The romantic mood was broken and Scarlett, aware their peaceful chat had been snapped in half, turned to Nick and laughed.

"I wonder what they're going to do with that sheep. I mean—"

Before she could finish, Nick had cupped her chin in his hand.

"I'm not a weirdo, I promise, but looking at you makes me feel that everything is going to be okay. I can't explain why."

They kissed and the gang of teenagers wolf-whistled before running away.

"I know what you mean," Scarlett whispered.

"Do you?"

She nodded, as he leaned towards her for another kiss.

"I don't know why but you make me feel the same," she offered, a little embarrassed by this sudden closeness. "I suppose on a biological level it'd be something to do with our scent, something familiar we can sense about each other's DNA."

He burst out laughing.

"How romantic."

She blushed. "Well. You know what I…"

He took her in his arms and made her tell him about her childhood. It took two hours. By the time she had finished, they were standing outside her university apartment, Scarlett exhausted from recalling the coldness and confusion of growing up emotionally impoverished.

"I can't imagine it," Nick said with a sympathetic sadness.

"But it's okay now," she cut in. "I mean, I'm okay." The last thing she wanted was for him to think she too was destined for the same fate. "I escaped. Oh, don't get me wrong. We speak, Mum and Dad and I. Dad came over not long ago, for a quick visit. It's not that we hate each other. It's just not… loving."

Nick nodded and shoved his hands in his jeans pockets.

"I know," his face lit up. "Come to mine on the weekend." Scarlett was surprised. "I know it's early days, but I live at home. There's nothing I can do about that. My mum is really chilled out. They'll love you. I promise. We've got a pool. I know you love to swim. I can pick you up at lunchtime. It's not far. Honestly." He paused. "Am I being too keen here?"

Scarlett giggled and kissed him on the cheek.

"No. See you at, what? 1pm?" She sauntered towards the dark concrete stairs that led to her third-floor room.

"Great. Cool. 1pm. Pick you up right here. On this spot. Or else. Got it?"

"Got it!" she called from the hallway.

"Maybe we can, you know, take out the canoe. Or we can go to the pub! Up to you!" She heard his voice echo off the low brick wall at the side of the building.

* * *

It was fun, she and Nick. It was fun for more than twelve years, four jobs between them, one pregnancy scare, several jealous tiffs and four rented apartments. More love and happiness than Scarlett ever thought possible for someone who used to suffer from crippling shyness, shoulders hunched by an irrational dread of being noticed by other people.

But then, aged thirty-four, she travelled to meet him when he was working for an orphanage in Tianjin, China. Three days after she'd arrived, he was killed, knifed for trying to stop the traffickers from preying on innocent children.

There had only ever really been one person in Scarlett's life, one who managed to unearth her dormant capacity to love and be loved – and it was Nick. Once he was gone, she would do anything to get revenge.

Absolutely anything.

CHAPTER FOURTEEN

The University of Hong Kong, Pokfulam.

Wang walked into his former university lecturer's office and sat down on a broad leather armchair.

"Tough week?" Professor Rider said.

"You could say that."

"Got the paperwork?" The professor pointed to the ceiling and widened his eyes; a warning of some sort. Wang cleared his throat. The professor flicked at the papers Wang had handed over. "Your dissertation looks good," the professor said boldly.

Wang nodded slowly.

"Yes. I worked on the, um, dissertation all night."

"Glad you're back studying again, Wang," the professor said earnestly, offering Wang a subtle wink over his desk. "You can only do so much with your bachelor's degree, not that you weren't a good student, but it's always handy to have a master's if you want to make a real go of a new career."

"I do. I *really* do," Wang said, holding back a smile.

The professor read a few lines of the paperwork and placed it back on his desk.

"I tell you what," he said, standing quickly, "I have to be at a lunch meeting in ten minutes. How about you walk with me over to the café and we can talk? I've got an idea for a debate you might be interested in joining."

"Sure thing."

The two stood and left the room. Professor Rider locked the door with a handful of jangling keys. Neither said a word until they reached a winding stone path that ran along the outer edges of the whitewashed academic offices.

They came to the middle of the path.

"Sorry, Wang," Professor Rider finally said. "I just don't know if I might be bugged in there. It's probably silly, but at this important juncture, we can't be too careful."

Wang kept walking. He didn't want to be heard either.

"I know. I get it. If I didn't think they might tap my phone, I'd call you to warn you I was coming round. But as it is…" he shrugged, "I have no idea if they're watching me anymore or if they've given up. That gold-toothed guy who came to Shek O hasn't paid me another visit?"

Professor Rider, who had a Chinese mother and gigantic Canadian father, stood at six foot four, and with his long and fast gait, Wang hurried to keep up with him. When Wang and his colleagues were undergraduates, they used to call their revered instructor Professor Strider. Now that he and the professor were in regular contact again, Wang had to regularly stop himself from using the nickname.

"I have been in touch with the other universities," the professor whispered into the middle distance as they walked. "And it's all good timing. Nothing's changed. The only thing I need you to do is harness more numbers via the usual channels the day before."

"I can do that," Wang said, trying to look nonchalant as they reached a small, grimy pond with a few myna birds twittering at its edges. "I came here last week and unlocked the safe you told me about. The address for the speech was in there and since then, I've… um…" A young woman walked past and gave the professor a giggly grin. The professor, known for his wandering eye, bellowed a hearty good morning to her.

"I see you still have a way with the ladies," Wang said, hoping he hadn't overstepped the mark.

The café was directly in front of them.

"One cannot help it if they are attractive to the opposite sex," the professor smiled knowingly, "no more than one can stand losing their voice. If anyone should know that, Wang, it's you."

"Well, maybe the last part."

The professor stuck out a hand.

"Pleased you didn't get scared off."

Wang nodded. "Not a hope in hell."

"Good boy. Cheerio." The professor turned to leave, then spun around on his heels. "In two weeks, there will be a note left in the same safe with the final timing. I have to speak with Archie Chang from the democracy forum first, but either way, it will be there. Let's say, fifteenth of September."

"Got it," Wang said, making a move to leave.

"In the meantime, be careful. No phone calls, no meetings with others related to this. Nothing. Go surfing. Work hard. Anything but looking like you're busy working on a… well, on *this*."

He walked away without saying goodbye. Wang turned and headed for the bus stop. Just a few more weeks and *this* would be a reality. All this time, all these months, all this dreaming. He felt the nerves flutter through his stomach and knew he had to call Alice. He hadn't seen her for three days and was already feeling a huge sense of loss. *I'm in love with her*, he said to himself, not for the first time. As he boarded the bus, he actually laughed out loud.

* * *

It was 2002. That year, Ben Affleck was named *People* Magazine's Sexiest Man Alive, the euro began official circulation in twelve European countries and North Korea admitted to developing nuclear arms in defiance of a treaty.

But, of course, there were other dramas going on then too, the smaller, heart-wrenchingly sad, yet day-to-day, ones that don't make the news.

2002 was the year Alice Carmichael arrived in Hong Kong, aged twenty-two, and was having the time of her life. Before leaving England, she had contacted Torquil, Cosy's cousin, and the two spent every night trawling the bars, every weekend hiking, every Sunday evening eating Thai noodles and drinking Tsingtao.

Within three weeks, Alice was sleeping with Torquil. He'd had a long-term girlfriend, a proper type, home counties and well-connected back in the UK. But they'd broken up, so Torquil had explained.

Alice didn't question him. She was so excited to be in Hong Kong, to have a new job, to be making some money, to be true to her promise to her dead friend. And being with Torquil? She could see Cosy beaming up there, having a real laugh at that one.

But 2002 was also the year that Alice's life tumbled out of control.

Sadly, Torquil went back to his girlfriend and, not long afterwards, left Hong Kong for the UK.

"It's work, you see, Al," he'd told her, head bowed and sloping shoulders on a Wan Chai street corner, incense from the temple behind him stinging her already reddened eyes. She was reminded of her father and felt a lump of misery settle in her stomach.

"But you asked me out to that restaurant opening this weekend. How can you have changed your mind so quickly?"

Torquil shook his head, his fringe still floppy.

"I... um. Well."

* * *

Alice, her tears dry a few days later, went to the opening anyway. She knew one or two others going. No break-up was going to dampen her spirits, she told them as she grabbed a glass of vodka cranberry.

And this was the day she met the then thirty-something Johnny and the slightly older Phil.

Alice, excited, naïve and recklessly joyous, drank the night away, danced until dawn and then threw her brand-new Ferragamo shoes out of a taxi window, just for a laugh. She'd awoken the next day wondering how she got home, her hair stringy and wet and a lamb souvlaki sitting unexpectantly on her chest.

This was the same Alice Carmichael, the same bookish red-headed girl, who once wore round green-tinged glasses and spent her weekends planting bulbs and listening to Chopin with her father.

Hong Kong then was an almost alien land to Alice, a menagerie of honking horns, thronging pavements, steep stone stairways, wet markets selling Jurassic-looking fruits, luxury marble lobbies, stormy harbour winds, late-night bars and the constant waft of opportunity. Alice, no longer trapped by her class or her background, arrived bursting with a pent-up excitement she could barely contain, her promise to Cosy firmly planted in the back of her mind at all times.

It seemed the pressure cooker was ready to explode.

Once the Torquil drama had fizzled, Alice realised she was again the master of her own destiny. She had never felt so free, so alive, so full of hope. Hong Kong was everything she expected it to be and more, apart from the pollution.

To compensate, Alice started smoking. At the time, she puffed away, reasoning the bad air outside was going to get her, so why not enjoy a few gaspers? Yet smoking was just the beginning. Whatever new thing was offered to her, she took it. Experience was her mantra and everyone was happy to help her gain it. Smoking, drinking… what else could she get up to now that she was free?

The one thing that kept her out of trouble at first was her new job – a trainee solicitor job with a respectable British legal firm – and one in which she was paid well and above what she could have brought in back home. She rented a room in a three-bedroom apartment on a quiet and leafy street in Mid-Levels, minutes from the famous outdoor covered escalator that took her directly down to her harbourside office every morning and then back up the steep slope every evening. The apartment was damp and smelled of polished parquet floors. Cerise bougainvillea bushes grew vigorously across the iron window frames, giving the space a sense of tropical splendour. Her work hours were long, but the partying in the evenings and on weekends was equally as epic. Alice worked like a Trojan and partied with the same enthusiasm. Anything to forget that Cosy was not with her. Or maybe, she wondered, to pretend that she was. In a sense, even she knew she was channelling Cosy's vibrant personality. She inadvertently became Cosy, without meaning to. But as one realises over time, living a life that is not yours – or not the one that suits your true self – cannot be sustained. Alice would find this out the hard way.

"This is for you, Cosy," she often said out loud, when charging a toast in a bar on a particularly thirsty Thursday night.

"Who's Cosy?" someone always asked.

"A friend. Ignore me. Come on. Drink up, everybody!"

* * *

One evening, just before her fourth Christmas living on the Island, Johnny called to ask her to Chez Diamond, a flourishing new rooftop establishment with clear views across to Kowloon and balconies festooned with oversized sofas and mountains of pearlescent tea lights. It was legendary around Christmas time – crisp fir trees decorated in the transparent gold, silver and white theme of the bar itself competed with dangling "diamonds" across the soaring ceilings. The constant tinkle of jazz-inspired Christmas carols and the popping of champagne corks in the background added to the festive atmosphere. Alice agreed to be there as soon as possible. She tidied her desk, applied some lipstick and caught a cab to meet her new friends, a smug smile, as always, exposing the self-satisfied state of her mind. She had not visited home once. She wrote to her parents and promised a trip back soon. But, in all honesty, she had no intention of getting on a plane to the UK in the foreseeable future. So far, she'd spent her holidays in Phuket, Bali and the Philippines, swimming, snorkelling, gorging herself on seafood and being massaged under palm trees. Trudging along the dreariness of grey, wet London streets and being forced to endure a rigid, sober lunch with her estranged father or her mother's latest squeeze held little appeal.

Alice, conversely, felt like a Hong Kong local already. By then, she had mastered conversational Cantonese. She had always had a knack for languages and this ability to converse in the smallest of ways helped her fit in even more quickly. Nothing was going to force her back home to the UK. She was there to stay and loving every minute of it.

Johnny and Phil were waiting at the bar, a bottle of bubbly at the ready. They greeted her eagerly and poured her a glass. Phil was not yet portly, although he had the telltale signs of someone with a propensity for a future wide girth – he unwittingly stood with his hands on either side of his hips and pushed his stomach out slightly, his core muscles obviously unable to hold him upright without assistance. He still had most of his blond curly hair and Alice fluffed it a little as he teased her for being late, again.

"I'm only late because I work so hard," she smiled, flirtatiously.

"We all work hard, Alice," Phil said.

"Some more than others," Johnny cut in, clinking his glass against Phil's.

Alice marvelled at Johnny. Everything about him had its place – symmetry, Alice had heard it called. Almond eyes, a square jaw, high cheekbones, thick dark hair he brushed neatly to one side, a straight back and broad chest. He laughed readily and when he was addressed, he focused on you and you only, giving the impression you were the most important person in the room.

"Which is why we all need some downtime, you know, to switch off. Cheers." Phil winked at Johnny.

Behind them, a raucous group of expats and locals, an office party maybe, broke into Christmas songs. One of them stood and pretended to be a conductor. The dutiful staff stood back and continued to pour champagne.

"I hope this city doesn't lose itself, as we get further from the Handover, I mean," Johnny said, without a hint of emotion.

"Could be a disaster one day," Phil replied. "They say they're going to come in here with tanks and rid us of our freedoms."

"Rubbish," Johnny scoffed. "There's too much money to be made here. They know that, we know that and the world knows it too. The Chinese will keep it just as it is. You'll see."

"I'm a bit nervous about it to be honest," Alice piped in. The champagne had already gone to her head. "People are already planning on leaving, which is depressing."

"They're idiots," Johnny snapped.

"Who are idiots?" The voice came from behind Alice and, as she turned, there stood a man, a bit older than her, smiling broadly and wearing jeans and an open-necked white shirt. Dark tendrils of hair protruded from his shirt and his cheeks were scratched pink, possibly from shaving. He smelled of a musky lavender and he rocked back and forward from his toes to his heels, as though excited. At the same time as he stuck out a long-fingered hand towards Alice, he leaned close towards her and kissed her cheek. He lingered there for a minute. "I am so glad to meet *you*," he muttered into her ear. Alice enjoyed the compliment.

"Oh. Thank you." She smiled.

Johnny, she noticed, turned to survey the room. Phil, however, was as overjoyed by the appearance of their new friend – whom had been introduced to Alice as Charlie – as

Charlie was to see Alice. Phil slapped him on the back and guffawed and asked Charlie several questions about his property business, all the while Charlie sideways-glancing at Alice, as though she were some precious jewel he was about to snaffle at a Sotheby's auction.

The four of them drank more champagne, the music changed from preppy carols to Rihanna. The crowd pushed against each other at the bar to bellow out orders and the lights dimmed to the point where everyone looked like teenagers and ten times more attractive.

It was Charlie, whispering in her ear again.

"Come with me," he was saying. Alice, drunk and happy, let him take her by the hand to the restroom at the back of the bar. It was a large room with a soft velvet armchair and luxury soaps and hand creams. Charlie kissed her as he closed the door and she let him, falling into the embrace without meaning to, as though it was all predestined, or so she told herself.

"Your skin is so soft," he purred into her hear as he stroked her arms. "Do you bathe in buttermilk?" She giggled. He had an American trill and it sent a shiver down her spine.

Charlie pulled a plastic bag from his pocket and lined up the white powder on the ledge above the toilet. They took turns snorting it – a new experience for Alice but one she was sure Cosy would have wanted to try – and started laughing. Laughing so hard she had to hold her belly.

"Oh God, stop. I don't even know why I'm laughing."

"Neither do I," Charlie said, and kissed her again. He was dangerously attractive, for reasons she couldn't fathom, and this made it all the more exciting.

"I tell you what," Charlie whispered, "I've got a whole heap more in here." He fished a large packet of cocaine from his pocket and waved it in front of her face. "How about you keep it? My gift to you. I've got plenty. It's been a good night so far. I can't keep it all." Alice had no idea what he meant. "It's good stuff. Go on. Take it. God, you're gorgeous."

He placed it into her jacket pocket and reached around and stroked her back. He kissed her for a long time until someone banged on the door. "We're going to have a lot of fun, you and me. Don't you think?"

She threw her head back, laughing, her cheeks aching with amusement, and followed him out the door, past the frowns and stares.

"Nothing to see here!" Charlie called to the people waiting, as Alice giggled into his back.

She was stupidly high and drunk and thrilled to be holding his hand, as they walked back to the bar. His grip was firm and secure and she clung to it, as he shoved people out of the way, basking in the wash of euphoria and overinflated self-confidence she was suddenly experiencing.

Alice had no idea she was carrying a substantial amount of cocaine. Later, in the police station, she was told what it was worth – more, they said, than could be reasonably for personal use. She'd no idea until later that Charlie was not really called Charlie, that it was his nickname, a moniker he created as a joke, to do with his side business of being a dealer to his friends and associates. Phil told her so, the day he appeared to bail her out of jail. He said something to the cops, who dropped all the charges. Alice never knew what he said or did. She was so grateful, so tearfully apologetic, that she promised Phil she would do anything to stay in Hong Kong, to not have a criminal record, to not lose her job.

The day after, when she was at home, hung-over and overcome with self-loathing, Phil – she remembers it all so clearly – had called by and stood tall in front of her, stiff as a soldier, arms crossed. He had tilted his chin down slightly, as though lost in some deep, unattainable thought that he was processing as quickly as possible.

"Actually, Al," he said quietly, "there is something you can do."

As he looked up, Alice saw something in his piggy little face she had not noticed before. It was a look of fury, like a steaming bull before it charged, nostrils flared and eyes squinted and piercing, as though boring a hole into an invisible enemy. Perhaps this look was an aberration, or perhaps it was always there and had been well-hidden. To this day, Alice would never really know. Either way, it gave her such a shock that Alice heard herself gasp and Phil, seeing her distress, smiled. It was forced and the two of them watched each other, Alice suddenly sensing her apologies were potentially not necessary.

"It's not much," he said with a forced casualness.

"Okay." She nodded and looked at her shaking hands. The day before, Alice had found out from Phil that the police had raided the bar on a tip-off. Someone had told Charlie the cops may raid the place later that night – it was known as a drug dealer's paradise. But he didn't want to lose such a big stash, so he passed it to Alice, thinking he could get it back later if a raid never happened. The police had headed for Charlie and Alice, no doubt having been pointed out by a bartender who knew Charlie or by an annoyed patron who had been waiting in the queue outside the bathroom. But after the police quickly chatted to Charlie, it was Alice who was hauled out of there – alone – and searched. Johnny had tried to intervene and blame Charlie but, by then, he had disappeared. Alice had stood wide-eyed, stony-faced and wasted throughout the entire process. It took a couple of hours for the coke to wear off and the reality to set in. Before he had skulked away, Charlie had glanced over at her from where he was being questioned by police and smirked. Alice spent the entire trip to the police station staring at the polish of the officer's black lace-up shoes, a high-pitched whir in her ears.

"I have a friend," Phil said slowly, pacing from one end of her living room to the other, which only took a few small steps. "And he needs help."

"Sure," Alice said, wiping at a tear.

"There's an envelope that needs to be taken to a colleague

of this friend, but, to be honest, this guy does not like me. The feeling's mutual."

Alice was beginning to see the real Phil. She tried to breathe slowly. The anxiety was rising.

He shrugged, lit up a cigarette and battled with the latch on a window before blowing out a gust of smoke. The usual thud of concrete being drilled greeted her ears and, in a strange way, its familiarity briefly comforted her.

"Yes. You see, we go way back. He's a prick – was then, is now. Used to work together in the old days at the police station. But I've been asked by… um… the boss, to pick up this document and take it to him, but I'd prefer if you could do it for me. It won't take long."

Alice composed herself a little and stood to walk towards the kitchen, a sorrowful room at the side of the apartment with no oven and just a kettle placed on top of a bar fridge.

"No problem. Can I go in my lunch break? And how did you get me off those charges anyway? I mean, I know you used to be a cop, but…"

Phil stubbed out his cigarette on the window ledge and rubbed at his temples. Alice flicked the switch on the kettle, just as a flick seemed to switch on Phil.

He snapped his head around, catching her by surprise. Her mouth opened to speak but was – seeing his red-faced frustration – rendered mute.

"Because, for fuck's sake, Alice," he roared, "I have contacts and that's all you need to know!"

She felt tears prickle again and a cold nervousness shimmer across her skin, the body's internal warning system to run.

Phil walked towards her, one arm outstretched. "Just take the fucking envelope, drop it where I tell you and shut the fuck up. The boss doesn't like questions, or mistakes."

"Phil, I…"

He stood over her and bit at his bottom lip, right fist clenched.

"Don't worry. You're safe. You can keep your little job

and go back to shagging blokes for free. Or maybe, you should start charging. You'd make a fortune."

Alice shrank into herself and tried not to meet his eyes.

Phil stomped back to his briefcase, pulled out a yellow A4 envelope.

"Here are the pick-up and delivery addresses. Tear up the address after you've delivered it, or even better, burn it. Do not tell a soul about this. Ever."

Alice said and did nothing. All she could hear was that ringing in her ears.

"When someone helps you out with a big favour, you pay them back and never breathe a word. Got it?"

She stayed still, crouched with her back pressed against the stiff handle of a kitchen cupboard.

"HAVE YOU GOT IT?" Phil screamed. Somewhere in the background, a door slammed.

She murmured a yes.

"Good girl."

His leather shoes made an ominous tapping sound on the floor, as he walked to the coffee table and placed the paper on top of it.

"See you on the weekend then," he said in a sing-song voice. "I hear it's going to be glorious weather."

He let himself out. Alice didn't move until his shoes click-clacked their way down the stairwell.

Two days after Phil's visit, she had called in sick and furtively caught a taxi to the address, a seedy apartment building in the bowels of a side street near Yau Ma Tei that stank of dirty socks and clogged drains. She had knocked – her face awash with silent, terrified tears – on a door with shoe marks etched into its base. She knocked again. After what seemed like ages, a guy covered in tattoos answered. Alice spoke to him in basic Cantonese, her voice quivering like a child on its first day at school.

The tattoo guy called for a friend, who appeared a few seconds later. Alice told him why she was there, taking in his smart leather shoes, neatly pressed suit, sparkling gold watch and imposing height, the antithesis of his eerily inked mate.

When the well-dressed man smiled, Alice noticed all his back teeth were gold. For no reason at all, she thought of Cosy, the day they sat on a hill out near Whitestone Park and drank beer until they both threw up. And with that, she ran down the hallway, flung open the door to the stairwell and emptied the contents of her stomach, the yellow envelope still in one hand while the other held back her hair. It was her breakfast – fruit and coffee – all over the landing, a rainbow of liquid and pips. The vomit slowly dripped from the top step, to the second, then on to the third. She stood to wipe her mouth.

She walked back to the apartment door.

"Here." The tall, well-dressed man was standing behind her, holding a grimy green towel. She took it and wiped at her chin. "Thank you for coming all this way," he said, in perfect English.

Alice remembered why she was there and, with shaky hands, handed over the envelope.

Alice took one last look at his face – slightly pockmarked cheeks, hair cropped to within an inch of its life – and edged her way down the stairs, avoiding the orange melon she'd eagerly scoffed only an hour or so before.

Later, she had many sleepless nights wondering what Phil would do if he found out what she'd done to the envelope seconds before the guy had opened the door. Over time, she tried to forget about it. Until Scarlett came along.

* * *

The Phil experience changed Alice for ever, as though something in her was switched off, or on; she couldn't be sure. For an entire month, Alice worked, ate nothing but takeaway from Oliver's, walked languidly along Bowen Road on weekends and slept. She didn't go out, she avoided the phone. One by one, her friends came over to check on her.

Every time, she told them her flu had been the worst she'd ever experienced.

Johnny called. She was sour.

"What's wrong?" he finally asked, when she refused to laugh at his jokes.

"I think you know."

He'd snorted.

"Er, I don't, to be honest. Is it the Charlie thing? I never forced you to snort bloody cocaine with him, you know. He's an infamous fool. I was going to tell you, but then you were all over him like a rash, so I—"

"Shut up!" Alice screamed down the phone line. Johnny, she assumed, was Phil's boss. "The boss", Phil had called him. If this was the real Johnny and Phil, she wanted nothing to do with them.

That night, she decided never again would she be taken in by anyone, particularly anyone with surface charm and an amplified sense of their own importance. The city, like many others, was bursting with the entitled and the arrogant and, finally, her radar was beeping like a metal detector in a gold mine.

From then on, Alice went to work with a mission to take charge of her life. Her ready smile was less forthcoming, her social calendar fussier, her work schedule increased in a bid to inflate her salary. In the evenings, she sometimes ran into Johnny. It was hard not to, working in buildings so close to one another. He was always friendly. They chatted amiably, but he always seemed confused as to her coolness with him. He asked her a couple of times why she seemed so aloof, but she just smiled, nodded, took on her new air of indifference.

But Phil? She would run in the opposite direction to him – across shards of glass barefoot on a forty-five-degree day – if he came near her.

Eventually, life went back to a kind of normality. Alice dated, sometimes. At thirty, she started a long-term relationship with a newly divorced man who had three children and no intention of ever marrying again. At thirty-six, she fell pregnant but had an abortion after he wept inconsolably over the news. Nearly fourteen years after that night with so-called Charlie and after Alice had witnessed Johnny fall in love, swoon over and then dump at least forty women, Johnny met Scarlett. Alice wanted to warn her new friend, but by then, so much time had passed she was unsure what to actually say. Furthermore, she'd vowed never to utter a word about it.

But things had changed. The world had changed. The time had come.

Until Scarlett asked Alice outright, Alice thought that'd be the end of that chapter of her life. And then, to help out Scarlett – or maybe satisfy her own curiosity – she had agreed to arrange to have Johnny followed. Looking back, she should have let sleeping dogs lie. But she'd promised. Furthermore, couriering those documents had haunted her for years and she felt it was time she worked out exactly who Johnny and Phil were. Alice would love to throw them to the wolves. Sure, she may have to admit they had got her off that charge at the time, but anyone would be able to see why she went along with it.

As it was, the guy at the Mandarin bar had found nothing on Johnny. He followed Phil too and all he reported back was that Phil frequented girly bars, bought bags of cocaine on a regular basis and took his simpering girlfriend out for expensive dinners. The whole thing had been a waste of time. Alice hoped it would stay that way.

It didn't.

CHAPTER FIFTEEN

Central Psychology.

It was 2.30pm and Carolyn still hadn't had any lunch. She felt her stomach growl and threw down her pen in childish anger. The air was on full blast but she was still sweaty and fanned at her shirt as she stood to leave the office. *Horses sweat, men perspire and women glow*, her mother used to tell her. *No, mother, this woman sweats, like a horse*, Carolyn said to herself as the lift clunked its way to the ground floor.

"Mrs Moorehouse is here," Koffee announced, as she reached her office door. Carolyn jumped. She hadn't heard Koffee's footfall behind her and Carolyn inadvertently frowned. "Why are you so grumpy?" Koffee barked. "I'm only doing what you asked." Carolyn sighed and wiped at a sudden prickle of tired tears.

"Because, Koffee, this is your last day as my assistant and..." Carolyn stood, "I don't know what I'll do without you."

Koffee smiled, Carolyn smiled, and the two found themselves embracing.

"You've been an amazing support and I know you'll be a brilliant therapist one day," Carolyn said.

Koffee walked back to the doorway. "I'm glad you got rid of Captain Loser," she said. The two women laughed. "You're better off without him."

"Too true." Carolyn steeled herself. "Okay, please send in

Mrs Moorehouse. To be honest," Carolyn whispered behind a cupped hand, "I'd forgotten she was coming."

Koffee turned to leave. "Oh, I forgot, Mr Humphries. He called. He wants to talk to you as soon as possible. I told him to call back in an hour."

* * *

Shaw Hotel in Tai Koo Shing had a rooftop bar – Caramel – that overlooked the eastern end of Victoria Harbour and over to the rows of white apartment buildings piled up like Meccano on the water's edge in Kowloon. It was Alice's new favourite, being so close to her home in the village of Shek O.

It was Saturday. It was steaming hot and Alice had been for a hike with Wang.

They were sipping fresh lime soda on his terrace when her phone rang. It was Scarlett, in a panic. Alice reluctantly agreed to meet her, but only at Caramel.

"Sorry, Wang," Alice had called over the open top of his convertible blue MG as she inched her way into the passenger seat. Wang's dad had restored it himself when Wang was a boy, working on weekends at his best friend's garage the year before he died. "She's, I hate to say it, a very troubled person. Increasingly so."

"I know. You need to be there for her, blah blah blah. We all do for friends. Come on, let's put on some music." He pressed at the tape player – his pride and joy – as they roared along Shek O Road, bypassing the double-decker bus and a weaving minibus in the process. "I found this tape in a box at the back of a cupboard at my mum's place. Forgot I had it."

David Bowie's dulcet tones flew through the early-evening sky, rising up to reach the soaring kites, the rocky green hills looming imposingly on either side. Alice smiled and gripped Wang's left hand as he changed into second gear on the steeper section of the road.

212

"Thanks," she called out over the music. "For everything. I mean it."

Wang sang along, his hair flipping back in the breeze. She laughed. Life was good. She hoped it would stay like that for ever.

* * *

Scarlett was waiting, a bottle of Sauvignon Blanc and platter of cheese on the table in front of her.

"Alice," Scarlett whined as soon as Alice's bum hit the seat, "I'm planning on leaving Johnny. I mean it this time."

Alice hurriedly munched on an olive.

"Okay. Well. Good on you. Good plan."

"But there's something else."

"Go on." Alice was hungry. Really hungry. She stuffed a thin slice of mortadella into her mouth and poured herself a glass.

Scarlett crossed her arms, almost defensively.

"Did you ever look inside the envelope you couriered for Phil that day?"

Alice nearly choked on the ham and then swallowed hard. She thought all these lines of questioning about Johnny were done. As she'd told Scarlett that night at the Albemarle after Bobby left, she'd asked for someone to follow Johnny. She'd since explained the guy had found nothing.

Alice wished she'd never told Scarlett the truth. In one moment of weakness when Scarlett's relationship with Johnny was showing the strain, Alice had explained about the cocaine bust, Phil, the fact he got her off. She had hoped Scarlett would see who she was living with, move on, dump Johnny and let it be. Scarlett was the first and only person she'd ever told.

"Not this again. And why? What does it matter?" Alice shrugged.

God, Scarlett had been so persuasive. She had seemed so

213

confused, so lost. Alice had agreed, partly because she also disliked Johnny and partly because Scarlett was her friend. All she did was get some bartender to keep an eye on him for one night.

If Alice had known how happy she would be with Wang, she would have run a mile from the drama of it all and never got involved with Scarlett's problems.

"It matters." Scarlett batted her eyes.

Ideally, all Alice wanted was a life with Wang, by the beach, her dog, her quirky little ramshackle house and a glass of Chardonnay on a Saturday night, maybe marriage? She felt a small flutter in the base of her stomach. Sure, he was following a difficult political path, but his passion for the democratic movement was part of the attraction. She would support him, even if it meant she worried constantly.

"Listen, Scarlett, I was so scared, so kowtowed by Phil at the time."

Scarlett nodded, her direct stare urging her to go on. "I, um…"

"It's important, Alice," Scarlett urged. "If I told you lives have been lost because of Johnny and Phil, would you help?"

Alice placed her glass down. The wine tasted sour all of a sudden.

She closed her eyes.

* * *

It'd been a warm start to winter, that much she could remember easily.

She recalled trudging along pavements with rubbish piled up in the roadside drains near where she had been forced to go.

She had walked slowly to the delivery address. It was up five flights of stairs and loud Chinese opera was booming from a tinny radio on the bottom floor, the screeching high notes sending a shiver down her spine as she sweated her way to the apartment. She knocked, but there was no answer. She knocked again and waited. Five minutes passed. Maybe ten. She knocked again. Nothing. Now what? She sat down with her back against the door. She was afraid of failing to deliver and wondering what Phil would do.

It was unseasonably humid. Alice was getting agitated waiting outside the apartment door. She had slumped down, the envelope sweaty in her palm. She fidgeted with it, fretted at it, and before she knew it, the humidity had caused the sticky end to come unstuck. She had slid her fingers through quite easily, knowing full well it was crazy but unable to control her desire to peek.

"What was in it, Al? Did you see? I promise I will not implicate you in anything I find out. I have your best interests at heart, I promise."

Alice hated that it had got to this, but she was tired of running from it too. So what about the cocaine? Fuck the past, the police, that stupid arsehole Phil and his boss Johnny. Maybe Scarlett was right. Maybe it was time to nail the bastards for whatever it was they were up to.

"Okay!" Alice spat. "I looked. They were passports." Alice choked a little. "Hong Kong passports," she whispered as tears sprang to her eyes. "Two men, maybe a woman. I can't remember anything else, I promise. Suddenly, I heard footfall coming up the stairs and this guy appeared. I don't remember him. I was terrified. I muttered something, handed him the envelope and ran. I threw up. He spoke good English. I'm sorry."

Scarlett turned grey. Alice reached for her hand and apologised, not that she knew why. Sorry for what? Exposing her boyfriend as someone involved in something unspeakable, whatever it was?

"Oh God," Scarlett mumbled. "I've got to go. I'll call you later."

CHAPTER SIXTEEN

Central Psychology.

She wasn't going to do it, but Carolyn couldn't help herself. They agreed Johnny would come to see her at 10am. Carolyn got to work early, saw her first client at 8.30 and then bought a large espresso. She tapped her fingernails on her desk as the clock approached 10am. She hadn't called Felicity. She wouldn't call Felicity. That was bad practice. It was bad enough she had not said no to Johnny.

She scoured the newspaper to calm her mind. A huge typhoon was predicted in a few days. The biggest yet, they said, although this was a common headline in the late summer months. The previous summer, they'd had two typhoons, both T8s, which were powerful and resulted in closed offices, schools and the cancellation of ferries. The city hotel bars, however, were packed at such times. Typhoon parties popped up all over town. Carolyn had managed to make it home on foot before the storm hit and found her two children curled up in front of the TV in the middle of the day, excitedly regaling her with the fact their classes were cancelled. A T8 day was a boon for kids. Another one this summer wouldn't bother Carolyn either. She could spend the entire day in her PJs and binge-watch *The Handmaid's Tale*. But with this typhoon, the newspaper continued, there could be storm surges. People living on outlaying islands were advised to find safety wherever they could in higher areas. The typhoon shelters would be full to capacity for all the junks and pleasure boats. This was the big one. It was coming from China and had already wreaked havoc in several heavily populated cities. This thought briefly distracted her from her impending appointment and by the time Johnny walked in, a little haggard to be honest, she had managed to settle her nerves enough to appear as unbiased as a professional psychologist should be in the early stages of a client relationship.

He was in suit trousers with no jacket, his rolled-up tie hanging from a pocket. He smelled faintly of, God forbid (Carolyn almost laughed to herself), sweat.

"What a day," he huffed as he sat down. This was not the same man she had met just over a month ago. "You won't believe it."

I bet I do. Carolyn tightly pressed her lips together, to avoid saying the words.

* * *

Three days before the typhoon hit, on the western side of Central and not far from the fishy odours of Aberdeen Harbour, Wang and Alice were making love in the cabin of a friend's junk. Their bodies were drenched in sweat, which made the whole thing seem sexier, or so Wang thought. Then again, anything he did with Alice was nirvana. Alice was, to Wang, the most perfect creature, pale and long-limbed with a sensual fluidity to her movements, gentle but not feeble. He lay back on one arm and watched as she stood straight-backed in front of the free-standing fan placed in a corner of the musty cabin.

"I... am... boiling," she said. Wang smiled, admiring her smooth-skinned nakedness. Her thick red hair hung in ringlets to her shoulder blades and despite just having had his way with her, Wang felt the urge to do it all over again. She saw the look on his face and laughed. "No way. I'm about to expire."

"Do you like this junk?" he called out, as Alice threw on

a beach towel she'd fetched from the galley. "Could you live on one?"

"No. A firm and undeniable no. Never. I went sailing, twice, and I went surfing, twice. I am done when it comes to water."

She plonked herself down on the hard mattress.

"Even with me?"

"Even with you. Besides, I like my house."

He pulled her closer. "I like mine too, which leaves us in a conundrum."

Alice said nothing. She hoped that what was coming was what she had been thinking of as well.

"You see," he said finally, "I'd like us to live together, like a real couple. Perhaps sooner rather than later."

"You're not pulling the 'I could be in jail soon' thing on me again?"

"Well, I could be. It's any day now."

Alice pulled away. "So you keep saying."

"I'll be okay. It's all going to plan."

"I don't think I'll be able to watch any of it on the news. And what about the typhoon?"

"I'm not doing this alone, you know. And we're going to be indoors, if all goes to plan."

"I know. But it's still so risky. What if it becomes violent?"

Now it was Wang's turn to pull away. "Being peaceful got us nowhere."

"It kept you alive."

"I'm only half living if I am not doing what I know is best."

"Half living?" She stood, walked into the tiny bathroom and slammed the door. "And to think I was hoping we could live together!"

Wang reached down to the floor for his boxers.

"What have I said wrong?" he called through the door. "You make me want to make things better! Without you, I…"

"You what?" she called back. He could hear water running, the toilet being pumped to flush. "I waited, for many days and nights, hid away from prying eyes, only saw you in strange and mysterious places. I mean, I have tolerated quite a bit of mystery and menace and now, I have to watch you possibly get pepper-sprayed, or worse, beaten with batons." She opened the door slightly. "I love you, Wang. I have not really ever loved another man, not since my father, when I was just a child. I can't lose you. So, yes, I am angry."

"It's going to be okay. They won't kill anyone. This is Hong Kong. The world will be watching."

Alice sat back down on the bedcovers. "Most of the Western world thinks Hong Kong is a part of Japan. They don't give a shit what political dramas we have here."

"They will if there is violence against a bunch of earnest students, church officials and democratic politicians."

"Maybe. But I doubt it. This is some rock in South East Asia. They think we have geisha girls. It will make the news once, and then they'll go back to talking about Megxit."

He knew she had a point, but nothing would stop them this time. Not even a Typhoon 10.

"I love that you're a man with purpose, some kind of depth. God knows, I'd seen enough empty heads during my childhood, the weak and witless my mother brought home. But with you, Wang, with all that you are trying to achieve, all I feel is pride. Pride that you care, pride that you're mine."

"So you will support me, despite the dangers?"

She wrapped herself around him, her legs pressing against his back as she held tight.

"Of course. I wouldn't be with you if I didn't. I'm just scared that—"

Wang's phone rang. As he answered, Alice dressed. She always wore the same thing to work when it was this humid – a cotton dress in a plain colour – and sandals. In the air-conditioned office, she threw on a jacket and changed into a two-inch sensible heel. But once outside, she let the breeze in, otherwise she said her skin would turn the colour of cayenne pepper.

He hung up and turned to face her and knew, plain as day, what was written across his face. *Nervous excitement.*

"We have to get going," he said.

"Why?"

"The information is in the safe. It's ready for me to pick up. Professor Rider just called, pretended he was discussing my dissertation, but he explained what I had to do, a while back. It means we're doing this. Finally. Any day now." Wang beamed into the middle distance, lost in his own thoughts.

Alice scowled and stood to leave.

"Well, I'm ready. If we have to go, then let's go. I assume this means I won't see you until you're either in hospital on life support or shirtless and bloodied in prison."

Wang took her in his arms. Breathed her in. He'd been sailing that morning and had called her at the office and asked her for lunch on a friend's junk. They hadn't eaten a thing.

Outside, the sun tried in vain to push through the murky grey skies, its faint, white glow barely visible behind the increasingly inky clouds above.

"If the typhoon's too big," Alice said hopefully, "you might have to cancel the protest, you know, to protect the university kids."

Wang squeezed her hand.

"It's never that bad. They always say it's going to be the 'big one'." Alice lowered her gaze to the pavement as they waited for a taxi. "I'll call you tonight. Maybe I can pop in for a drink after I've been to this meeting. Okay?"

They kissed goodbye, a few tears threatening them both. Wang smiled as he wiped at his eyes. Somewhere north and at some distance, they both heard a deep roll of thunder. Wang turned towards it, then turned back to Alice. She was looking up at him like a frightened child.

"When I was scared by thunder as a little kid," Wang said, "my dad used to distract me by asking me questions, you know, how many drops of rain did I think had fallen? How fast was the wind? If I had to name it, what colour would thunder be? It got me in a state where I was looking forward to the next thunderclap, so I could find the right colour for it. He had a knack for calming me down."

Alice clung to Wang's arm. She didn't want to let him go.

"And what colour *is* thunder?"

Wang saw a taxi, hailed it and edged Alice towards the door as the driver jerked to a stop.

"It depends," he half-smiled, "on the mood I'm in. When I was with Dad, I saw it as white, but now, whenever thunder's very close and very loud, I see it as black, the darkest black possible."

"How cheery," Alice said from the back seat.

"But when I'm with you, it's gold."

"Oh please." She smiled despite herself.

He leaned in, kissed her and waved goodbye.

"I'll grab the next one," he called to her through the open window of her cab.

* * *

Back in her office, with the door closed, Alice tried to call Wang to make sure he was okay, but her hands were shaking so much she couldn't dial the numbers. She waited, sipped at some water and breathed.

Her phone rang.

"Scarlett?"

"Al. Can you meet me in an hour? I've left him. There's lots to tell you."

They spoke for another five minutes. Scarlett gave her an address of an office in Central.

"I'll see you there in twenty minutes," Scarlett urged. "And don't tell anyone else. Just come."

CHAPTER SEVENTEEN

Central Psychology.

Johnny tried to sit upright but, within seconds, he was slumped back in the chair. Carolyn pushed the box of tissues closer to his side of the table and he took one, noisily blowing his nose. It was red from crying. Carolyn briefly felt motherly towards him; this man who Felicity was convinced had been involved in her incarceration and had potentially had his own father murdered, if Felicity's research had any substance to it. Carolyn again sucked on a mint and waited. In the background, she could hear Koffee fussing over the photocopier, no doubt trying to peek inside to take a look at Johnny. She stood and closed her door.

"Now," Carolyn said as she sat down, "let's start from the beginning."

For the first thirty minutes, Johnny talked exclusively of his early childhood – the modest home he shared with his mother in East London, her obsession with getting Sir Robert to pay for him to go to a good school, her constant complaints combined with an intense love for her only son, whom she felt had missed out on opportunities he deserved. But it was when he started to talk about Brian that Johnny's tearful, quivering voice changed into one of almost elation, as though the mere mention of Brian were enough to dismiss the unhappiness with which he was battling.

"Tell me why Brian brought you such joy," Carolyn asked, interrupting his monologue.

"Hmm?" Johnny uncrossed his right leg and re-crossed it with his left. "It's an age, I suppose, when boys – especially boys like us, you know, from difficult homes – when they form bonds, bonds many of us lose over the years. Well, Brian and I, we never did. That bond remained. We were both lost, both angry. We had good reason."

Carolyn felt her heart race and imagined that Felicity was there, hiding under her desk. In a way, she wished she was.

"Why was Brian so angry?"

"His father," Johnny said with a venomous sneer towards the window. "He was a violent drunk. The worst kind. To his mother, to him. The last time I saw what he did to Brian…"
Carolyn waited. Johnny slumped again in the chair. He was exhausted at the memory. "Let's just say we both vowed to get revenge on our fathers."

Carolyn nodded. She pushed another thought of Felicity from her mind.

"Why did you want revenge, as you say, on your father, Johnny? Yes, he was absent, rich and did not pass his wealth on the way your mother wanted him to. Furthermore, he denied all acknowledgement of you as his son publicly, which must have been hard. But, as you say, he did send you to Bramar Hall and he did house you and your mother, a time when you were relatively happy."

Johnny let out a bitter little laugh, reached for a glass of water and slowly took a sip.

"That's the thing, Carolyn. You see, I think he had my mother killed. I was away at school, she was home alone, as she always was. They said she had fallen down the stairs and broken her neck. My mother never fell, drank twice in her life. She was lithe and swift on her feet. She ate well and walked everywhere. We didn't have cars, of course. So, ever since, I have been convinced, absolutely convinced, that he had her done away with. Even as a child, when I met him, I couldn't trust him. He was a man of loose morals, someone who thought of only himself."

Carolyn nodded.

"When Brian and I were fourteen, we turned detective, you see. We asked around the neighbourhood. Had anyone seen someone near my house that day? Was there any suspicion? Who knows, people might be hiding something. They might be afraid. Don't get me wrong. Sir Robert didn't actually kill her. He wouldn't know how to. He would have paid some low-life to do it, which is why we were asking around."

By then, Carolyn's next client was waiting outside. She buzzed Koffee in and told her to cancel the woman; her next appointment would be on the house. Nothing was getting in the way of Johnny's story that day.

"What did you discover?" Carolyn almost whispered.

"The old bloke who ran the bakery, Bill his name was, took me aside the morning I came to talk to him. He'd been serving out front and when I went in and asked him straight up, he called to his wife and got her to take over. He told me…" Johnny took a moment, his eyes watered. "He told me that he and two others in the street had seen two young guys walk towards my house that morning, minutes before she supposedly fell."

"Is that strange? I mean, to see two men?"

"Well, these guys, Bill said…" He shot a hand to his fringe and pushed it from his glistening forehead, smiling. *"Bill the Baker, best bread on the High Street."* He snickered a little. "Well, what Bill said was that they were walking, very slowly, looking around, dark sunglasses and heads slightly bowed. No one had ever seen them there before and they seemed a little lost. They walked towards my street but no one saw them return. They were gone. Headed there and somehow disappeared. It was a cul-de-sac. Must've jumped over the back fence."

"Did you ask other people directly, if they saw it too? Not just Bill?"

"Yes. Brian helped me. By then, I was convinced, so was Bill. He knew my mother and he knew all about my father. Communities like the one I grew up in, well, they band together. They know all there is to know about each other and they're always watching."

"Why didn't they say anything to the police?"

"I went to the police. They spoke to Bill too, and the others. But a week or so later, they came back to tell me that the ruling was accidental and without concrete proof of foul play – they told me that sightings of a couple of leather-jacket-wearing blokes on the street was hardly a lead – there was nothing they could do. My mother had fallen. No signs of a struggle. Case closed." He shrugged.

It was getting dark outside, not because it was so late but because the weather was turning, gusts of angry wind whipping at the windows.

"And Brian?"

"Well, his father had to die."

Carolyn tried to stop her hand shooting to her mouth.

"What do you mean, Johnny?" She licked at her lips. They were as dry as her throat.

"Men like that don't deserve a family. They don't deserve to be breathing the same air as you and me and poor Brian." Tears welled again and Carolyn reached for more tissues and handed him a few. Johnny composed himself and slowly lifted his head to look her directly in the eye. "Do you have a duty of care, Carolyn, to report a crime to the authorities, if a client confides in you?"

She nodded and kept her mouth closed, fearful of what she might say.

"I see."

They were silent for a very long minute. Johnny stood and paced and then sat back down, holding on to either side of the chair as he lowered himself in.

"To be honest, I am actually here, sadly, to report that

225

my girlfriend – you know, Scarlett, whom I came here about recently – has left me. Yesterday."

Carolyn had been taking notes when these words were uttered. By the time he had finished the sentence, she felt her heart was pumping behind her eyes.

"What do you mean?" she stuttered.

"I got home yesterday and she has packed all her things and gone. She left this." He reached into his jacket pocket and took out a leather photo wallet. In it was a photo of a tall, blond man, broad grin. A blue sea with white-capped waves blurred in the background. It was particularly sunny. "It was lying on the ground. She must have dropped it." He widened his eyes. "Shocked." He absent-mindedly hugged himself. "Well, not sure why I'm shocked. The woman had turned on me, as you know. I suppose she must have held very little regard for me after all."

"That's difficult, Johnny. I'm sorry."

"Phil always told me not to put so much time into her. Brian did too. He always told me I had a weak spot for the needy ones."

"Well, our friends can sometimes be right and sometimes completely wrong. We can only trust our own judgement and, often, we're wrong. Not just you."

Johnny scoffed.

"I feel like I've been wrong quite a lot in life. Oh, don't worry. I got a few things right – the business, Brian. But, of course, there's Phil. He's proving to be more of a problem than I thought. It's time to… move on from him. Get rid of him."

Carolyn felt her throat constrict. "What do you mean, get rid of? From the company?"

He let out a huff of air.

"I'm sick of him. He has become a liability, with his underhand ways and dirtbag friends. I want to, you know, get him out. I am just unsure how to do it." Johnny turned his gaze to the floor, his mind ticking over.

"Are you the sort of man who will take matters into his own hands, then, Johnny?"

He didn't move his head but raised his eyes towards her. "Possibly."

Carolyn tried not to respond physically.

"And Scarlett? Will you contact her? Or at least try?"

Johnny sat back and crossed his arms. He shook his head very slowly and kept his eyes trained on the ceiling.

"No. Why?"

She said nothing. He was angry. Very angry. She'd seen it in clients before – the inability to meet her eye, the crossing of arms, the puffing up of the chest and holding their breath. It was her life, watching her client's idiosyncrasies.

"Just curious. You did just mention something that could have been against the law and then thought better of telling me. That's all."

"Sure. But I can assure you now, I would never hurt a woman." He glanced at his watch. "Not personally."

"How do you feel about losing Scarlett?"

He threw both arms in the air. "Sad," he spat.

"Does it make you…" Carolyn flicked at some papers on her desk, "angry at Scarlett? Does it make you want to, you know, punish her for doing something so deceitful?"

Johnny winced. His tears were now dry and his features replaced with a permanent scowl.

"No, Carolyn. Scarlett is a troubled, hurt and confused young woman. I can accept she is gone, as much as it hurts. I do, however, want to know who this bloke is in the photo."

Carolyn guessed by now she had turned a little pale, a little washed-out. She had been nervously rubbing her eyes and forehead throughout the conversation. But she was too damn curious to call the session quits just yet. Not wanting to push him, she stayed quiet for a few seconds, to let Johnny gather his thoughts.

"*Phil*," he finally whispered. "It's all because of Phil. And, unfortunately, *that* goes back to Brian." Carolyn swallowed hard and tried to cement an unemotional expression on her face. "But that's all I can say."

"I see." She dared to meet his eye. "Did you and Brian take revenge for your fathers' sins? Did Phil somehow help you with that? Is that why you owe him?"

Johnny's mouth hung open, just slightly. Carolyn's right hand fluttered to her eyes.

"I'm very sorry," she said into her hand. "I didn't mean to ask that. I suppose the whole story sounds like a, you know, like a great mystery and I got carried away. Please, don't answer it. I don't want to know if you were involved in something like murder. I—"

Johnny held up a hand, as though in surrender. "Please," he hissed, "let's stop there."

They both shifted in their seats.

"Johnny. Be honest here. Are you seeing me because you want to talk about Scarlett and you? Or did you come to see me to work through your past. I mean, either way it's fine, but for me to get to the bottom of it all…"

Johnny closed his eyes, very briefly.

"Okay, Carolyn, I suppose I'd like to continue to chat every now and then; about my *past*, as you say. I'd also like to talk a bit about how to deal with women, going forward. You know how it is. I'm obviously rubbish at this male–female thing. A series of bimbos followed by a highly intelligent nutcase."

Carolyn nodded and tried to smile.

"Sure. I will do my best to help." She doubted it. Her dealings with Felicity had made it all too close for comfort. Furthermore, she had realised something. Johnny wanted love, he wanted a wife, but there was something missing in his approach. He didn't want connection with a woman; he wanted a vision. Scarlett's inability to stay in his life for long, her difficulty living in his world, made her all the more alluring, like a painting he coveted but could never convince the owner to sell.

With red pen, she wrote on her notebook one word. *Psychopath?*

Johnny leaned forward and tapped his index finger to his lips. "You're frowning, Carolyn. What did you just write down?"

She flushed. Her hand automatically covered the word.

"I'm sorry, Johnny. My notes are private."

He sneered. She instinctively sat back in her chair.

"Okay, then," he snickered. "I see I'm intimidating you. Oh, well. You will realise one day, it's not me who's the big bad wolf here."

"Oh, Johnny." She tried to make light of it. "I make no judgement. I am here to listen and advise best as I am able. Got it?"

He raised one brow. She turned her notebook over and placed her pen on top of it.

Johnny stood. They shook hands and said their goodbyes.

"Please call again for your next appointment," she called, her voice high-pitched and shaky at the end.

After he left, Carolyn sat down on her swivel chair and swung sideways slowly, back and forward, for fifteen minutes straight, letting this information whirl around her head. She refused to look at her phone, but when it did ring, it was Felicity.

"Hi. Listen, I'm a little—" Carolyn started.

"Can you meet me tonight? Scarlett has asked me to a friend's office in Central at five and I could meet you afterwards."

"Isn't there a typhoon on the way?"

"So what?"

"Whose office?"

"Some friend of Scarlett's. She's holed up with her for a few days. She's left Johnny. She's walked out on him. And she's called me and told me she wants to talk. I don't know what about, but thought you might want to be there."

Carolyn heard Felicity light up a cigarette and take a puff. *Finally, she lit the damn thing.*

Carolyn uttered something meaningless and hung up. She went to the M&S Food Hall, bought a bottle of Cabernet and walked home in a light, warm drizzle, the pavements steaming with bullet-sized raindrops. Felicity texted her five times. She ignored them all.

Carolyn had dinner with her children, drank most of the wine in front of some trashy TV and slept for eleven hours straight. The next day, she woke and, as soon as she stepped into the shower, knew what she had to do.

CHAPTER EIGHTEEN

The Head Office of Stealth PR, Central.

Four women seated around a table sipping champagne would usually be considered a joyous affair.

But not for these four women.

As though suspects in a whodunnit, they sat furtively glancing at each other around a circular marble-topped table in Vivian Ma's twenty-fifth-floor office. Outside, the steady thump of water on the windows kept up a regular drumbeat in the background.

They were an unlikely group – Alice, Felicity, Scarlett and Vivian.

Alice sipped at the bottle of soda Vivian had handed her, a rising nausea threatening. Again, thoughts of Wang clouded her mind. In a few hours, the typhoon could make landfall not far from where they were standing, Wang could be immersed in some violent protest and her world could come shattering down around her. The last thing she wanted was to talk about Johnny and his past antics. She was done with Johnny and Phil and hoped the others would be soon as well. She'd been coerced there by Scarlett and was already regretting it.

Considering it was her office and therefore her domain, Vivian was perhaps the only one who showed a sense of confidence. This was heightened by her glamorous attire – bright red stilettos and a navy-blue wool wrap dress and hair that hung long and bouncy around her shoulders. From both ears hung two egg-shaped diamond earrings. They swung like heavy breasts as she stood and walked from the wine bar in the corner towards her gargantuan glass desk, past the Picasso sketch of a contorted horse and back towards the three other women perched on the edges of green velvet dining chairs. Vivian fluffed a few red gladioli in a mammoth vase – more than two dozen – and placed one elegant hand around her throat before coming to her senses and sitting down, a narrow smile forming as she placed a file on the table, her nails a citrus orange. Vivian saw Alice glance at them.

"In honour of Bobby Ling," she said to Alice. "It was his favourite colour."

They all nodded, stupidly.

Felicity couldn't take it anymore. She stood and moved herself back from the bizarre claustrophobia of the table.

"Can I just ask something? I don't get it. Didn't you used to work for Vivian, Scarlett? And she sacked you, for no apparent reason? That's what you told me. I am feeling a little weird about this chat. What's going on here?"

"Listen. I am really tired and really worried about this typhoon," Alice piped up. "I might have to go home. Now. Before it's too late. While I can still get a cab back to Shek O. I'm sorry, but I don't know why I'm here. And I don't know who you are, Felicity."

Scarlett turned to face Alice and glared menacingly at her friend.

"Not yet."

Alice sat back down, shocked by the coolness of Scarlett's voice, so unlike her usual tone.

Felicity held her breath. Where was Carolyn? She would love this. She checked her phone. No reply.

Vivian placed both hands on the table and inhaled.

"Ladies," she began, "not long ago, a document arrived for me. It will clear up much confusion – not all – but much of it. And, Felicity, I believe you have made some discoveries of

232

your own. Johnny's father? His best friend's father? Scarlett has told me all about it."

Alice and Felicity looked from Vivian to Scarlett.

"Our main problem, for all of us, is Johnny Humphries," Vivian said dramatically. "All of us have been affected by him and by the work of his business partner, Phil." She blanched. "Just saying his name makes me shiver."

Scarlett uncrossed her arms.

"However, we have known little of whether it is Johnny or Phil who is the main culprit, until this document arrived on Vivian's desk from a contact in Beijing. It is a letter that exposes the lies either Johnny, Phil, or both of them told many years ago. The man who sent this letter has since killed himself. He was dying, but he wanted to go without a guilty conscience, a burden he had carried for decades."

Vivian sat back and placed a hand on Scarlett's forearm.

"There's much more to tell." Vivian rubbed at one of her massive diamond earrings. "Many years ago, something happened that changed the course of my life for ever. I was the eldest of two children, my father had passed away and my mother worked long hours as a teacher. My younger brother had an inherited illness that required medical care. It was so expensive and my mother was pushed to breaking point. I did what I could and became a translator, a job I loved. But the work was sporadic and so I took a job in a bar part-time. It wasn't great, but it was temporary, I told myself, until I could get more experience as a translator. Well, my brother's health worsened. I told my boss at the bar and he organised for me to borrow money from a business partner, someone who was also his friend. Turned out, this was a loan shark. They prey on young and desperate people like I was then, and they demand big interest on the repayments. I was terrified I couldn't pay him back and it haunted me day and night." Felicity and Alice both froze. Neither dared look at the other. "One night, not long after that, this guy called Phil came to the bar and spent a fortune. We talked for hours. Well, he did.

I listened. The night seemed to go on for days. He told me a lot about his work. He told me about an incident he had been involved in the year before. He told me their names and the money he made. I had his secrets. Not that I wanted them, but that's how it goes in the bar business." Outside, thunder ricocheted off the island and the building shuddered. Vivian cleared her throat. "But as the night wore on, more drinks were consumed and everyone else left the bar as Phil snorted plates full of drugs." She paused, her eyelids fluttering as she inhaled, "He attacked me. It seems to be a weakness in Phil. I wouldn't go with him to whatever place he wanted to go to next and I was badly beaten. I still suffer from post-traumatic stress. I have several scars that will always remind me of that night." Felicity gasped. Alice shook her head knowingly. The howling wind and constant police sirens barely registered. "Some time later, in the police station, just after I had made my statement and as I was getting ready to leave, Johnny arrived. He was kind, handsome, gentle. He explained that if I changed my statement about Phil – especially the bit about Phil being involved in some kind of kidnapping – if I let him take me to the hospital and then just go home quietly, he would give me an amount of money the likes of which I never thought could be mine and mine alone. I was desperate, tired, in agony, worried about my brother and mother. I wanted a way out of my life and Johnny handed it to me. I changed my statement immediately. Johnny told me his business partner, Phil, was once a cop and he knew people. After a few phone calls, they handed Johnny all my paperwork and said they'd dealt with it. Johnny kept all these documents – my statement about Phil and the fact that, in a cruel twist, when the police had turned up, the loan shark at the bar told the police I was a sex worker, as a kind of punishment for not having paid him back. So that's what they put in the report. Johnny had shown me in the station. Even though I wasn't. Not even close. I remember Johnny being wide-eyed with shock when I told him it was a fabrication, but looking back, of course, that little act of revenge from the loan shark suited Johnny just fine. And there's photos. I've asked for it all a million times and Johnny said no – and all because he knows Phil told me what they'd done all those years ago. As for the loan shark, he was killed in a knifing incident in Wan Chai not long after I started Stealth, so I never had to worry about him exposing me. So the deal was that I keep my hard-fought reputation as a serious businesswoman in this town and Johnny keeps his. And, for the record, I worked my butt off to build this business. The money Johnny gave me went to my family and started Stealth off, but from then on, it was all me and me alone. The problem was that, over time, I couldn't accept it anymore. Occasionally, Johnny asked me for contacts I have in big business; people they wanted me to introduce them to. And I did, because I had to. I had taken Johnny's money. I've stayed quiet, but what I know about their past crimes has haunted me more and more. Sure, I've wanted my documents back, so I can destroy them. I've asked him many times. Recently, I asked to meet with him, ostensibly to ask again for them. But," she closed her eyes briefly, "it was really a ruse. I wanted to see what he was thinking, where his head was at, and to make him think that I was still at his mercy. Why? Because things have changed. The world has changed. *I* have changed and so have attitudes towards women. Years ago, I would have simply kept things the way they were, relieved I have this life, despite knowing the reality of what Phil and Johnny were involved in and feeling controlled by them because of my past." She stood, walked back to the wine fridge and pulled out a bottle of vintage Krug. "That was, until I met Scarlett."

"What do you mean?" Felicity half-whispered. *Some PI I am*, she thought to herself.

Scarlett dabbed at her lips with a white linen napkin and squared her shoulders slightly.

"I think it's time, Madeline, that I told you who I really am."

CHAPTER NINETEEN

Stealth PR office.

"You see," Scarlett was pacing the room, a new Scarlett, raging as powerfully as the storm outside. "Thanks to a man in Beijing named Simon Gu, we now know so much more." Scarlett placed a letter down on the cold marble. They all read it slowly.

I, Simon Gu, do swear that in 1995, I was paid by the boss of Phil McComish to lie about a meeting between myself and his employer, Johnny Humphries, during the kidnapping of Madeline Chung in Hong Kong. I was scheduled to dine with him at my offices on that date, but it was cancelled by Mr McComish. Mr Chung was my former employer and – like Mr McComish – I despised him. I never advised police of this, nor the fact that I did not dine with Mr Humphries after all. I also benefited financially from this subterfuge. I am not proud to say that this has since been a source of much shame. Later, in the mid-2000s, I was contacted directly by Mr Johnny Humphries' himself, asking me to speak with the Sunflowers Orphanage in Tianjin. This had to do with a donation in the mid-1990s, when I had arranged on behalf of Mr Humphries and his boss to transfer a large sum of funds to the said orphanage, one which later became embroiled in a trafficking scandal. Mr Humphries' name was mentioned to authorities as having been a large donor and the authorities had contacted me to ask about his donation. Nothing more was ever communicated, and I have no idea what came of this. I can't elaborate more, other than to say that I never heard from the authorities again. However, when a Ms Beverly Wong from the above orphanage contacted me recently, seeking to speak with Mr Humphries, I wanted nothing more to do with it, and instead provided her with the contacts of a mutual friend, Vivian Ma, in the hope she instead may be able to enlighten Ms Wong about Mr Humphries' involvement. As I said, I am unclear about what that was. However, I am very clear that Mr Humphries and his colleague, Mr McComish, were somehow involved in the Madeline Chung kidnapping – and I helped them escape prosecution. Sometimes, one finds themselves in a situation they believe will be a passing phase to quickly elevate them to a life of ease – a short interlude, a one-off. Yet once you're in it, the ball keeps rolling. A few months ago, after being contacted by Ms Wong from the orphanage, this shame became too much of a burden. I am now dying of lung cancer. I don't have long to live. My wife has passed on and my children live in the US. My dying wish is that Mr McComish and Mr Humphries be investigated for the crimes they and I had committed, for hurting innocent people. I write this to assist Ms Wong and other friends and family of any other victims. I am sorry to say that I do not have information on Mr Humphries, other than knowing he was somehow involved in the Madeline Chung kidnapping. But I am unsure as to why he was involved in funding orphanages.

Scarlett continued: "We – Vivian and I – believe that Johnny and Brian wanted to fund the murders of their fathers and – strangely – then donated handsomely to an orphanage in China, one that then became embroiled in a child trafficking scandal. Why they did, we simply don't know. But, to organise the murders and choose to donate to such orphanages, they needed money. News reports in 1995 say that Mr Chung – Madeline's father – reportedly paid US$10 million directly to the kidnappers. Well, to someone who controlled the kidnappers. That's more than US$16 million in today's terms. We also know now that Gu lied to the police about actually meeting Johnny on that day all those years ago, Madeline. You thought you heard a British man's voice, smelled Johnny's scent, had seen him near a teahouse you visited regularly in the days beforehand. You thought that he ordered for your finger to be cut off. Gu didn't mention any of this. But he did confirm he was coerced to lie by Phil. That Phil, acting for 'the boss', he said, told Gu to lie and take a big wad of cash as payment or face the consequences. You see, Gu was a former employee of your father, Madeline. But your father sacked him, as he found him to be untrustworthy, not long after Phil was let go from the company. Gu and Phil felt, no doubt, bonded by this, bitter and seeking to make as much money as they could to compensate for being fired. Johnny, once he had left working for your father and was on his own, possibly arranged for Phil to involve Gu. But Gu wasn't cut out for it and became eaten up with the guilt. He had children of his own and could never live with what he had done for money."

"What does this have to do with you, Scarlett?" Felicity asked, deeply confused.

Scarlett continued. "A new Westerner, Nick, was working at Sunflowers Orphanage earlier this year. He had also been looking into the practices of child trafficking from years before. He had started asking a lot of questions, trying to get to the bottom of it. He had a personal mission to bust the process all together, as his own adoptive sister could have been one of those children many years before. But someone – maybe a gang – sent a representative over to scare him off. The guy did much more than scare Nick. He killed him, knifed him in front of me and the children. Nick was the love of my life, and I watched him bleed to death on a dirty concrete driveway."

Alice was hungry. She was tired, but she was transfixed by Scarlett's tear-stained face as she paced the hushed carpeted room. Felicity sat on the edge of her chair, both hands gripping the sides. Scarlett continued.

"Well, Gu. It's laughable. Yes. He's the bad guy too, although he says he was not involved in Nick's death. But Beverly, who ran the orphanage, once she started asking around the neighbourhood about the guy who killed Nick, someone who used to work at the orphanage pointed her to Gu. He had visited some time ago *and* once arranged a large donation. People were trying to put the pieces together and he was the only name they had. So, she told the police about him. They told her that her information was wrong, that Gu was not a criminal, which was true. But still, Beverly felt that Gu was hiding something and, after a while, she took the matter into her own hands. She contacted Gu again, and started with a few angry threats. But by then, he had been diagnosed with cancer. He simply told her to contact a woman called Vivian Ma in Hong Kong; that she would tell her all about a man named Johnny Humphries. That's all he would say and that was all I knew. He said he'd give more information later, but first, he asked us to give him some time to get his life in order, then he could put it all in a document, one he would sign. In the meantime, all he would do was put Beverly – and subsequently me – in touch with Vivian. I begged Beverly to support me to handle things and a few days later I was in Hong Kong, sitting right here, in this office, listening to Vivian's story. We both wanted something badly and that's when we came up with our plan."

As though issuing a massive round of applause, a sharp lightning crack startled them all. All four of the women jumped before settling back down to monitor each other's reactions.

"How did Gu know you, Vivian?" Felicity asked. The champagne had gone to her head and she picked at some pastel candied almonds in a pewter bowl, the loud munch as she ate drowned out by the rising winds outside.

"I've been in Hong Kong business circles a long time now." Vivian shrugged. "Gu was well known around this town in the old days when he worked for your father, Madeline. He knew I hated Phil. He didn't know why I did – I was hardly going to tell him about my past and that Phil beat me up – so when he wanted to put his wrongs to right, he knew I wouldn't hesitate to throw Phil and Johnny under the bus."

Alice, slouched in her chair, finally spoke.

"But how did you know that Felicity was really Madeline?" Alice glanced at Felicity. Despite having seen and heard about it in the news all those years ago, she never would have put two and two together. The old Madeline – from what she remembered of the photos at least – was weak and feeble. This Madeline was bullish and prickly.

Scarlett sat back down. She too was tired. After this, she would have nowhere to go. She would simply get on a plane and hide. Maybe go back to Perth and stay with Nick's devastated parents. She roused herself.

"We spent a lot of time on it," Scarlett said, briskly, her eyes a little glassy. "I'll get to that in a minute. First, I want to explain, about Vivian and I. Of course, I was never really working in PR. We were working on finding out who Johnny really was. Vivian took me on as a way of making my appearance in Hong Kong look legitimate, so I could get an ID card and so on. But I was getting nowhere with Johnny. Furthermore, Vivian knew what Johnny liked in a woman – hot one day, cold the next. Vivian knew that he never liked the independent ones either. He was more into the needier types. So I simply became that. Vivian 'sacked' me as a way to give me more time to get into his safe during the day and to make me seem… in need of saving, so he could rescue me. I'd noticed he'd been backing off a little and so I confused him, became distant. I needed him to open up. I needed him to feel like my hero again." She scanned the others' faces, her chin raised, a look of defiance. "Vivian had already explained Johnny's foibles when we first met. In the beginning, of course, it had to be romantic, which is why it took me a few months to make a real move. I couldn't have him being suspicious. He's very coy about personal things. But then, just recently, he had started trusting me." Scarlett half-smiled. "I was not really cut out for PR anyway. Was I, Viv?"

To Alice, their subterfuge seemed to be the act of the unhinged and her skin tingled as she watched.

She was jolted back to reality by a surge of wind outside, the storm rising as fast as the nausea that had once again settled in the base of her throat.

Now, it was Felicity's turn to start pacing.

"Was it Gu who worked out who I was? Did he have contacts in Hong Kong Immigration or something? I mean, if you know who I am, who else does?"

Scarlett sat straight. She and Vivian, she explained, had started with Felicity's most recent public web profile when she was still called Madeline Chung.

"I realised through a few internet searches that you had worked in HR for a US company for three years. Then, two years ago, you were no longer employed You'd gone off the radar. I rang your old company and they said they thought you had moved to New York. Vivian did some digging, using her well-heeled New York contacts and one of them knew your mother. After a few weeks of emails and phone calls – thanks to Vivian's network – we got a confirmation you had returned to Hong Kong. At the time, I thought about contacting you, to talk to you about Johnny. But—" Felicity winced. *Her mother*. She had told someone. *People talked*, her mother had warned her. But did it have to be her own mother?

"How did you find me here? Here in Hong Kong? I am now Felicity Cussler and I have no web presence. Nothing. *Fuck!*" She kicked at the wall, not caring about the pain.

Scarlett turned and spoke calmly.

"You're right. I asked Gu to help. He had a cousin in Immigration. He asked around, we checked, then rechecked photos, your age and, of course, once I met you up close, I could see it in your eyes." Felicity smirked. "It's sad, I know. People will do anything for money. But you see, by then, Gu would do anything to help us out. He felt that his cancer and his wife's untimely death was punishment for him having consorted with Phil and Johnny all those years ago. He took a while, but he got the confirmation of your name change, your details. Sorry, Felicity, but it's all been in the name of nailing Johnny and Phil."

Felicity hung her head in her hands.

"Why, then, didn't you just come to me, Scarlett, instead of pretending you didn't know who I was?"

Vivian shrugged, her earrings shimmering in the low light above her.

"That was our initial plan, but we had no idea if you wanted to have anything to do with Johnny or to continue seeking the truth. So it was a matter of not knowing you, not knowing how to tread, at first. You might have baulked at the idea if you knew we knew who you were. You were a loose cannon. And we really wanted to see what you could find before we told you the truth. And through your seriously good PI work, you got the info on Johnny's earlier history. Scarlett and I were more focused on dealing with Johnny. And Gu didn't know any more than what he told us."

Scarlett stood and straightened her pleated skirt.

"It's Carolyn, however," Scarlett almost growled, "that we're not sure about."

Felicity flinched at the mention of her friend's name.

"Leave her out of this. Please. She's done nothing wrong. We're friends and she happens to be my shrink."

Vivian smiled weakly. "But she's also treating Johnny."

"Only once," Felicity replied. "God. How did you know about Carolyn anyway?"

"He's been back to see her since," Scarlett enunciated very slowly, as though Felicity were being foolish. "Just yesterday, actually." Vivian paid Bobby Ling's old driver to keep an eye on him sometimes. Because guess who was the last person in Bobby's car the night Bobby died?"

"Johnny?" Felicity's eyes widened.

Vivian narrowed hers. "Phil."

Felicity sat back hard in the chair.

"Phil killed Bobby?" Felicity asked.

Alice nodded. "Don't doubt it. The man is violent."

"We don't know if he killed him," Vivian added. "But we will find out."

Felicity shivered. Then, in frustration, she slammed a hand on the table. It stung more than she expected.

"None of this officially links Johnny to my kidnapping," Felicity snapped. "I mean, he has to be involved, but how? Why? Johnny's father was murdered, yes. His best friend's house was burned down, his father killed. Johnny's mother died years before, which got this whole ball rolling. I was kidnapped *and* I have a jumble of small reasons to link Johnny to that event. All we know from Gu is that Phil asked him to lie about meeting Johnny that night in Beijing. Gu said Phil explained the directive had come from 'the boss'. Having said that, Johnny was actually still in Beijing, so why didn't he tell Gu himself? So that leads me to…" she reached into her oversized bag and pulled out a packet of Marlboro Lights, "Phil? Why would Phil be running the show?"

Scarlett emptied her champagne glass.

"He isn't," she sighed. "We all agree. Most likely, Johnny wanted money to have his father and his best friend's father killed. Perhaps Bobby provided the contacts to go ahead with the kidnapping. Gu then helped out with the lie about having had dinner with Johnny that night. End of story. And, they all made cash from it. But none of this confirms Johnny as the unknown factor when it comes to your kidnapping. What we do know is that Phil told Vivian all those years ago that he had been involved in a kidnapping in Hong Kong, acting as a liaison – and that all the orders came from 'the boss', whom we assume – but only assume – is Johnny."

"Who else could it be?" Vivian glanced pointedly from one woman to the other.

It was Alice's turn to finally speak up.

"So I've got to ask this again. Why fund the orphanage?"

Alice had had enough with this conversation, but this was the sticking point for her. Johnny and Phil were no Triads. Johnny was Eurasian and, yes, well respected for his business success, but he was not a local Chinese, not even close. And Phil. Forget it. He had plenty of questionable social friends, many of them involved in illegal businesses, but he would never be included in their business deals. He was a drug-addled *gweilo* who liked to live on the edge. Yes, Phil had been involved with the passports she had couriered all those years ago, but surely it had been in a very minor way. Maybe he was the guy who knew the guy in the British Embassy. But a serious human trafficker? No way.

"That's what we don't know," Vivian said, her lipstick still perfectly glossy. "Neither did Gu. All Gu knew was that 'the boss' made the orders, then he paid Gu into his account. And he paid well."

Vivian went to rub at her shiny hair but lowered her hand to her champagne glass instead. "You see, we need this missing piece of the puzzle in regards to Felicity and Scarlett. So now it's all out in the open, can we help each other? If we can find that one last connection, we have a better case."

They all spoke at once: would they go to the police? If so, Vivian's past may be made public. Vivian was past caring about that. She'd own it. It was time. Would Felicity's identity be revealed by the press if they went to the officials? Did Felicity care?

Finally, Vivian rose.

"We don't know what we will do once we have proper evidence. Gu's letter may be enough, but I'm not sure I want to go to the police yet. I am thinking there might be a better way of dealing with these two."

Scarlett laughed. "Well. Maybe. I mean, Gu's letter does mean Felicity and *I* could go to the police."

"Well…" Vivian started.

Felicity held up one hand and tapped her cigarette again.

"Hold on. Where are the documents and photos relating

to Alice and Vivian – the ones you found in Johnny's safe, Scarlett?" Felicity shot a look at Scarlett. She felt intimidated by her now.

"I took them, and Vivian and I burned them. I left the safe locked and empty. I changed the code to 'Sunflowers', the name of the orphanage where Nick was killed. Johnny will never get it."

"And how did you get into the safe?" Alice said quietly. She was clutching at her belly, a headache around her eyes that pulsed.

"I can answer this part too," Scarlett replied. "The safe had a code. Vivian had seen the safe some years before, long before we met. She didn't have the nerve to try it. She never got close enough and, naturally, felt she was still in Johnny's debt, so didn't want to rock the boat back then."

"So what made you think you could do it?"

Alice looked at Scarlett. Her small hands were placed comfortably on her lap, as though relaying a political decision. Alice realised how much of an actress Scarlett had been. Were they really friends, or had Scarlett suspected Alice knew something from the second they met?

"I spent months searching for some kind of clue as to his code," Scarlett started. "It was a mixture of letters and numbers, ten digits in all. Very complicated." She laughed and looked out the window. A flash of light hit her cheeks, making her face briefly ghoulish. "I would flirt with him when he logged on to his laptop and his desktop, to see what password he used. And, yes, I learned one computer password, but it wasn't the same code for the safe. After I went swimming in the mornings, I often snuck past his study, through the basement of the house, to see if he was opening the safe. It was under his desk, like a concealed drawer. I thought that, at the right angle, I could have made out at least the first few numbers or letters." She stopped and took a sip of her champagne. No one breathed. "I tried to see if the maid could answer it. But she had no idea and, to be honest, that was a long shot. But then one day, I was at home, thinking, thinking, always thinking."

Alice felt her stomach churn.

She cleared her throat and shot Scarlett a piercing glare.

"Were you ever my friend? My real friend? Was I some pawn in the process?"

Was it real? Alice could no longer tell.

Scarlett explained that when the two had met on the junk that day, she had no idea about Alice's connection to Johnny. They had become friends simply because that was Hong Kong – people of the same age working in offices near each other, professionals all hanging out in the same bars, the same restaurants. They were part of the same group in the city, Scarlett stressed. Their friendship stemmed from being in the same places at the same time, the same cafés at 11am on a Tuesday, the same streets on the way to work. It was plain old luck that Alice had information that helped paint a broader picture of who they were dealing with.

"Recently," Scarlett said, "Johnny and I had talked. My behaviour prior to this had been somewhat erratic. I was in mourning and living this bizarre double life, trying to play an emotional game with Johnny. But I realised, just in time, that to get him to trust me, I needed to open up a bit. I'd tried this game in a small way when we first got together but it was all too new then and I hadn't wanted to push him. So I gave it one more try. This time, I inferred I was thinking of leaving him. No one had ever left Johnny. It worked."

"How?" Felicity snapped.

"On his bedside table at home there was a framed photo. It was the only framed photo he had in the house. It's of Johnny and a man whom I now know is his best friend, Brian. They're standing next to a letter box and the house number is 25B. The house is burned to the ground, the roof collapsed into a pile of bricks. I'd asked Johnny a couple of times about it and got nowhere. He said it was just a random photo. He doesn't have photo albums. He doesn't leave old letters lying about. But then one day—"

Alice thought of Wang again. She didn't have the headspace to stay in this room anymore. Her life was moving on. She would make sure it stayed that way.

"I have to go," Alice grimaced. She walked to the door, her bag slung haphazardly across her shoulder, gaping. Something was happening out there and it wasn't just the storm. In the past twenty minutes, there had been many police sirens.

"Alone?" Scarlett barked.

"Yes. I'm fine. I want to just… go home."

"Please don't, Alice. You need to know what to do if Johnny contacts you about me leaving him."

Felicity stood.

"Forget Alice!" Felicity snapped. "Then what happened, Scarlett?"

Scarlett took a long, slow breath.

"I asked to meet Johnny for a drink and, finally, he opened up about Brian, about his past, just a little. He also told me about Vivian – without mentioning her name. But it was funny. After he spoke about Brian, I noticed a change in his features. Saying Brian's name made him happy. So then, I realised something. If there was only one photo in your entire house with you and one other person in it, then that person held a special place in your life, as did the burned-out house they were standing next to, for reasons he wouldn't explain."

"So?" Felicity rubbed at her stubby finger.

"The code was *25BLillian*, the number of the house and the street name in the photo. Ten digits. Johnny was at work, the maid was cleaning the pool house. I tried a few different versions of *25BLillian* before I got the right one, and as soon as I discovered everything inside, I took it, packed and then rang Vivian. Not long before, Gu's letter had arrived on Vivian's desk. So there you have it. Nick was up there, watching after us all along." Scarlett gazed at the ceiling, as though Nick were sending a halo of light back at her.

One very broken person, Felicity observed. Maybe worse than she was. After this, she'd never question her sanity again.

Alice, swaying a little near the office door, surprised them all by spinning on her heels. For once, her easy grey eyes that spoke equally of sarcasm and boredom were focused and bitter.

"I've got a life I want to lead. I've got a future that doesn't involve this shit about the past!"

With that, Alice yanked open the office door and stormed down the hallway. As soon as she got outside, she could feel it. The eye of the storm. The rain had calmed, the wind had settled. Above her, a large neon sign announced it was a T8 and rising. That meant it was likely to go to T10 – a super typhoon. She was running out of time. Minutes away, she stumbled into the closest Watsons Pharmacy. It was closing, the aluminium doors being rattled shut by a shop girl dressed in a bright pink tunic, her hair whipped around her face in a frenzy.

Alice accosted her in friendly Cantonese and the girl reluctantly let her in. She purchased a pregnancy test and ran to the Mandarin Oriental bathroom. She was forty years old. The signs were all there. She just had no idea she'd ever get that lucky.

She shakily unwrapped the stick.

Minutes later, she knew.

Alice left the pharmacy. She walked towards Admiralty with a strange spring in her step, despite the hovering darkness and moody skies.

It was only when she reached Wan Chai, aiming to grab a cab, that she saw the throngs emerge. Sirens wailed from right behind her and voices, too many voices, singing "Glory to Hong Kong" and yelling, mantras that merged into one cacophonous football-stadium roar.

Behind her, around and in front of her, came a constant flow of bodies, dressed in head-to-toe black, marching from the MTR station exits on every angle. Those in front were holding placards. They were unsmiling, their war cries strident, fists pumped. Alice felt herself carried along with it, reflexively hugging her stomach, following them in the vain hope that somewhere among the protestors was Wang. She would find him. She would tell him and she would stop him.

* * *

Johnny was watching the storm from his office, the TV news relaying every second of the unfolding protest.

He stood facing the harbour window with one hand in a pocket, a whisky-and-water in the other hand. A part of him wanted to laugh, another to cheer. He couldn't help but see the irony. A storm of protestors forcing their way into the PLA Headquarters in Hong Kong in the midst of one of the city's biggest typhoons. He almost felt proud of these young guys and girls, draped in black, linking arms in the foyers and offices. They were refusing to budge, knowing full well the drama of the protest during a typhoon would get the world's attention.

So far, the police had pepper-sprayed the first wave of protestors, but a second, much angrier lot came along and managed to get inside. There were apparently thousands of them sitting cross-legged in every corner of the building, safe from the storm on each floor, flooding the forecourt along with the rain and ready to wait it out.

Meanwhile, Typhoon Pareshan reared its head, roaring into life while the harbour water surged and thudded against the cement typhoon barriers that encircled the building. On the hills behind them, the lush, tropical greenery was ripped from the ground, flung along steep roads, the drains filled with leaves, broken chairs, clothing, bicycles and tree branches.

Cars parked in villages in the New Territories were carried away in low-level flooding. The seaside village of Shek O was under threat of storm surges and anyone living at sea level was forced to sandbag their properties.

A few of the town houses closest to the beach were already flooded and emergency crews were on standby for potential landslides throughout the island. Two surfers had been rescued from rocks in Big Wave Bay, both bloodied and bruised. In Mongkok, on the Kowloon side, household items were strewn about the streets, becoming weaponry for anyone stupid enough to be walking around. There were a few injuries from the waterways – people trying to rope-in their vessels and falling – and two teenagers who dared to venture out onto the pier at Stanley were washed into the water by a giant wave, the alert sounded by onlookers from a nearby local restaurant.

But Johnny? He was busy hatching a plan to start a new life.

CHAPTER TWENTY

Hong Kong, Beijing and Tianjin, Mainland China.

September, 1994.

Brian hadn't wanted to come. Well, he'd wanted to – he'd been reading about China for years – but he was a nervous flyer and considering what he'd been through lately, didn't think he'd manage it alone. Yet Johnny was worried enough to send Brian a ticket, a chance to get away from the past for a bit, he said. Johnny told him that his business partner, Phil, had decided to take some time off, being summer, and was out of town for a while. Johnny wanted to get out for a bit, too. Johnny promised Brian he'd be fine in the nice Cathay Pacific jet, that the airline knew he had a mild disability – a limp and intermittent pain in his back – and would assist with a wheelchair if he wanted it. Brian felt he couldn't say no to such a generous offer, so he took an anti-anxiety pill and finally arrived in Hong Kong, staying in Johnny's two-room flat on Seymour Road for a week. Johnny, keen to cheer Brian up and show him the world he himself was coming to know and love, then flew them both to Beijing. "For the adventure," he'd told Brian. "The one we always wanted as kids."

Johnny was conscious of not babysitting Brian, but the man had been seeking psychiatric help since he was sixteen and Johnny had to tread carefully. Brian had worked hard, they'd told Johnny when he rang the only doctor who'd helped him, to get to the point where serious medication and talk therapy had supported him through an accounting degree. Now Brian could start afresh, get strong again, they said. He told Johnny that Brian was doing well and would come out of this with the right approach. Now, Johnny was there to help. This holiday seemed like the perfect solution.

In Hong Kong and Beijing, Brian seemed like his old self. Talkative and excited about the foreign sights and smells of such vastly different cities from London, his eyes actually sparkling as they wandered through Kowloon Park and then, in Beijing, the eye-wateringly vast expanse of Tiananmen Square. After more sightseeing in Beijing, they'd got a driver to take them to Tianjin where Brian had expressed his desire to take a look at an orphanage. He'd been reading about such places in news magazines and – as he had a strong desire to help children in need, as he once was – Johnny agreed to go with him.

Afterwards, nursing a cold beer in the hotel bar, Brian was quiet. In front of him was an English-language newspaper the hotel had left in their room with a feature story about a kidnapping in Hong Kong a few years before. There'd been another in 1992.

"The 1990s: the decade for Hong Kong kidnappings!" Johnny said, his attempt at a joke falling flat.

Brian sipped at his beer, his now pale yet clearly visible facial scars never ceasing to send shivers down Johnny's spine.

"Maybe that wasn't such a good idea, mate," Johnny said, "to take you somewhere like that. Those poor kids, eh?" Brian had nodded. Still quiet. Brian's recent happy mood had turned suddenly sour. "I mean, if you want to donate to the orphanage or something, I might have a few bob left after this holiday. After you've cleaned me out." Brian didn't smile.

Finally, Brian cleared his throat. "How do you feel about it all?" he asked Johnny.

"About what?"

252

"About what our fathers did to us? About how so many children in the world never find the happy home they deserve?" Johnny went cold. The last thing he wanted was for Brian to fall apart again.

"Brian. I think we should just get something to eat."

"No, seriously. I've had a lot of time to think about this." They both said nothing for a few seconds. "A lot. And I've seen how hard you're working to get Berwick up and running and you could've stayed on with Chung. But he was an abusive bully and now you have to start all over again. And somewhere, in London, our fathers swan around enjoying themselves while we struggle."

"Okay, Brian. I hear you." Johnny was getting nervous.

"When we were kids, you said you'd do anything for me. Anything. And I know, I just know the time is right. I can't handle it anymore and I don't want to go back to the... the hospital. If I can do this, if I can make this plan work, I'll feel better. Stronger." He'd hung his head in his hands and Johnny was reminded of the day in Brian's bedroom, the smell of disinfectant, his best mate's face mangled. "No one would suspect us, either. We're nobodies. I... we... can move on for good. Never think about them again. Maybe help out the orphanage as well, as part of it, to make it more worthwhile. Don't you think?"

Johnny shook his head. "Mate. What *are* you talking about?"

* * *

It was nearly 6pm when Johnny turned on the news in his office. Breathy reporters in pointless raincoats standing on the forecourt of the nearby Immigration Tower, righting themselves against pillars in the wind, were getting agitated with anticipation. The police were trying to escort the press away, but they kept coming back. Someone was going to get seriously hurt, the police repeatedly stressed.

He stretched, went to the bathroom and showered. He brushed his teeth and tried to stay calm about Scarlett. It didn't work. Still, he felt some kind of relief in the knowledge that he was now in the mood to pass on the reins of Berwick. He'd leave Phil some cash and move on for a bit, see what was out there in the big wide world. He'd miss Hong Kong, but he'd be back. He just needed a breather.

* * *

The news ticker at the bottom of the screen kept screaming out the words: *T10! Offices closed! Extreme Danger!* The screen flashed to reports from global news desks about the ins and outs of the democracy movement. The question they all asked: "Would the police go too far?" Possibly, Johnny thought, but only if the protestors did first.

In the news today, Johnny mused, *forgotten about tomorrow.*

Johnny lay back on the sofa and watched the TV with his arms folded above his head, listening to the winds rage.

This recollection was just fading from his mind when the on-screen camera shuddered. On the TV, some of the protestors' chants turned to screams. Everyone turned to look above them. As Johnny stood to peer from his rain-lashed office window, a deafening thunderbolt cracked through the sky, shaking the building. Johnny leaned on the edge of the sofa to stay steady.

"Fuck," he hissed. He turned back to the screen. It had gone blank, completely blank. The room plunged into darkness. He picked up his desk phone. Nothing. "What the hell is going on?" Johnny yelled in Cantonese, to no one.

Johnny threw the receiver onto the desk and ran from the office. The lifts didn't work either, so he ran down the stairwell and was in the lobby in minutes. It was completely empty. Even the doorman was gone.

Outside, about four hundred metres to his right, the Chinese

People's Liberation Army Forces Hong Kong Building was a darkened box against a soaked skyline. The lights had all gone. Every street light along the main roads was gone too. The centre of the city was in blackness. But was it lightning that had caused this, or was it something more sinister?

Johnny ran back to his office, pulled out his Nokia burner phone from a bottom drawer and inserted another pay-as-you-go SIM card, simultaneously trying to find out information from local websites on his usual smartphone. Nothing as yet.

Johnny dialled a UK mobile phone number from the Nokia. It answered after three rings.

"Big day in Hong Kong," the man on the other end said with his usual slur.

"Something's gone on with the protests. Thunder? A bomb?"

The man paused.

"No. Got it here on the BBC. Lightning strike."

Johnny clicked through to the headlines on his own laptop, which had now sparked back to life.

"Yes. Lightning strike. Oh, hold on," Johnny said, cocking the phone to one shoulder. "You there?" Johnny said. "These old phones aren't too clear."

"Yes. I can hear you quite well, as always. I'm not deaf, only crippled and deformed."

"Seems the blackout incited panic. Shots fired… no reports of injury or death, but it's early days."

"That'll be the end of the protest," the man said, before coughing heartily off receiver.

"Where are you?"

"At home. Just had a stroll. Taking it easy."

"And how is it all going? Feeling good?"

"Perfect."

Johnny paused as he read through more of the news reports coming in. *Two shots were fired. People ran. Some have been trampled. No reports of death. Emergency crews already at capacity because of the typhoon.*

The boss had only communicated with Phil and Johnny over old pay-as-you-go burner phones. If there was ever a concrete link to Brian, *then* they would be in trouble. After they spoke or messaged – which wasn't that often these days – he and Phil always ripped out the SIMs and dumped them in public bins. The boss sometimes redialled the numbers once or twice, to make sure Phil had actually removed the SIM. He always had.

"Not going so well for me here with Scarlett."

"How so?"

"She's left me."

"I'm sorry to hear that."

"She just disappeared. Yesterday. Took all her things, all except one photo. I found it on the floor in the bedroom, near the bathroom door. Blond kid, in his twenties."

"Right," the man said, very slowly.

"I know." The TV newsreaders continued their concerned babble.

The man on the other line made a startled sound.

"Did you check the safe?"

Johnny reddened. He hadn't. He'd been too upset she'd gone. Too upset and confused about the photograph she'd left behind.

The other man fell silent for a while.

"Get on the next plane out of there," the other man finally whispered. "Who the hell was she?"

"I don't fucking know, mate. Why are you so worried? She obviously left the photo by accident. In a hurry or something. Vivian said she was just a nobody. She did a background check."

"No. She could be involved with Madeline. I'm sorry, but you were always useless when it came to women. You see danger everywhere unless there's a blonde hovering nearby."

"No way, mate. Scarlett is an innocent. She's new in town. Knows no one. Vivian sacked her. Promise, mate. If you had met her…"

The man on the line sighed deeply.

"Well, if she got into the safe, big deal?" Johnny paused. "All I had in there were Vivian's documents. Oh, and Alice's police file." Johnny thought of Vivian. The scar near her right eye. Maybe it was fair enough she finally had them. Brian was right. He should have just given them to her when she'd asked. Johnny felt panic rise and pushed it down. "She's no idea about you, so don't worry. Anyway, I was thinking of having a holiday anyway. How about France? We could go on a road trip, hire an Aston Martin?"

"You've been promising that since I can remember."

"Well now I finally have the time – and the need to get out. Berwick can manage without me for a while. If shit hits the fan, Phil will be the one with all the footprints. Phil was always going to be the fall guy. That was our plan, all along, remember?"

"You might not have *any* freedom, if Scarlett is on to you."

Johnny sniffed. "Come on. It's impossible." *She couldn't have found anything*, Johnny said to himself. "The only people who would talk are now dead," Johnny insisted. "The kidnappers were paid off when they got out. You know that."

"The dead can talk, Johnny."

"Do you think Gu talked before he died?"

"Listen. I know nothing. I'm going to just say it one more time: get on a plane as soon as they put one on the tarmac."

The other man coughed again.

"You okay?" Johnny asked, genuinely concerned with the cough.

"Yes. Feeling a million bucks. Your Aston Martin plan sounds great. Just let me know when you're here. Call me when you actually get on the plane."

"Sure. Fair enough, mate."

"Speak soon."

Johnny went to hang up.

"Oh, Brian?"

"Yes?"

"It's been a long road. But we got there."

"Thanks to you. You kept your promise. I never doubted you, Johnny. You really are a one-off."

Johnny smiled.

"Any regrets?"

"Sure." They laughed. "But then, I remember why it came to this." Johnny sighed. "I heard Tchaikovsky's Fifth the other day."

"Ah. Yes. It does bring it all back, doesn't it? Reminds us of how we got here."

The two smiled into their phones before saying their goodbyes and hung up. Hearing Brian happy made him happy. Their childhoods had forged an unbreakable alliance. One's happiness was intertwined with the other's.

It would stay that way.

Thinking of their impending car trip made him smile. He picked up the Nokia again and wrote a message to Brian: *The Madeline thing was worth it. I'm okay with it. I'm not angry with you and I understand. We were in it together. It wasn't just you. See you soon.*

Johnny turned off the phone, tore out the SIM and placed it in his briefcase. Later, he'd put it in a bin in a laneway when the storm passed. He and Phil never left the SIMs in the office or at home. Well, he hoped Phil didn't. Recently, they'd messaged Brian quite a bit about Gu and Bobby's deaths, referencing the two men's involvement in Madeline maybe, too? Oh well. The SIMs would be landfill soon.

As soon as he could, he'd book a flight to London and be gone. For how long, he had no idea. The thought was a small bolt of bliss, in spite of Scarlett's hurried departure, and he smiled at his milky reflection in the window, just as the TV flickered back on.

Protests Come to a Thunderous End!

* * *

Looking back, *had* it all been worth it? Sometimes, it felt that it was, others not so. But in a way, the whole Chung kidnapping thing – which had started as a nightmare – ended up as a perfect scenario for Johnny.

Johnny had secretly hated that fucker Albert Chung – Madeline's father – for weeks beforehand. One week, Chung had been stressed as usual, angry about a hotel land grab gone wrong. And then, when Johnny failed to secure the deal, because of a missed phone call of all things – a one-off failure, mind you – Chung hurled abuse at him, humiliated him in front of the entire team, the way his own father made him feel. The team didn't let him forget it either. Oh, yes. Johnny remembered it well. *He* would never forget it. Chung tried to calm down afterwards. Said he didn't mean it. That he was angry about the deal going sour. But as if Johnny would ever be able to pretend that didn't happen. Chung might have been a savvy businessman, but he was a spoilt, self-indulgent snob who had only pretended to respect Johnny.

When Brian's plan was hatched all those years ago, Johnny was torn. Sure, he wanted to help, but would it work? This was where Phil came in. Johnny knew Phil could be useful for what he and the Brain – or "the boss" as Johnny told Phil he was called – needed, to ensure they got what they wanted going forward. And he had been liaising with Bobby, who had second cousins who were happy to make some money fast. But poor old Bobby. Not that anyone actually killed Bobby. Bobby did that himself. All Phil had done was, acting on advice from the boss, hop in Bobby's car to scare him. Bobby was so smashed he'd fallen, stumbling down a stairwell not long after Phil had left him. The doctors reported that Bobby had hep-C and was on death's door anyway. And Gu. Well. Gu obviously had a guilty conscience. He was always a bit of a weak link, as far as the boss was concerned – hated having to lie to the police about meeting with Johnny not long after the kidnapping apparently, especially since his wife had died. Johnny had been in Beijing, just not with Gu.

In recent years, Johnny marvelled at their original boldness, their devil-may-care attitude. Who did they think they were? In today's technological, interconnected world, they wouldn't have even entertained it. Still, as he and Brian always said, it worked. Brian gave a shitload of funds to the orphanage via Gu and after a quick word with Bill the Baker in their old neighbourhood, they got Phil to liaise and make contact with the shady figures who got the ball rolling. They paid them a handsome sum to set fire to Brian's father's house when he was out of his mind drunk inside it. Soon after, they shot Johnny's father. Brian bought his old mum a house in Surrey, himself a cottage near his place of work out in Essex and Johnny set up Berwick. The only downside with the orphanage funds was that Johnny and Brian didn't understand what they were getting in to. They were young, idealistic and didn't have the faintest how it all worked. In the mid-2000s, Johnny got a call from Gu to say authorities were looking into how child trafficking was affecting such orphanages and someone at the orphanage had mentioned Gu's name due to the fact that a considerable amount of money had come via him some years before. Anyway, Brian's donation wasn't related to trafficking of course. But who actually benefited from the funds was anyone's guess, which was a real shame for Brian. There was not much they could do about that now. But Johnny was firm with Gu: go and talk to the orphanage and tell them all Brian had done was send a donation directly years before. Nothing more, nothing less, which was true. Maybe he was a bit rude to Gu at the time, but the thing with Simon was that he had always felt bad about benefiting from the Chung case. Johnny could almost feel Gu prickling when they'd spoken over the phone.

Brian and Johnny never thought about Tianjin again.

Johnny had to admit that Gu had done a good job of lying about meeting with him at the time of the kidnapping, just to have a second back-up that Johnny was where he said he was. Sure, Gu got paid for it, but he had helped them out when they needed him. Gu hated Chung as much as Phil and

Johnny did; Chung had screwed him in some kind of hotel property deal, although Johnny suspected it was the other way around. Bobby Ling's only involvement in the whole thing was to initially involve the gang members who did the actual kidnapping. Bobby's second cousins had known those guys since childhood. Bobby was desperate for extra money to start up a few more bars and restaurants, so he became the link. The things they did in those days were the stuff of cowboy movies. Times were different, that's for sure. And Bobby simply thought that the demand for the kidnapping had come from "the boss". Johnny knew Bobby would've thought that meant the boss was Johnny. But that was the beauty of it.

And throughout it all, if somehow the shit did hit the fan, it was always Phil who had the bad reputation. The only other name Phil could throw around was the faceless boss from whom he took orders. A man in the UK with a lisp and a husky voice. A Mr No Name who always paid generously and on time. Johnny snickered to himself at the thought of Phil trying to explain that to the cops.

When it came to Scarlett, he had truly loved her, or thought he did. He had genuinely wanted it to work. Deep down, he wanted a family of his own, a chance to make the change to normalcy. But it seemed she had a dark side too. Johnny would have to go back to having no one.

Well, he had Brian.

Just the two of them, all over again.

* * *

Johnny turned up the news. The cameras were trained on a group of protestors, singing songs of solidarity and freedom. Johnny shrugged his way into a crisp white shirt he kept hanging in a cupboard and squinted at the TV screen. Everyone in the picture was yelling, singing or barking orders. The protestors – plenty of them just kids – had the determined look of do-or-die. The police officers standing around them were outnumbered. The storm battering at the windows no doubt heightening their sense of fear.

The cameraman couldn't get that close and the people's faces were grimy, but for a split second, he thought he saw the back of what looked like Alice's head. Her red hair was pulled up but was damp and stringy. When the camera got close to her, she turned and Johnny leaned in to get a better look, noticing her trademark pale cheeks and upturned eyes. What the hell would Alice be doing there, in the lobby of the PLA Hong Kong Headquarters? No. It couldn't be her. Alice. *Jesus.*

To this day, Johnny never did know why she hated him so much. Johnny had been the one who had asked Phil to use his police contacts to get her off the cocaine possession charge. Whatever it was, she truly hated Phil – and Johnny by association.

In those early days, Johnny had been too caught up in his own work to notice what Phil was doing every minute of the day, but he suspected it wasn't always above board, considering Phil's expensive habit.

And when Johnny asked about Alice's coldness towards him, Phil had shrugged.

CHAPTER TWENTY-ONE

Essex, United Kingdom.

Brian walked with a stick but he was strong. He'd done years of rehab and had a fabulous osteopath who helped with his gait. He had a speech therapist too, but nothing seemed to make his lisp better.

His dad had done him in good and proper the last time he'd beat him. Johnny was already away at school then and couldn't do anything about it. Brian's mother never would have dared to go to the police. She knew his father would kill them both if she did. She could have left, of course, but apart from the fact they had no money and nowhere to go, they worried he'd find them. *Different times.*

When Johnny had visited him one summer when they were teenagers, they'd talked for hours about how they'd love to deal with their fathers. By then, Johnny was convinced his father had organised to have his mother killed and Brian agreed. Johnny's mother was in good health and hardly ever drank, so was highly unlikely to have simply fallen down her own stairs. Plenty of local people had seen those guys cruising down the street that morning, trying to look inconspicuous and standing out like sore thumbs. It all added up. Even Brian's drunken father reckoned two lads at the pub said they saw the same blokes shoving open Johnny's mum's back door, seen it from their top-floor windows. Could have been talk, but where there's smoke…

It was a beautiful day. Brian ambled slowly, as always, down the stone path to the garden with the feature pond and the flower beds filled with late-summer flowers.

It was 9pm and the sun had just set, a few wisps of pink and orange still visible in the night sky.

As he often did, he thought of Johnny and the sacrifice he made for him. Brian would never have dealt with the horrific emotional fallout of the violent childhood he'd suffered if Johnny hadn't helped him kill his father – and his own – buy his mother a house, himself a home and then fund something close to his heart, despite the fact that orphanage donation was a complete fiasco. People who haven't experienced such violence, maybe they can't understand it, can't comprehend what it does to the brain. Maybe his was addled, maybe that's why they chose to go ahead with the kidnapping. But at the time, he hadn't a penny, he'd been in and out of psych wards and he didn't have a proper home. Johnny was going to do well with a bit of a leg-up financially speaking – another reason to bring money in quickly – but he was young and broke too.

There'd been a couple of high-profile kidnappings in Hong Kong. In fact, a real crime wave. It'd be unthinkable in today's Hong Kong, but that was reality then. The ransoms had also been paid.

And there was Chung, a sitting duck for people like them.

After Brian had brought it up with Johnny that day in China, Johnny took a while to come around to the idea, being so fond of Madeline. Still, as they discussed it further, Johnny told him he didn't doubt that Madeline's father would pay the kidnappers directly, that he'd ignore the police not to negotiate. Chung was a law unto himself who always did what he wanted and got what he wanted. And he and his wife adored Madeline, their only child. Chung was the perfect target, hated by Johnny and Phil and others in the business world. A bully, Johnny said. Brian knew all about bullies. The

Chung family would get over it, Madeline would be fine, and the job would be done.

Brian had stressed to Phil and Bobby to tell the abductors not to hurt her, just to scare her. Brian was not a violent man. Maybe he was a mad man, a damaged man. Why else would he have gone down that path? But he didn't resort to physical violence. It just, regrettably, happened.

And then in China, Gu had done the groundwork of funnelling the orphanage payments to Tianjin, although looking back, that was obviously a rookie error, as they say in the movies. Over the space of a couple of years, they had given millions to that place, something Brian had wanted to do from the start, even though Johnny told him not to overdo it. It wasn't until they were advised the funds were being misused, most likely by gangs preying on the orphanage, or God knows, vice versa (Brian never really understood it all, there were so many unanswered questions), that they asked Gu to alert the authorities. As far as Gu could tell them, Sunflowers was later temporarily shut down. That was the last he heard of it.

Shuffling inside to his comfortable, warm cottage, Brian hoped that some child, somewhere, benefited somehow from all that money that went to the orphanage. Impetuous young men they were. He shivered.

Brian had to admit, Madeline was certainly right about one thing. Her kidnapping did involve Johnny and Phil, although they never physically got involved in it.

The problem for Madeline really started because of Phil. He had trusted Bobby Ling to speak with the guys who abducted Madeline. After all, they were friends with Bobby's family and all of them were going to make a pretty packet out of this. And they did. But as time wore on during the kidnapping, Phil was panicked and rang "the boss" with concern. Nothing was happening, Phil had advised him. Brian, thinking it could fall apart, told Phil to put the word out to scare her family a bit. That day – six days after Madeline had been abducted – Phil had been hanging out with Ken in the old, two-room Berwick office, pretending to be working and therefore giving them an alibi, when Brian gave Phil the go-ahead to put the wind in Chung's sails a bit. The kidnappers didn't have a phone, so they couldn't be traced. One of them had had to call the Chungs from a payphone on day one, to make the demands and tell them how to send the money. The only way for Phil and Bobby to communicate with the kidnappers was to speak to them in person. Phil knew the kidnappers were expecting Bobby – they wanted news, so it was safe for him to approach them. But when Phil tried to contact Bobby, he wasn't in his office. Later, they found out he was incoherent at some event luncheon. In the meantime, Phil grew impatient. He knew he couldn't show *his* face in that part of town and not be noticed.

So, Phil asked his completely unconnected, non-descript assistant and old schoolmate Ken Chen to go to the seedy basement storage room in Kwun Tong on Kowloon side and talk to the kidnappers about hurrying it along. Ken was fresh over from the UK and had needed a job, so Phil and Johnny had agreed to help out, give him some work. That's what you do when an old friend arrives in the city. Ken was eager, but lacking a bit of confidence, desperately trying not to show it. In a panic, Phil got Ken involved. Ken. A guy, then, with no real job other than "assisting" Phil, no real personality and nothing to do with the greater picture. And he couldn't even speak Cantonese! Ken either didn't listen to Phil or Phil never passed on the message about not hurting her in the first place. Brian would guess the latter. Either way, Ken went and screwed up with the finger debacle. Ken came up with that order all by himself, so Phil said. Rubbish, Brian knew. But once they had Ken and Phil involved, they were stuck.

Just thinking about it made Brian sick to his stomach. Turned out Ken simply wanted to please the boss. He thought that by being the tough guy, he'd win favour with Phil and Johnny. The problem was, he was then involved and would be for ever. So Brian made sure he never talked, thanks to their old friend "money". Shame Johnny had to bear witness to Ken in the office on a regular basis, but it was safer that way.

Brian also made sure the kidnappers were paid out when their sentences were up about seven years later. He'd set up a series of shell companies around the world that had no connection to anyone in Hong Kong. That's why the kidnappers left Ken alone. He just took his monthly payment and hung back, didn't ask questions. Brian made sure Ken had an old Nokia phone too, but he hardly called him. Ken stayed in the background, chastened by overdoing it with the Madeline thing all those years ago. But, Brian mused, what a prize fool, dabbing on a liberal dose of Johnny's bespoke scent before heading off to order a young woman's finger to be cut off. Phil confirmed he'd watched Ken open the bottle and steal a bit, no doubt aspiring to be that kind of man. Brian had almost bellowed with laughter at the farcical situations they'd found themselves in.

But his dad was dead. Johnny's father was dead. His mother had died happy. Well. Happier and not violently. The young kidnappers got busted, as Brian knew they would, but long before, the ransom money had come in. It was a massive stash paid into a Swiss account Brian had set up the month before the kidnapping. He'd had a false Russian passport done for himself too, Boris T. Sharakov. He and Johnny had a good laugh about that. Fake Russian passports weren't that hard to come by when you had people like Phil to ask around, Bill the Baker too. And the Swiss bank didn't seem at all suspicious of a disabled man limping into their offices with a stick and a lisp. Luckily, Brian also knew some Russian. Well, he'd practised a few words that he threw in to pepper a thick accent.

After the kidnapping was done, the account was gradually emptied and swiftly closed. The money was filtered around to those they owed and into various other offshore accounts. He was an accountant after all. Brian then got Phil to ask around his old stomping ground in London and, *bam*, his and

Johnny's fathers were dead. Johnny flew over to London and they took that photo outside Lillian Street.

Johnny, of course, knew about the Russian passport, but he didn't know Phil later dabbled in similar antics to make extra cash, even years later, a side business to pay off his drug debts, namely. Brian only found out because Phil once called him begging for a helping hand, debts mounting after doing business with a nasty crowd. Johnny was tiring of Phil even then, but Brian agreed he wouldn't tell Johnny if Phil continued to keep quiet and calm down. And Phil had. He really had.

Anyway. *C'est la vie*. Brian had survived his father. If he had to end his days in jail, he'd knock himself off before they got him. He doubted they would. They still used old Nokias to call and sometimes sent text messages. But they dumped the SIM cards. No emails, no letters. Johnny said he was always careful about which bin he used; never on a main road, never near the office.

Yes, the reverberations of his initial plan were, sadly, felt for years to come. Maybe if he'd known that, he would've done it differently. Maybe not. Brian felt like a lone star in a crowded solar system, overseeing but always invisible. He let a moment of guilt wash over him before focusing again on the fact that what was done was done. And, let's face it, he knew Johnny was a fighter. If the worst happened, Johnny would somehow make it okay for himself.

Despite the joy of such a marvellous sunset, Brian realised he was tired. Tired of fighting back against a system that had allowed him to be maimed for life. Now, it seemed, Johnny was tired of it too.

The two of them needed a break. Just a couple of old mates, cruising down a clear highway, the sun on their backs and no one to get in their way. Well, that was the fantasy. Brian sat down at a smooth panelled oak desk and started writing a very long letter.

＊ ＊ ＊

Johnny grabbed his passport, took a few shirts and trousers from the cupboard in his office and rang the driver. The roads would be empty now. The typhoon was still raging but the worst was over. He bent down to close his suitcase and, as he did, caught a reflection of himself in his office window, the rain creating a sea of tears across his distorted features. He looked hard at himself. Who was he? Who the hell was Scarlett? He felt his knees buckle a little and before he knew it, he was weeping like a baby, head buried in his arms on top of his suitcase. He missed his mother. *I'm damaged*, he told himself before trying to picture Brian, their car trip, their unbreakable union.

After a few minutes, he sat up, wiped at his nose and dabbed his eyes with a tissue from his desk. As he often did, he sat down and focused on listening to the incessant hum of the air-conditioning units. The steady white noise calmed his mind and, in seconds, he was in the bathroom, splashing his face with water. In the mirror, he smiled. He'd better run. The driver would be downstairs any minute.

＊ ＊ ＊

The driver always waited behind the Mandarin Oriental. Through drizzling rain, Johnny could see him in the front seat as he walked briskly to the service entrance of the hotel. There was a driveway and, alongside it, a row of overflowing skips. Johnny grabbed the plastic bag with the SIM and this time, the old Nokia too, glanced around and threw it towards the back of a row of two skips. He checked behind him. A flurry of waiting staff was lugging a few dining chairs towards a rusty lorry, smokers in uniform were hovering near the door. *Just a bunch of service lackeys*. Johnny lowered his head and marched towards his car.

CHAPTER TWENTY-TWO

Shek O Village, Hong Kong.

Wang was asleep. He had a broken elbow from falling in the crush, a lump the size of an egg on his head and a few scratches on his arms and legs. On the night of the protests, Alice hadn't been able to find him in the madness that ensued after the massive lightning strike. All she could recall was that her legs had been pulled from under her as the crowd panicked and surged towards the exits. Further thunderclaps and lightning strikes that shook the foundations were confused by the protestors with more gunshots and fear had taken hold, the screaming and pushing and bellowing made all the more terrifying in a murky blackness. She had waited for hours in a hotel lobby down the road alongside hundreds of protestors. By morning, the storm subsided and was downgraded to a T3 and she had tearfully made her way back home to Shek O, unable to get through to Wang on her phone and concerned he was the guy the police had shot, or so the rumour went.

He wasn't.

Wang, however, was as yet unable to speak about it. He'd been home from hospital for twenty-four hours – briefly questioned by police first – and his stony face made it quite clear he was devastated the protest had failed so spectacularly. Alice was relieved. No one else had contacted him to ask about his involvement in the protests. Yet. The creepy guys spying on Wang had not paid them a visit – yet – no doubt pleased they had got what they wanted, despite the protests going ahead.

Alice sat by his bed and wiped at his brow, his skin damp and cool in the late-summer mugginess. As he wasn't talking, she did it all for them – made plans for him to discuss becoming an official Democratic Party candidate, to make the most of his intelligence and leadership qualities instead of going underground again. He listened silently, staring out the window towards the prawn fishing boats, their white-hot spotlights lighting up a clear post-storm sky.

"Are you hungry?" she asked him, as he made a move to sit up, wincing as he held at his elbow. He shook his head no. "I've got noodles from downstairs. Or there's Thai soup. I've got pizza from Cocos if you'd like."

It wasn't true. Alice had already eaten it all, alone, just a few hours before. The hunger was overwhelming. She could imagine that if a bacon sandwich were waiting for her when she woke in the morning and the only way to get to it was to run over hot chicken-wire fencing, she'd do it. It shocked her and pleased her at the same time, the constant joy of salivating when the Thai restaurant brought out steaming plates of Thai pineapple fried rice. "You've got to eat something, Wang."

He finally looked at her. With a slow hand, he reached up and pushed a lock of hair from her eyes. A single tear edged its way down his cheek and stuck on to his chin stubbornly. Alice wiped at it.

"Come on," she said. "I read in the paper today that the Hong Kong government is prepared to listen to the protestors next week, under some kind of organised meeting in Victoria Park, you know, an olive branch to the students."

Wang shook his head.

"I'll believe it when I see it," he said, his voice hoarse.

Alice bit her bottom lip. It tasted of pizza sauce.

It was time to tell him, but she wanted him to be happy, not briefly excited before slumping back into a state of depression about the protests.

"Have they arrested anyone?" he asked her. Wang had refused to look at the newspapers or watch TV.

She shook her head.

"Not yet. Some guy I've never heard of has his name all over the news, considering he was the one with the gunshot wound, but as far as arrests go, it's all a bit... confused, I think."

Alice would have to make an appointment to see an obstetrician – and soon. God knows how long she had been pregnant. But she'd done it. She felt superhuman and tried not to smile in case Wang took it the wrong way.

"I can't turn myself in. It'll get Professor Rider into trouble."

"Of course not," she said, handing him a glass of water. He drank it and then reached for her hand.

"And you? How are you? And what the hell were you doing at the protests?"

Alice couldn't help it. She started laughing, a little snicker at first; a childish giggle.

"What's so funny?" Wang said, a slight smile forming. "Come on. Surely this," he raised his broken elbow, "isn't something to laugh about."

"Promise me you will try to change tactics," she said.

He opened his mouth to speak and thought better of it. "I just don't know what I can promise right now."

"Say you will try," she said, her smile fading. She had, he noticed, a flush to her cheeks, a doll-like roundness that made her seem younger. Fuller. He frowned a little.

"Okay. I will try. I don't know how, but if that's what you want to hear."

Alice reached for his hand and placed it on the base of her stomach.

"I don't want you to give up your hopes and dreams," she said quietly, "but you will need to approach them more sensibly, because soon, we're going to have a baby. You're going to be a father, Wang. You. Us. A family."

Wang sat up, threw back the bedcovers and buried his head into her chest. She felt wet tears through her shirt.

* * *

Phil woke on Shania's sofa, his mouth *Sahara dry*, a joke he used to bandy about with the lads at the station. They had been a tight bunch, and thank God for that. Helping each other out here and there. He plodded to the shower.

"Shania?" he called. No answer. She must have gone to work already. He'd never get used to calling out the name Shania.

He showered, drank a litre of water and walked outside to hail a cab. The typhoon had passed and all was kind of back to normal, save for branches, plastic chairs and broken umbrellas all over the pavements.

Two cabs passed, both full. He tapped one foot, checked his phone. Nothing from Johnny. *Good.* To pass the time, he took out some papers from his briefcase. There was the Taiwan deal to go over, the meeting with that shithead from compliance. He looked in his briefcase.

"Fuck." Phil remembered that he hadn't thrown away the SIM from his last phone call to the boss. "Forgot about that." He fiddled with the back of the dinosaur of a phone and chucked it into a bin a few metres away, just as a taxi pulled up behind him. "Good stuff," he groaned, as he eased himself into the back seat.

About twenty metres down the road, Bobby Ling's driver sat watching. He checked Phil's cab had gone, hopped out of the Mercedes and quickly walked towards the bin.

* * *

After dinner, Wang mercifully slept and Alice now needed some exercise. She had eaten almost half a cow and felt sluggish. She put on her rain boots, grabbed a light raincoat and took off for the beach. It was empty, the sand hard and wet and the sharp grey rocks under Cape D'Aguilar rising clearly from the low tide. Just the way she liked it. As she reached the end of the bay, and she looked back to admire the lit-up rainbow colours of the village houses at the base of the headland, her phone rang, a mobile number she did not recognise. Should she answer it?

"Hello, Miss Alice?" the man on the other line said. "It is me, Chang, from the Mandarin hotel." Alice opened her mouth but found nothing came out. "Hello?"

"Yes. Hello. I'm sorry. Chang?"

"Yes. You paid me to watch Mr Johnny Humphries. Some months ago now."

Alice switched into Cantonese.

"Oh, yes. I am sorry. I did. Long time ago now. I should have told you that there's no need to do so anymore."

Chang was somewhere busy. Traffic roared in the background, the city coming back to life after two days of typhoon recovery.

"No," he continued in English, despite Alice's command of his own language. "It's not that. I was coming home, from work, after the typhoon, and it had been very busy. It was outside the hotel, in the evening."

"Okay." Alice pulled the raincoat tightly around her waist.

"And just my lucky day, right? I saw Mr Johnny with a bag, a large bag. I was smoking a cigarette on the corner, you know, just hanging out, and then I spotted him. So I watched."

"Yes, yes."

"Well, it might be nothing, but he stopped, took out plastic bag and threw it in a bin." Alice couldn't think of what to say. She had no interest in Johnny anymore. After all, she had gone ahead with this idea to have him followed, at the time, to appease Scarlett's concerns, or – in a small way – the hope they might find something and Johnny and Phil would get their comeuppance. She never thought it would come to anything. "So, after he left, I went over, took it out. Inside were three old Nokia phones and some SIM cards. But I put together again. If you want them. Okay?" A truck rattled noisily in the

274

background. "I will leave with the concierge at the Mandarin. His name is Man, Mr Man. Tall guy. Got to go."

Alice walked back along the sand, feeling a few bites of hot rain on her cheeks. She smelled the pungent odour of fish sauce from the Thai restaurant, watched a few excitable teenagers taking off into the grey surf at the far end of the beach. Alice felt comforted by the seaside calm-after-the-storm and although she was initially torn about the phone call with Chang, by the time she reached the empty playground that fronted the sand, she knew what she would do.

Then, she'd be done with it. Her life would be quiet, untroubled and filled only with family, work, new friends. She couldn't risk being involved in anything to do with Johnny, Vivian and Scarlett, not if it went public, certainly not with the role Wang was still no doubt going to play.

But if Scarlett, Felicity and Vivian did nail Johnny and Phil for something… Alice let the sweet sensation of revenge run through her veins.

She pulled out her phone and dialled Scarlett's number.

CHAPTER TWENTY-THREE

Central.

Carolyn, too, was on her way out of Hong Kong. She was in a snaking queue at the Airport Express, a Central-based check-in service, where, afterwards, a fast train whisked passengers to the actual airport twenty-three minutes away. The metal trolley holding their suitcases kept being shoved this way and that against her ankles, as people pushed through the lines, going God knows where, doing God knows what. How, she mused, could so many people – including herself – want to get on or off a plane at the same freakin' time? To make matters worse, her children were growing agitated from waiting and were bickering with each other.

"Stop that." Carolyn pulled them apart. "It's going to be a long flight. So get used to waiting. Okay?"

"How long?"

"To Charleston? Just over seventeen hours."

Both kids groaned and kicked at each other's heels.

"Well, that's life. Your grandfather's so excited to see you."

She'd made the decision to get away as soon as she'd woken up after the typhoon. It'd been too long since she'd had a break, she was too caught up in Felicity's dramas, she felt that something darker was going on with Johnny and she didn't want to be around for that. When they returned in a couple of weeks, she planned on quitting her business and going back to full-time study, maybe do something a bit off-centre in the health realm. She'd always been fascinated with alternative medicine. Either way, she had just sent one final text to Felicity.

Sorry, but I have behaved unprofessionally. I wish you the best in your endeavours. Please be careful – and for both our sakes – don't communicate with me anymore. I will no longer be treating you or Johnny. Lots of luck.

A few people in the queue behind her stood a willowy blonde in a simple white T-shirt. On her back was a small leather backpack and she was carrying a battered leather overnight bag with a red plastic luggage tag; nothing glamorous at all, but she had bone structure of natural beauty nailed, that was for sure. Her hair was brushed and pulled into a low and loose ponytail. By way of make-up, all she had slapped on to her face was clear lip balm highlighting a generous pout and a shiny sunscreen that gave her high cheekbones a nice sheen. Carolyn briefly mourned her blink-and-you-miss-it youth as she rubbed at her tired, red eyes. But, Carolyn noticed, the girl seemed edgy. The businesswoman standing behind the girl became quickly annoyed with the blonde's jiggling and shifting. She clicked her tongue a few times to show she was irritated and affected a serious resting bitch face, but the blonde was oblivious, her attention divided equally between the check-in desk and something – or someone – over her shoulder.

Then her phone rang. The blonde let it ring a few times, sighed and answered.

"Alice."

She listened to her phone. Carolyn listened to her.

"I'm going there now," she said very loudly.

Seconds later, the girl hung up, grabbed her leather bag and ran from the line to the escalators behind them. A massive queue was edging its way ahead of them and the woman who Carolyn didn't know was Scarlett threw her hands in the air in frustration. The typhoon had caused untold damage and delays all over town. Every inch was heaving with sombre faces atop slumped shoulders.

* * *

Scarlett turned and ran for the taxi rank outside. A domestic helper with a small child was being dropped off on the corner and, despite the queue of people waiting for taxis a mile long, Scarlett forced her way to the front and hopped into the back of the cab.

"Hey, you!" the people called. "Hey! How dare—"

Scarlett closed her ears to their protestations.

"The Mandarin Oriental," she said, out of breath.

The taxi roared into life.

POSTSCRIPT

Three years later.

Johnny's lawyer sat on a plastic chair in the sun, a few feet from where Johnny sat on a thinning lawn under a tree, hunched and smoking. He'd never smoked, and yet, there he was, puffing away. If you can't beat 'em…

"Any chance at all?" Johnny sighed, squinting into a weak afternoon sun.

"There's a very, very small chance," the lawyer pinched his forefinger and thumb together. "But this is Hong Kong. Kidnapping, coercion. Then there's the UK, um, murders. I'm—"

"Don't say you're sorry," Johnny hissed.

The lawyer recoiled a little.

"I suppose there is one thing."

Johnny took a long drag.

"I'm hardly busy, so talk away."

The lawyer bought some time with a cough.

"It's a long shot. But we could go try the mental incapacitation road again. It'll take a—"

Johnny nearly doubled over laughing. A gardener in a conical hat sweeping a concrete path nearby stopped and stared.

"Why not," Johnny replied, trying to straighten up. "What have I got to lose?"

The lawyer noticed the guards had moved under a covered quadrangle nearby.

"Rain," the lawyer said, as though to himself. Johnny looked to the sky. "Typhoon coming."

"I have a psychologist friend, who might help me," Johnny offered. He'd had a good rapport with Carolyn. It was worth a try. The lawyer gave him a pitying false smile.

The harsh dinner bell rang and echoed off the Dragon's Back Hills. As he often did, Johnny pictured Alice just a few hundred metres below, walking along the beach, holding her new baby. He pictured her husband, Wang, arriving home from his busy day as a divisive politician, a Localist, who had an inch of reluctant respect of the government officials. Maybe... just maybe, Wang would know someone who could garner some support for Johnny's appeal? After all, Alice now knew he had no idea that Phil had asked her to courier those documents all those years ago. He had only tried to help Alice, not hurt her. He went to tell the lawyer this idea, but the rain had started and they had to move under cover.

Sometimes, he had dreams that Scarlett was on the beach too, cooing over Alice's baby's cute little toes, regaling Alice with tales of her new life campaigning to find Nick's killer. Scarlett had spent some time in a specialist hospital, considering she had a breakdown. No wonder. She'd falsified why she was living with Johnny, among other things. Anyway she'd moved back to Australia, but was often in his dreams, crowding out the others, who seemed to float menacingly in the background – Gu, Madeline, Ken, Vivian.

And then he thought of Brian, a man who could have done so much were his early days not so dark. Had he not taken matters into his own hands, Brian also would have been destined for a harsh sentence like Johnny's. You see, the "Witches of Stealth", as Johnny had come to call them, went to the police with Gu's confession, and soon after, Ken and Phil were arrested. Ken caved first, Phil followed suit and then they came for Johnny. The SIM cards had recent damning messages and Brian's number was top of the list as the one most called. As soon as news got out that Johnny was arrested, Brian had set off in his restored Aston Martin at top speed and driven it off a cliff in Devon. What a grand way to go. Johnny found it a fitting end for someone who had endured so much. And Phil? Well, he was in the shit with Johnny too. Once they'd found Johnny's old Nokia SIM cards in the bin near the Mandarin, they located two more through Bobby Ling's driver, who was proud to say that he had liberated them not long before the other ones were found. Phil had always been hopeless about getting rid of them. The trail was unmistakable. At least, though, the world knew he – Johnny – hadn't been the one to order those morons to take a knife to Madeline's finger. You should have heard the gasps in the courtroom when the pieces were put together – the British voice, the scent, his fallout with her father, the fact that Johnny had been scouring for a new office to rent near where Madeline would hang out after college and she'd seen him twice before the kidnapping – it had been enough for Madeline to paint a picture in her head that led to Johnny. Phil pleaded guilty. Finally, he owned up to something.

Yes, sure, the kidnapping had been Johnny. But not the finger. He'd not been involved in *that*. But he did lie about one thing during the trial. He hadn't been scouring for office space before the kidnapping. He had been watching Madeline. She was an easier target than her father, who had a bodyguard. That was why she was the perfect victim. In the court, they were told that Madeline refused to be followed by one; wouldn't let the driver take her, either. But the truth was, Johnny had only spied on her once, so he could tell Phil to tell Bobby to tell the kidnappers – with conviction – where she most likely went. They didn't want to waste any more time. Phil had watched her for days and she always ended up on this narrow lane. But Johnny had wanted to see for himself. The second time she'd seen him, he was genuinely walking back from a lunch, not even thinking about the fact he was near her favourite teahouse. *So shoot me.* She probably would.

Phil was locked up somewhere on Kowloon side. Phil had written to Johnny a few times. He wrote a cheesy diatribe about how he had lost ten kilos and found God. Johnny scoffed before tearing the last letter into tiny pieces, figuring Phil's reformation was most likely a ruse to work towards an early release. Phil was considered more the small-time guy, not the mastermind. Suppose that *is* true, Johnny almost laughed. But still, they were both in serious trouble.

And then he thought, again, of Vivian and Scarlett. He clenched his jaw hard, something he had done so much of late, he had nearly bitten a hole in the inside of his cheek. They'd banded together during the court case and Johnny didn't have a chance, even though he hadn't personally hurt either of them.

Vivian was still running Stealth, an empire that Johnny had originally funded, thank you very much. She was newly engaged to her long-time boyfriend, Tom Jamieson (too pretty for a grown man), and had quite the upstanding appearance. The joke? Since the case, her past was publicly revealed and – guess what? – no one gave a shit. In fact, she was being hailed as a kind of heroine, a victim of male repression who rose above and took control. All those years hiding it and being ashamed and now she was apparently doing agony-aunt columns for *Marie Claire*. It drove him mad to keep up with her life, but he needed to know what she was doing. One day, he'd be out of this hellhole and get back on his feet. *Just watch me*, he whispered at a photo of the smiling face of Vivian dancing with some corny B-grade celebrity at a charity dinner. What a fake.

Scarlett. Talk about a goose chase. Johnny and Phil had nothing to do with her boyfriend's death. Not one little bit. And at least that was something that came out at the trial. Scarlett would probably spend her life on a fruitless search for that killer. The contact with Gu and the orphanage about that initial funding in the 1990s was an unfortunate link that came back to bite them big time. If Gu hadn't been on death's door and his guilty conscience about the kidnapping hadn't motivated him, they wouldn't be in this mess. Gu never would have pointed Scarlett to Vivian, she never would have contacted Felicity/Madeline and Johnny would now be driving along a country lane in France in Brian's Aston Martin.

In other vivid dreams, Johnny pictured Scarlett laughing, walking along Lugard Road with his dog, the fresh wild jasmine bushes framing the path as she strode purposefully. This peaceful scene would be disrupted by Phil, perhaps Gu running along beside him trying to stop him, the ghostly faces of Bobby, sometimes Ken, Vivian with crossed arms and a bloodied face walking down some stairs to his right, Brian waiting for him at the end of the path and Felicity pointing at him with her mangled finger. God it was horrible. He, Brian, Phil, Ken, Bobby and Gu were like some twisted family, stuck together for all those years because of one favour Johnny agreed to for his troubled friend.

Well, that's how the prosecution painted them. The image haunted Johnny almost every night.

But it was a joke. You'd have to be blind not to have seen that the Witches of Stealth had all behaved badly at times too. Drug dealing, spying, breaking medical laws by sidling up to his psychologist for God's sake, faking who they actually were, thank you very much, Scarlett. Why weren't they being punished?

Madeline, aka Felicity, was living a quiet life. So quiet that Johnny had no idea what she was doing. To be honest, hearing it all played out at the trial about Phil and Ken and who said and did what during that kidnapping was frustrating. To Johnny, it was a story he had pushed to the back of his mind for so long that when he heard it, it was almost illusionary, someone else's life, and while he felt a few pangs of guilt about Madeline, he also felt removed from it all. There was so much more to what happened before all this, and *that* reality – that story – was all Johnny could see. No one in the courtroom experienced Brian's father, his violence, Brian's injuries. None of them knew what it was like for him – Johnny – growing up having to pretend he didn't have a father because, to anyone and everyone, his father pretended he didn't have a son. His lawyer tried to explain all this, but no one really cared.

But he had to admit, Madeline was a nice kid. Yes, she was that bastard Chung's daughter, but that wasn't her fault. Anyway, she'd got her answer. Last time he saw her, she was in court, with a sickly pallor and a bit too skinny. He wouldn't have recognised her if she'd stood in front of him and screamed out her name.

The protests had died down, but there was always the threat of more. That sickeningly earnest Wang was turning into quite the politician. Good luck to him. He'd need all the luck he could get. Johnny held little hope for Wang and his cohort, but that wasn't what occupied his mind most days. It was how he was going to get out, no matter what his lawyer told him. What would it take? he wondered. War? A pandemic? Maybe then, the prisons would be rife with some disease that meant they had to move them into hospitals. Johnny would be the sickest person around if that was the case. Refuse to leave hospital and work something out, like Julian Assange. *Yes. Well... you can only hope. Pray for me, Phil*, he laughed to himself, and took a final drag of his cigarette.

Johnny stomped on the butt with unnecessary force.

"Bring on the case. You watch me."

The lawyer nodded and opened his mouth to speak, just as a deafening thunderclap trumpeted across the sky. The lawyer jumped. Johnny raised his eyes to the heavy clouds and saw it. A perfect black. He closed his eyes, and all was clear.

ACKNOWLEDGEMENTS

I would like to express my immense gratitude to the roller coaster of romantic love, the demands of small children, the daily grind and the process of making and enjoying friends (and the resultant hangovers) without which – or even without half of the aforementioned – I would have finished this book many years sooner.

Of course, I wouldn't have had the material to write it without the aforementioned, thus my sincere thankfulness. Especially you. You know who you are.

More specifically, I would like to thank the wonderful Lauren Parsons from Legend Press, alongside Lucy Chamberlain and the rest of the impressive Legend team, for taking me on as one of their authors and fulfilling a long-held dream, as well as those kind early readers who said they finished my manuscript in its most messy form but may not have, and said they did so as to not hurt my feelings. Special thanks also to Nan-Hie In and Clare Halifax, for their wise manuscript insights.

I also extend my heartfelt gratitude to my husband and three wonderful children, my Shek O and Perth tribes, friends thankfully made when living in London and Sydney and parents who told me to "read a book", a pastime that was and still is my first real love.

Last but not least, to that jutting rock of soaring concrete and green hills, sampans and spas, giant cobras and equally giant rent, gloriously safe streets, stinky tofu, fragrant hotels and an anything-goes attitude – the city of Hong Kong. I hope you continue to shine in all your neon-lit glory.

If you enjoyed what you read,
don't keep it a secret.

Review the book online and tell anyone who
will listen.

Thanks for your support spreading
the word about Legend Press.

Follow us on Twitter
@legend_press

Follow us on Instagram
@legendpress